Worth The Lies

He smiled. "Haven't you ever done something pretty stupid?" He knew he had. Pretty much weekly since he'd been fourteen. And it almost always involved a girl.

She looked down at their entwined hands, then further down the sheets, and Huck regretted asking her the question. It was obvious whatever she was thinking about pained her.

"Only once," she whispered, and although Huck desperately wanted to know what could bring that haunted look to her pretty face, he didn't ask her to elaborate.

"Listen, Kelsey, we don't have to do—"

"You were right, though," she said.

"About what?"

"About wanting something—someone—badly enough that you stop thinking about what's right or wrong, or stupid."

"Me and you?" he said, hope in his voice.

"Yeah. Me and you. You. I want you, Huck Beck, very badly."

"I want you too. For a long time," he added.

A soft smile crossed her face, parting those full, sumptuous lips. "A whole week?"

He took a deep breath and let it out. "Longer," he said.

He knew the second she got it. And it didn't take her long. She knew that he knew. Still, she didn't call him on it, so he didn't push further.

"Huck?"

"Yeah?"

"Done talking?

"Yeah."

"Start kissing?"

"Oh yeah," he said, then moved across the bed toward her.

OTHER TITLES BY MARA JACOBS

WORTH the LIES

The Worth Series, Book Six

MARA JACOBS

Published by Mara Jacobs
©Copyright 2016 Mara Jacobs

ISBN: 978-1-940993-04-1

For more information on the author and her works, please
see www.marajacobs.com

For Jules

Prologue

—⚏—

Four Years Ago

"OKAY, FOR THIS EXERCISE, WE'RE GOING TO DO something a little different," the instructor said. That was already obvious to Kelsey Cameron. The big divider down the middle of the room had been the first giveaway. The neck-high, covered openings at three-foot intervals along the divider were the second giveaway.

But mostly, Kelsey knew this part of the training process was different because she could hear the buzz of people on the other side of the divider. So far, her small, elite training class had come into zero contact with other people.

"Okay, find an opening, making sure that when you open the door, you will be able to see."

Kelsey walked down the divider wall—which went right up to the ceiling of the classroom—until she got to a spot where the little door was at her eye level. The door—hatch?—was about seven inches wide and about a foot in length. Basically the size of a human head, if you included some of the neck.

Which, she guessed, was exactly what she would see when she opened the door.

"So far, we've been working on peripheral vision, seeing things all around you, and retaining that information," the instructor continued as the others in her class found the door slots that worked best for their height. Kelsey was the only female in the class, but was not necessarily the shortest. "We've been pounding it into you that you always have to be aware of your surroundings, that you need to be able to describe *every* detail of a crime scene."

Each trainee had now found a spot and were all looking at their instructor. They'd been together every day—and many nights—during their intensive training course, but Kelsey hadn't exactly been embraced by her fellow trainees.

Which was fine with her. At the end of the day, they were all her competition anyway.

"But now," her instructor said, "I want you to concentrate on something very close up. In particular, another human being. When you're face to face with a perp, or a suspect, or—and this is sometimes even more important—a witness, you'll need to rely on your instincts. Is that person lying? Are they telling the truth? Are they nervous? It goes beyond being able to physically describe or identify them. Sometimes, it's about *knowing* them. *Feeling* them."

One of the trainees down the line—most likely Jenkins, that asshole—made some comment under his breath (probably about the *feeling* directive), and a couple of the other students tried to swallow laughter.

The instructor gave Jenkins a censuring look, but continued. "So, when you open your door, you're looking at the physical, yes. Always. But you're looking deeper. Much deeper. And you'll have just one minute to do it."

Right. No problem. Kelsey had aced every other part of the FBI training. There was no reason to think she wouldn't blow her competition away with this exercise as well.

"You will not speak, nor will they. There is to be no interaction other than your observance. Okay, open your doors."

Kelsey did, and behind hers was a man she quickly began cataloging: chin-length dirty blond hair with haphazard lighter highlights that came from the sun, not the sure hand of a stylist. Blue eyes. No, gray. No, definitely blue. Before they could change color on her again, she shifted her focus down. Straight, almost patrician nose. Full—*very* full—lips framed by a goatee, which was also dirty blond with just a tiny, tiny gray spot at the fullest part of his bottom lip. He had a thinner beard, which looked like two, maybe three days' growth, but the goatee had been around. It wasn't neatly trimmed, but it was shaped.

In fact, nothing about him was neat. He had an air of neglect about him, but an almost practiced one, not the pure inept disarray of a true junkie or homeless person.

Kelsey briefly wondered if they brought people in from the local prison or from off the street for this exercise.

She took her focus off the various parts of him and concentrated on the whole. Which was when she realized he was staring back at her. Of course, that would be the case, and yet his steel gaze studying her as she tried to decipher him was a bit off-putting.

But that's what it would be like in an interrogation. The suspect would be trying to read and play her all while she was trying to do the same to him.

I wonder if he's another trainee?

I wonder if he's single?

Whoa. *So* not what she should be thinking about. *Focus!*

Right. Blue eyes. Were they laughing at her now? His mouth hadn't moved, not even a twitch of that oh-so-full bottom lip.

What had the instructor said? Deeper than looks. Go deeper.

God, she'd like him to go deep, that's for sure.

What the hell?

She hadn't had a physical thought about any of her fellow trainees for weeks. It had never even occurred to her that they were...well, *men*. There was no way she wasn't going to do well (for her, that was being the best) in this exercise simply because she'd realized that there was someone actually sexy in her vicinity.

But *was* he sexy? Really?

Yeah, he had that motorcycle bad-boy look going for him. She even thought it might be the top of a leather jacket she saw at the bottom of the opening.

But no, it wasn't…real. It was someone he'd created. Was it for this exercise or did it go deeper than that?

He was about her age—twenty-six—or perhaps even younger, based on the clear, unlined perfection of his skin, which looked so soft when everything else about him screamed (perhaps too loudly?) hard.

Was the gray in his beard real or were those few hairs dyed to give him the appearance of being older?

Feel him.

Usually Kelsey was ruled by logic, not emotion, but she was smart enough to know that sometimes a good agent had to trust their instincts and gut. The only way to do that was to open herself up.

So, she dropped her shield, the one she'd had firmly in place ever since she'd been recruited for the Bureau while in grad school at Harvard, and let herself *feel* the man who stood with his face so close to hers.

Brave. Reckless. But more. Afraid. Unsure. But trying mightily to cover that up. (Wasn't everybody?)

But the problem with dropping your guard to see others more clearly was that they too could see you. She felt his gaze upon her more intensely, as if he could feel her, and not in the existential way her instructor suggested.

Her skin prickled and heat rose up her neck, though she willed it to stay out of his line of sight. She stared straight into those blue eyes, watching as his pupils dilated, as his nostrils flared ever so slightly. And then, just as she was thinking this had to have been the longest minute ever, his lips parted to reveal perfectly white, supremely straight teeth. The corners of his mouth turned up slightly in a poor excuse of a smile, almost a feral growl without any sound.

But the effect it had on his face made her emit a tiny gasp.

"Doors closed," the instructor said. Before Kelsey could lift her arm, the man slid the door shut with a hard "snick."

"Okay, I hope you paid attention. Now you're going to each meet with a sketch artist and see how well you can describe the person you just studied."

Hmm. Would a sketch artist be able to do something with the description of "crazy handsome, but I think he might be the devil?"

"I hope you can remember well, because you won't meet with the sketch artist until three days from now."

Not a problem for Kelsey. She would remember everything about that man for longer than three days.

Possibly forever.

But she didn't see him again throughout the rest of her training. Nor for the next four years.

The next time she saw him was the day she married him.

One

HUCK BECK TRIED HARD NOT TO NERVOUSLY SHIFT IN his seat as he and Prescott waited for the others to join them. He was thrilled as shit to be there, and wondered if perhaps his being summoned to D.C. meant that he was back on Prescott's good side?

"Don't think that this puts you back in my good graces or anything," Prescott said beside Huck, pretty much shooting his theory all to hell. The older man didn't move a muscle, didn't look at Huck next to him as he spoke, just stared straight ahead at the empty chairs across the conference room table. "I still think you majorly fucked up four years ago."

"I know," Huck said. Because, really, what else could he say? Prescott was right.

But Huck was here now, and he was going to make this—whatever this was—count.

Okay, so he was still on Prescott's shit list. So why was he even here? And more importantly, why did he even care?

But he did. He wanted this. Badly.

"Exactly why do you—"

Huck was interrupted by the opening of the door and entrance of three people in suits. FBI. They just had a way about them that shouted Bureau, even when they wanted to blend in. And from the looks of arrogance as they swept into the room, laid a couple of folders on the table, and then took their seats, they didn't want to blend in today.

They wanted Huck and Prescott to know exactly who they were. And that they were in charge.

Except for the one woman of the three. She had the look of an agent, but not the surety of the two men. She was about his age, as was one of the men. The other one was around fifty, with some graying at the temples. Very Scott Glenn in *Silence of The Lambs.*

So, was she Clarice? Not that she looked anything like Jodie Foster. She wore her dark brown hair in a short, choppy style that would have screamed no-nonsense except for the natural waves, which created a soft, flowy effect.

Her suit was navy and cut for a female, but she wore very little—if any—makeup, and Huck bet she was mistaken for a man from behind more often than not.

But not from the front. Not with those full lips and huge eyes. A brief flash of vague familiarity blinded him for a second, and he barely caught the introductions as the older FBI agent took control of the meeting.

"Agent Jenkins, Agent Cameron, this is Agent Prescott from the DEA and Huck Beck."

"Who is not officially with the DEA," Prescott was quick to clarify to the others as they all nodded across the table to each other.

No handshakes, just nods. And a very pointed stare from the woman—Agent Cameron.

"Huck, this is Agent Tarrington, Midwest Bureau chief."

Tarrington acknowledged his introduction to Huck with a slight movement of his head, opened a folder, and said to his agents, "Mister Beck will be joining us in a civilian capacity for this operation. It's a low-involvement, low-risk task. He will be used in a backup role only. Both of you will be." He directed the last to Agent Cameron.

"So, he's not in law enforcement? In any way?" Agent Cameron asked, looking at Huck with interest.

Not female interest. At least, not the type of female interest Huck was used to. Agent Cameron looked at him like a puzzle she was trying to figure out.

Being that he was the only one in the room not in a suit or with a super-professional air about him, he supposed that was normal.

But it seemed like more than that. The other agent, Jenkins, was barely paying him the time of day, his head stuck in his own folder.

There was something about her. Something so familiar…

"Not at this time," Prescott answered her. "He has been through extensive training, though, and is well equipped to handle this particular project."

"Which is what, exactly?" she asked, looking at Tarrington. Huck noticed a sly smile on Jenkins' face, which he tried—badly—to hide.

"You and Beck will pose as a married couple to provide backup to an ongoing operation in the Upper Peninsula of Michigan."

"What?" both Huck and Cameron said at the same time.

"You wanted to get into field work, Kelsey," Jenkins said, not even trying now to hide his glee at what seemed to be distressing news to Cameron.

"Shut up, Jenkins," both Cameron and Tarrington said. Jenkins looked down at his folder again, but the smirk wasn't fully wiped from his face.

He'd never met the man before, but Huck would sure love to forcefully wipe that smirk away.

"Okay, let's back up," Tarrington said, pulling a sheet of paper out and placing it to the side of his folder. "We have reason to believe that large quantities of drug-creation ingredients are being brought to the Upper Peninsula from Canada via Lake Superior. Mainly this would be pseudoephedrine for the creation of meth."

"Seriously?" Huck said, interested now. He'd lived in the U.P. his whole life. Had spent every summer working on boats on Lake Superior. He'd never imagined a drug ring—apparently big enough to be on the FBI and DEA's radar—could infiltrate the small tourist towns that lined Lake Superior. Although he had read about outbreaks of meth busts across the U.P. in the past couple of years. "You mean, like in Marquette? Munising?" Huck asked, naming the two larger cities that were along the lake.

"Possibly. But the one we're concentrating on has been feeding into your neck of the woods, Huck. The Copper Country in general, Copper Harbor specifically."

"Are you shitting me?" he asked, shocked. The Copper Country wasn't immune to crime or drug use, of course, but this seemed unreal to him. "What's the scope?"

"Small potatoes right now, which is why we want to shut it down before it can grow or get any real muscle behind it."

Huck felt a small sense of relief that it wasn't a large presence in his own backyard. Yet. His heart swelled with a desire to protect his home, the place he loved.

It was the same feeling he'd felt when he'd met with Prescott on the Northern Michigan University campus several years ago about going into federal crime prevention.

"We have an agent already in place. The two of you will be there to provide supplemental information and physical backup… *only* if needed."

"Which agent is in place?" Cameron—Kelsey, apparently— said.

"That is not information you need at this time," Tarrington said.

Another smirk from Jenkins and a slow flush rose up the neck of Cameron, though she only nodded, showing no other reaction to being shut down by her boss. Or to her coworker's obvious—and childish—amusement.

Jenkins. What an ass.

"Mister Beck is from the area and has worked on tourist boats for several years. He currently resides there doing…" Tarrington took a closer look at his paper, and Huck resisted the urge to lean over and read from it too. "Odd jobs during the winter months."

"Which is most of the year, right?" Cameron asked.

"Agent Cameron was chosen for this operation, even though she works out of the D.C. office, because she has family ties to the area as well."

"Really?" Huck asked, genuinely surprised. "From what area?"

She was shaking her head. "My mother is originally from Chassell. My father was a Tech student. They married soon after my father graduated. I visited my grandfather once or twice when I was child, but I haven't been back to the area since he died when I was six or seven." She looked to Tarrington as she added, "I wouldn't exactly say I have ties to the area."

Tarrington waved that away. "Enough for the cover story to work. You two met in D.C. while Beck was here visiting his mother. You bonded over your common ties to a remote area, and a relationship developed. Quickly."

He passed a second folder across the table to Huck. "Most of it is in there. We've kept it brief; less chance of you tripping up. We matched the dates with an actual weekend when you both actually were in D.C. There will be more coming to you this afternoon. We're working on those documents now."

He'd been here a few months ago visiting his mother and her husband, who lived in Virginia. They'd come into the city to see the sights. "How do you know when I was here?" Huck asked, looking from Tarrington to Prescott, both of whom only stared at him. Yeah, of course. These guys could find out anything.

Thank God Huck had nothing to hide.

Well, almost nothing.

"For now, the two of you will just establish yourself in the area as a newly married couple. Spring is upon us, and the boating and tourist industry will begin staffing soon. Beck will get work in Copper Harbor and will secure work for you too, Cameron. That's basically it for now. You'll be contacted when needed. Keep your eyes and ears open."

It looked like Tarrington was getting ready to leave, and Huck felt a moment of panic that his life was changing irrevocably in the blink of a file folder closing.

"Wait, wait, wait. First of all, I haven't actually agreed to anything." Tarrington and Prescott exchanged looks, and Huck continued, knowing that Prescott would probably be able to talk Huck into working on this operation. Would know how much Huck was dying to do something like this.

But married? In front of all his friends and family? "And if I do decide to do it, why would we even have to be married? If I can't do it alone." He looked at Prescott, who gave a subtle shake of his head. Yeah, Huck figured that was a no-go. No credentials, no authority. "Then why do we have to be married? Why can't Agent Cameron just act as my girlfriend? A live-in girlfriend."

"Several reasons," Tarrington said.

After a moment of silence, Huck said, "Such as?"

Tarrington, who obviously wasn't questioned often, and just as obviously didn't like it, sighed, pulled a sheet of paper closer, and read from it. "Huck Beck, aged twenty-eight. Attended Calumet High School and Northern Michigan University. Majored in criminal justice. Was accepted to law school when Agent Prescott recruited you for the DEA." Huck snuck a look at Prescott, waiting for the man to interrupt and set the record straight. That Huck had approached Prescott first. But something about Prescott's face had Huck wondering if that was how it had actually happened. Had he been played right from the start? Prescott, that sneaky SOB.

"Washed out of DEA training," Tarrington continued. Huck bristled, but didn't stop the man. That was what everybody thought? Yeah, of course they did. That he couldn't be a team player. That he wouldn't be able to work with a partner. Huck knew it had been Prescott's major concern, but that wasn't what ultimately had had Huck withdrawing from the program.

Another smirk from Jenkins, but Huck didn't look at Cameron, didn't want to see her expression. "Didn't put your degree to any substantial use, just doing boat crew work in-season and odd jobs in the off-season." Again, Huck inwardly bristled. He knew he was thought of as the family fuck-up, but that was within the family unit of his two older brothers who loved him unconditionally. To be thought it by these over-achieving, suit-wearing agency robots was something else altogether.

And was that what Prescott thought of him?

No. He wouldn't have contacted Huck out of the blue last week if he did. His career, and the agency, was too important to Prescott to go out on a limb with someone he thought couldn't get the job done.

"We were getting to the part where we had to be married," Huck said to Tarrington. He noticed Cameron nodded, with a wondering look. So, she thought it was unnecessary, too.

And why did he get a little bit pissed at that thought? Like she was turning down his proposal or something.

"You have been in and out of several relationships with women in the area, have you not?"

"I've...I've...dated some women. The same as any single man my age."

Tarrington raised an eyebrow, but continued to stare at his paper. He finally looked up, straight at Huck. "The fact is, another girlfriend, even a live-in one, will not be anything new. She won't be taken seriously amongst your friends or the people you work with. Wouldn't even be expected to be with you for very long."

"But isn't that better? That she fly under the radar?"

"Agent Cameron is one of the best information gatherers and analysts that we have. She is incredibly observant and has impeccable instincts. We want her around the docks, working amongst the boating community."

Huck looked at Cameron, who was obviously surprised by Tarrington's compliments. Huck guessed she didn't hear them very often.

"Tell me, Mister Beck, would that group of people be open to just another girlfriend that you were introducing them to?"

"No," Huck admitted.

"But, on the other hand, if you showed up with a wife whom you married after a whirlwind courtship, wouldn't they be inclined to spend time with her? Get to know her? See what kind of woman tripped up the town player?"

"I'm hardly the town player," Huck said. Yeah, he slept with women—who wouldn't? And he, so far, had shown no signs of settling down with any of them for more than a month or two, but… "Yeah, okay, they would. But I still—"

"And there is the factor of a husband and wife not being compelled to testify against each other."

"How does that come into play?"

"It probably wouldn't. And again, you two are the background on this operation. But if you are newly married, and you put it out that you and the wife are looking to upgrade from the small house you currently own…"

"You think someone will approach me about, what, muling for them? You really think it's people I know already?"

"Don't you, to various degrees, know everyone with a boat for hire in the Keweenaw Peninsula?"

"Probably."

"Then yes, you probably know the parties we're investigating."

"And you think if I show up with a new wife, saying she hates my tiny house and that I need some cash for a bigger one, that someone I know—and obviously have never, ever even remotely suspected was up to no good—is going to approach me and offer me drug-running work?"

"No. But it's a contingency we're prepared for. By being married, your wife could work with you. If that's balked at, you have the added bonus of being able to say she couldn't testify against you. Nor you her."

"That's kind of a weak argument," Cameron said. Huck nodded.

"We're not hanging much on it. If it comes up, it helps strengthen the reason for you being around."

"Basically, Beck has been through so many girls that only

someone he'd tied the knot with would be taken seriously," Jenkins said.

"Yeah, I got that," Cameron said to Jenkins, who only shrugged.

Huck started to argue, but Prescott placed a hand on Huck's arm, so he kept quiet.

"Any other questions can be directed to Agent Jenkins, who will be your point of contact going forward," Tarrington said.

"As in…I report to Jenkins?" Kelsey asked, shock in her voice. Jenkins sat back in his chair, not able to hide the gloat in his expression.

"For this operation, yes."

"But…but I—"

"May I have a word with you?" Tarrington said to Prescott as he rose from the table, ignoring Agent Cameron. He gathered his things and moved to the door. Jenkins got up and followed, as did Prescott. Prescott waved for Huck to stay seated, so he did, as did Cameron.

"Good luck, Agent Cameron," Tarrington said to Cameron, who started to rise, but he waved her to sit back down. "This is the chance you've been asking for. We expect good things." Tarrington held the door open, and Jenkins and Prescott walked out of the room. "Okay," Tarrington said dismissively to Huck and Cameron as he turned to leave. He waved a hand in a ceremonial way over his shoulder as he walked out.

"I now pronounce you man and wife."

Two

—⚏—

IGNORING TARRINGTON'S WAVE THAT SHE STAY BEHIND, Kelsey was out of her chair in a flash, following Tarrington and Jenkins out the door. "Sir, may I have a quick word, please?" she asked, hating that she was dogging the three men and also that she suspected there was a panic in her voice that she hated for them to hear. Especially Jenkins. Totally unbelievable that her first chance at undercover work was going to be with Jenkins in charge. It almost ruined the whole thing for her.

Tarrington stopped in the hallway, turning around to face Kelsey. "Make it quick, Cameron. I have a plane to Chicago to catch, and I need to talk with Agent Prescott before I do."

"So, this operation is being run out of the Midwest Bureau?" she asked. Well, of course it would be. That was the bureau Tarrington headed up and where Jenkins had been the last two years. And it was probably the least important question that Kelsey needed answered.

"Yes. I thought I mentioned that," Tarrington said, puzzlement in his face.

Had he? Kelsey wasn't sure. And Kelsey was usually so sure about everything.

It wasn't just because she was flabbergasted that Jenkins seemed to have risen farther and faster than she had in the two years since he left the D.C. office, although that was bad enough.

It was seeing Huck Beck again after four years that had

thrown her. Seeing him and his stupid gray, maybe blue, eyes.

The guy who she now had to play house with?

"Sir, I understand your reasoning for just another girlfriend of Beck's not being taken seriously…" Tarrington made a hurry-up motion with his hand. Prescott looked at his watch. Jenkins stared at her with a smile on his face. "But there's really no need to involve him at all. Especially given that he's a civilian."

Before he could say anything, Kelsey went on. "You said yourself that I have ties to the area. It would be perfectly natural for me to want to spend some time in the area, learn about my deceased grandparents. There's really no need to have Beck involved at all. I can insinuate myself into the boating world on my own."

Tarrington placed a hand on her shoulder. "I don't doubt that you could, Cameron. But by being with Beck you save a considerable amount of time. Time that you could be gathering information on these people, not spending trying to infiltrate their circle. You'd already be in."

"But I know the Bureau hates using civilians in its operations…" Which wasn't exactly true. Informants and contacts were used all the time during investigations. But to go undercover with a non-agent? As a married couple? Kelsey hadn't heard of that before. Of course, she'd only been with the Bureau for four years and had thus far been relegated to analyst work in the office, so maybe it happened more often than she knew?

Tarrington removed the hand from her shoulder, and Kelsey knew she would lose any argument she'd try to come up with for why she didn't want to be married to Huck Beck.

And saying she didn't think she could fully concentrate around him was probably not going to earn her points on her next review.

Besides, she was a professional, and if this was where the Bureau felt her talents could be best used, then who was she to argue?

Tarrington, no slouch agent himself, knew the minute

she mentally acquiesced and gave a firm nod. "Good. All the information you need to know at this point will be couriered to your apartment this afternoon. Go home. Pack your bags, because you're going to the U.P. as a blushing bride."

The three men turned and walked away while Kelsey stood in the hallway, dumbfounded. She looked behind her at the closed door that led to the conference room and Huck Beck. Her new husband for however long the operation took.

This was not going to end well.

THIS WAS NOT GOING to end well.

Huck sat in the small room for five minutes, maybe ten, trying to figure out how the hell he was going to explain showing up with a wife to his family.

In some ways, Tarrington had unfortunately pegged it— bringing home a wife would definitely make people curious and want to meet her. And, actually, his brothers might not be all that shocked after all. They'd probably think this was the kind of thing Huck would do. Yeah, impetuously marrying a woman he'd only known for a short time but was crazy in love with *was* something he'd probably do.

But not with Kelsey Cameron.

He couldn't imagine his brothers believing he'd marry a woman as…together as Kelsey Cameron appeared to be. In her no-nonsense suit with a no-nonsense hairstyle.

Not that every girl Huck was with was a bimbo or anything. They just usually were a bit more…feminine in their look.

But that could work to his advantage. That's why they might pull this off. People might believe that Huck would be rash and marry a woman who was so different from anyone he'd ever been with.

Yeah…it could work.

"You're already thinking of how to make this work, aren't you?" Prescott asked as he came back into the room, shutting the door behind him and sitting at the table, across from Huck.

"Maybe," Huck said, not wanting Prescott to know where his thoughts had been. He didn't fully trust Prescott's motives yet, didn't know if the agent was just looking out for the DEA, or if he had Huck's interests in mind.

Prescott nodded, as if knowing Huck would give nothing away. "Yes, you are. That's why I found you four years ago. That's why you're here now."

"Yeah, about that," Huck said. He leaned back in his chair, trying to act more nonchalant as he questioned Prescott about something that was anything but reason for nonchalance. "Tarrington said something about *you* recruiting *me*?"

A hard stare from Prescott and then a curt nod. "Yes?"

"But I was the one who sought you out."

"Were you?"

"You know I was. I came to see you after that lecture you gave."

"And why do you suppose I was giving that lecture? To your specific class? In the fucking nowhere Upper Peninsula?" He raised one brow in a move that Huck envied.

"No. No way. You're just playing head games with me now."

Prescott shrugged, like he didn't care if Huck believed him or not.

The truth was, it really didn't matter how it happened. Perhaps Huck had been singled out—he knew of at least two of his criminal justice professors who had personally mentioned that he had a bright future ahead of him if he applied himself. Maybe they had reached out to Prescott and the lecture Huck had attended had been a carefully orchestrated setup to get Huck to approach Prescott.

Yeah, that was the kind of fuckery the DEA did best.

Or maybe it had really happened as Huck thought and he'd been inspired enough by Prescott's talk that he'd wanted to work for him.

Back when he'd believed in doing good.

"Whatever," Prescott said, and Huck knew he'd get nothing

more on the subject from the man. "A package with more information will be sent to Agent Cameron's apartment this afternoon. You will leave with her now, go there, wait for the package, get her packed up. Then you'll be flying to Marquette, where you left your car."

"Yeah, why didn't you want me flying out of the Hancock airport?" When he'd gotten the summons from Prescott two days ago, the agent had specifically told him to report to the Marquette airport this morning, where a ticket in his name would be waiting, taking him to D.C. via Detroit.

"Too many people probably know you at the Hancock airport. We wanted to make sure we had your cover story firmly in place, so it was better if fewer people knew you'd flown out and back in on the same day. Was there anyone you knew on your flight out of Marquette?"

"No," Huck said, and the agent only nodded.

Prescott started to rise, and Huck felt a sense of panic that the rest of his life was about to be decided and he had a minimum of information available. And also a sense that it wasn't even him who would be deciding his fate.

"Wait—"

Prescott continued to stand, but stuck out a big hand, stopping Huck. "Listen, it's really not that complicated. You're being given a second chance. I saw something in you four years ago. You chose to piss away your opportunity then..." He waited for Huck to challenge that summation, but when Huck stayed silent, Prescott continued. "I rarely give second chances. This opportunity came up with Tarrington reaching out to us, and it seemed like an ideal way to see what you were up to. As it turns out, that was pretty much nothing."

Huck started to balk, but kept silent. Yeah, doing seasonal work at twenty-eight would be considered doing nothing to someone like Prescott. Honestly, it was to Huck, too.

"Anyway," Prescott said, heading for the door. "Cameron is waiting in her office for you to leave when you're ready. Tarrington was right—you and Cameron might not even be called into play. Just go about doing what you normally do every spring. Get a job on a boat, party with the Harbor crowd. Just keep an eye open and be ready if you're contacted by me or whomever the FBI has working on this. I think it's probably that Jenkins we just met."

"But do that all with a wife," Huck pointed out.

Prescott waved the words away, like he was getting rid of a pesky insect.

"What happens when this operation is over? Am I in the DEA?"

"We can discuss that when we see how the operation goes."

"Basically, be a good boy, do what I'm told, and *then* you'll let me know if I'm back in."

"Basically, yes."

"But to do that, I have to lie to my friends and family about a wife and then take their shit when, big shocker, we split up a few months later."

"Basically, yes," Prescott repeated.

Huck knew he was being tested. His commitment had always been questioned. By everyone. But not by Prescott. Not until Huck had walked away from the DEA just before his training was completed.

He knew Prescott had felt burned by Huck's decision to wash out. And he didn't blame the man for testing him now.

Huck was surprised how much he wanted to prove to the agent he admired how committed to something he could be.

Shit, he was surprised how much he wanted to prove it to *himself.*

"Honestly, Huck," Prescott said more softly, surprising Huck by using his first name. He'd always called him Beck before. "Yes, this a test for you. Absolutely. But I'm also getting the feeling from Tarrington that it's a test of some kind for Cameron, too."

"First time doing field work, it sounded like."

Prescott nodded. "I get that there's a lot at stake for her on this. And I don't think she's any happier about having a husband than you are about having a wife."

"Misery loves company, is that what you're saying?"

"I'm saying you're both people with something to prove—both to yourselves and to others. Work together. Accept your position. Make it work."

He wanted to ask more, wanted to know why Cameron didn't want to go undercover with him. It wasn't her family who would have a new in-law thrust in their faces.

"Her office is third floor, at the end of the hall," Prescott said as he walked out of the door, shutting it behind him.

Huck pulled out his phone, happy to see he got a cell signal in the building. He'd wondered if the FBI would have some kind of voodoo tech shit that didn't allow civilians to get cell service in their midst.

He punched in his brother Twain's contact and waited for the phone to ring. Part of him hoped that Twain wouldn't pick up, that he'd be in the woods with loud logging machinery going and not hear the call. But the other part of Huck knew that this was not something he wanted to leave on a voicemail.

"Holy shit, I was pretty much ready to call in the cops on you," Twain said by way of greeting when he answered. "You barely answer texts; you're never at your place when I stop by. What have you been up to?"

A perfect opening, and Huck took it. "Actually, I've been out of town a lot lately."

"Yeah? Doing what?" Twain asked. There was no suspicion in his voice, and Huck realized that Tarrington had been right—people would believe that the fly-by-night Huck Beck *would* show up with a bride that he'd never before even mentioned he'd been seeing.

"It's a long story, but it involves a woman," Huck said.

Twain chuckled. "It always does, my man, it always does."

"Yeah, but this time, this...*one* is different."

"Oh yeah?" Huck could imagine his brother, perhaps in his offices at T&B Logging, sitting up straighter in his chair, listening more intently to words Huck had never said before.

"Yeah, very different."

"Well, that's great, Huck. Really. Is she from around here?"

"No, but I'm bringing her home with me today."

"Great. I can't wait to meet her."

"I need a favor."

"Shoot."

"I need you to go to my house and get it cleaned up. Make it presentable, you know?"

"Got it. Remove all signs of any females that went before her."

Huck knew there weren't many remnants of girlfriends past at his place, but he just agreed with Twain. "Yeah, but clean it too. You know, make it look like a home, more than just a place where I crash."

"Okay if I take Liv with me? Get a woman's eye on it? She'd be better at that."

"It's got to be today. We'll be there tonight. I don't know if you'll be able to get a hold of—" He stopped when he heard Twain speaking to someone else and a very feminine response from, he assumed, Liv.

"She can do it with me. We took the day off anyway. We'll head over there now."

"You took a day off? You're with Liv?" Both statements seemed odd to Huck. Twain never took a day off. And though Twain and Liv were now civil after years of being divorced, they didn't exactly spend their spare time together. Unless...

"Is Matty okay?" Huck asked, concerned about his fifteen-year-old nephew.

"He's fine. Great, actually."

"But then why—"

"You're not the only one with news," Twain said.

"What—"

"See you soon," Twain said, gave a devious chuckle, and then disconnected.

Huck knew he'd make a great undercover agent. Had known it four years ago when he'd approached (been recruited by?) Prescott. He also knew it now. And he knew it because instead of wondering about Twain's news and why he and Liv were spending rare days off together, which he did, those thoughts took a backseat to the idea that with Twain's life being in a different state, Huck's own lies may be easier to pull off.

And suddenly, wanting to succeed in this, to get back into Prescott's good graces and have a career with the DEA, became very, very important to Huck.

And they felt good—these feelings of purpose. This…desire. Feelings he hadn't had in over four years.

Three

—⁓—

"SOMETHING STINKS ABOUT THIS WHOLE THING," Kelsey said to Huck Beck as they entered her Dupont Circle apartment. She led the way through the foyer, tossing her keys onto the side table as she always did when she came home.

Except there usually wasn't a husband in tow.

"Yeah? To you too, eh? I thought it was just because this was all pretty much new to me," he said. Kelsey waved him in, following him into the small but tidy living room.

"I kind of got that. How new is this all to you? What exactly is your connection to Prescott and the DEA?"

He turned from his surveying of the room to stare at her. Hard. With eyes that made her want to squirm, though she stood her ground. She hadn't been in on much questioning of suspects (okay, none), but she knew enough not to give up any kind of balance by looking away from him because his piercing eyes unsettled her.

"You heard Tarrington. I washed out of DEA training a few years ago."

Four. Four years ago. But she didn't let on that she remembered him from her own training. In fact, she wasn't at all sure why DEA agents-in-training had been used in her FBI class, though both the FBI and DEA did their new agent training in Quantico. She'd probably never know. Unless he'd already washed out by then and hadn't even still been in DEA training?

She mentally shook her head. Back to the case at hand.

The case that wasn't a case. A file of some sort was to be couriered over to her place soon, but Kelsey didn't feel very certain that they'd glean much more information than Tarrington had shared with them.

"Yes, I heard Tarrington. But I'm guessing the DEA doesn't keep in touch with former trainees. And not somebody at Prescott's level, that's for sure." She tried to turn the formidable gaze back on him, but he only shrugged and turned, continuing to look around her home.

She knew she should probably go to her bedroom and start packing, but she watched him as he shed his sport coat and tossed it across the arm of her big chair. She resisted the urge to go over and straighten it out or hang it up like she would have liked. Huck Beck looked like the kind of guy who was uncomfortable in something as formal (and it wasn't *that* formal!) attire of a tie, chambray work shirt, khakis, and a navy sport coat.

Skipping over his background (deflection, much?), Huck said, "While we're waiting, maybe we should start putting our background story in place."

Yes. Good. Business. She pulled a notebook from her messenger bag, which she'd placed on the console table that was along the wall. Clicking her pen, she flipped to a blank page. "Right. We'll probably have a marriage certificate in the stuff that's being sent over, so we'll know the date we got married when we see that. But yes, background. Let's see, we met…where?"

"A bar," he said, his back to her once more, his hands dusting over the framed pictures in one of the built-ins that ran across the shorter wall of the small room. One of the many neat little features that made Kelsey rent the place.

"I don't go to bars," she said.

"My wife would go to bars. Or, at least, that's where I would meet anyone from a different city. Anyone I would…" he said.

She opened her mouth to argue, but thought better of it. "Fine. We met in a bar. I'd been dragged there by a girlfriend who was having her bachelorette party."

He turned around, one of her photos in his hand and a teasing smile on his face. "Because there's no other way you would have been there."

"Right."

"You cut your hair."

She touched the ends of her hair, which just brushed her jaw line. "When?"

He raised the framed photo in his hand. "Since this photo. But how long ago? Did you have long hair when we met?"

She didn't need to get closer to know that he held the photo taken of her with her family the day after she officially became FBI. It was about a month before she cut off her waist-length hair in an attempt to seem more professional once she was in the D.C. office.

"No, not recently. I've had it short since I became FBI."

He nodded, put the photo back on the shelf, and continued to look at her belongings.

She was going to be in very close confines with this man in the weeks (months?) to come, having to pretend she was in love and deeply attracted to him. But something about having him looking at her personal stuff—even though it was things out on display—was unnerving.

"So, you were with your girlfriends, you and your short hair, in a bar in D.C., and I happened in."

She wrote the word *bar* down in her notebook. "Yes."

"I was alone, killing time before leaving to fly back to Michigan the next morning. We got to talking, and it went from there."

"Okay. What were you doing in D.C.?"

"Visiting my mom. She lives in Alexandria."

She wrote that down and then looked at him. "Does she really?" He nodded. "And you come to visit her often?"

"A couple times a year. I'll get the exact dates of my flights once I'm online. Second to last time was around five months ago, not too long after New Year's. The last time was two months ago, mid-March."

"So, we met in January. Kept in touch and then saw each other in March. Then married now, at the end of May." She wrote the dates down. "We can have flights added to old manifests, you know. Records created that have you visiting a few more times in that five-month period."

"Nah, let's not do that. Those visits can be corroborated by my mother. Any additional ones wouldn't be."

"Maybe you just came to see me, not your mother."

He tsked at her, a smile playing at the corners of his mouth. "Now what kind of son would that make me? Let's just stay with the two visits. In between, we Skyped like crazy."

Kelsey nodded, writing down *Skype*.

"Why didn't we invite her to our elopement, if you're such a dutiful son?"

"Ah, there we got lucky. She and her husband are on a three-month European cruise right now."

"That's convenient."

"Yes, it is. And hopefully this will be over by the time they get back, and she'll never have to know about my short-lived first marriage."

"Nobody from your hometown will tell her?"

He shrugged. "She's only in touch with my brothers in the U.P., and I'll tell them I want to tell her in person when she gets back."

"And what will you tell your brothers when we…split up?"

He sat on her couch, leaning forward, his elbows on his knees. The chambray shirt pulled tight across his shoulders, revealing a muscular back. "Well, it'll either be one of two things."

"Which are?"

"If we are successful, and it ends the way I hope it will, I'll tell them that I've begun a career with the DEA and my first assignment included being undercover as a married man. Then I'll pack my bags and head to Quantico to finish my training. And then to whatever field office I'm assigned to."

Kelsey was even more curious about what had happened four years ago with Huck and Prescott, and why he still wanted to be DEA, but she didn't ask. "And if it doesn't go that way?"

"Then you come back here, I tell my brothers you left me, that it was stupid to get married so quickly, which they'll no doubt already be thinking, and then I let some Yooper darling help me mend my broken heart."

"Yooper?"

"That's what people from the U.P. are called. U.P.ers... Yoopers."

"Ah," she said, wondering why she felt a bit irked at the idea of some Yooper *darling* comforting Kelsey's left-behind pretend husband.

"I thought Tarrington said your family is from the Copper Country?"

She took her suit jacket off, straightened it on the back of a chair, looked at Huck's tossed sport coat pointedly, and then sat down on the comfy upholstered chair next to the built-ins.

"They are. My mother was raised in Chassell. But she doesn't talk about it much. And certainly doesn't call herself a...Yooper."

"Blasphemy," he said.

"No. Just a woman who embraces her Westchester life."

"And denies her roots?" There was humor in his voice, but his eyes looked serious.

She shrugged. She wasn't about to get into her parents' relationship and her upbringing with Huck Beck.

Seemingly sensing he'd get no further with that topic, he rose and looked around the small room. "Okay if I look in the other rooms? Seems like I'd know this place if I'd been here on three occasions. Three memorable occasions for us to have gotten married."

She waved a hand for him to proceed and then rose to follow him into the kitchen. She wasn't much of a cook, and that was reflected in the neat, but Spartan, kitchen area. She ate most of her meals at her desk in her office, returning home usually after eight in the evening, getting in a quick run and then going to bed.

No wonder she'd had to be dragged to her friend's bachelorette party in order to meet a guy.

Which might have happened if she'd taken the time to make friends since moving to D.C. and beginning her tenure with the Bureau.

The only allowance to kitchen gadgetry was her state-of-the-art coffee maker, which, along with a seldom-used toaster, was the only thing taking up counter space.

"So, I didn't marry you for your cooking skills, eh?" Huck said after taking a quick peek into the bare refrigerator.

"I have other skills," she said. He raised a brow at her, and she felt a flush rising from her chest up her neck. Damn. That wasn't what she'd meant. "I can split an apple with my Glock a hundred yards away."

"Yeah, that's exactly why I came home with you the night we met," he said with a slow, deep chuckle.

"You *didn't* come home with me that first night."

"Oh yes I did."

"I would never have gone home with someone, or had them come to my place, on the night I met them."

"Exactly," he said as he brushed by her and exited the kitchen, heading down the hallway to her bathroom. "That's why I'm different from any other man you've been with. That's why you said yes to marrying me after only a few months." Just before he stepped into the bathroom, he looked at her and added, "With me, you break all your rules."

A weird chill ran through her, and she had a scary premonition that he might be right.

And that he hadn't even begun to break her rules.

Four

—⁓—

HER SHAMPOO SMELLED LIKE LEMONS. AFTER INHALING it, Huck handed the bottle, plus the conditioner, to Kelsey, who had followed him into her bathroom. "They're nice," he said. "Pack 'em."

She looked at the bottles he'd handed her with confusion on her face. He'd thrown her with that rule-breaking line, he could tell. Good. He had a feeling he'd need to keep her a little off-kilter for this thing to work. She was just too rigid otherwise.

He'd suspected it at the FBI offices, but when he saw her neat and tidy, nothing-out-of-place apartment, he knew he'd "married" a control freak. Possibly a neat freak, too, but the light coating of dust on the bookshelf in the living room made him suspect that she just wasn't in her apartment all that much.

He stepped out of the bathroom and across the hallway to her bedroom, sitting on the bed. She followed him in and seemed a little taken aback that he'd made himself at home so easily.

"We can keep talking while you pack," he said, taking in the room. Like her living room, it was sparsely furnished, but the pieces she did have (dresser, queen-sized bed, nightstand on one side only) seemed of good quality. No clothes draped over the one chair that sat in the corner of the room, fully visible only if the door was shut. No scads of jewelry, makeup, and scarves across the top of the dresser. Just one small jewelry box, the kind that a young girl might have. Huck suspected that if he lifted the lid, music would play and a little ballerina would spin around. It seemed out of place for this room. For her.

The comforter on the bed was a warm, deep green. Not masculine looking, but certainly not feminine, either. Not a ruffle in sight.

Kelsey Cameron was not at all like the girls he usually went for. But that might play in their favor as they tried to convince people that he'd fallen hard and fast and asked the woman to marry him.

Yes, they had a better chance of people believing that he'd fallen for Kelsey *because* she was so different than that competent, no-nonsense Kelsey had fallen so quickly for Huck Beck.

"So, we've got the logistics down. When, where, Skype and all that. Why did you say yes?" he asked as she pulled two suitcases, one large, one carry-on, from her closet and opened them on the bed next to him.

She looked at him for a second, her eyes running over his body, sending a shock of desire through him that surprised him.

"Why did you ask me?" she said, throwing his question back at him. She moved to the dresser and took out handfuls of undergarments and deposited them in the suitcase. Huck poked through them as she went back for another handful. White cotton bikini briefs and boy shorts. Not a color or thong to be seen. "Do you have any racier stuff? Stuff for date night? Because you'd probably bring that with you for your new husband."

She looked at him blankly and then down at the garments in her hands, also all white cotton. A small flush crept up her neck, barely visible because of the stiff collar of her light blue dress shirt. Huck instantly felt like shit. "You know what? Never mind. We need to stick as close as possible to who we are so we don't slip up. If this is what you normally wear, then that's what I've seen for five months and that's what I expect to see for our married life."

She nodded slightly, depositing the clothes in her suitcase, neatly arranging them along the bottom. She turned to the closet, but as she reached to start taking a blouse off a hanger, her hand dropped. Huck watched her back as she stood in front of the closet. Her hair in the back had many layers, the bottommost landing right at the collar of her shirt. Her body was lean and strong, but still had the hint of curves, which she seemingly tried to downplay with the severe cut of her slacks and blouse.

She expelled a sigh, and instead of reaching back into the closet, she moved to the dresser again and pulled open the bottom drawer, reaching deep inside to the back.

This time her hand was full of reds and blacks, and Huck couldn't keep the smile off his face as she dropped the bras and panties in the suitcase, covering the pile of white cotton underneath. "Shut up," she said, turning back to the closet and jerking several blouses from hangers.

"Didn't say a word," he said, taking the blouses as she flung them at him, folding them neatly before placing them in the suitcase, though he hated to cover up that red lacy bra.

Another blouse came his way, and then she stopped and turned to face him. "What do I need to bring? What's the weather like up there?"

He held the blouse in his hands and shrugged. "End of May in the Copper Country? Could need sweaters one day and a tank top the next. It's really unpredictable." He tossed the blouse he was holding back at her. "You don't need more of these. A few work blouses, slacks, and blazer is plenty. The rest of your stuff should be casual. If we're going to be working boats in Copper Harbor, it should be sweaters and sweatshirts, tees, cargo pants, and shorts."

"I don't have a lot of that," she said, moving down to the other end of her closet.

"Just bring what you have," he said. "You can always get what you need up there. Then you're sure to blend in."

"But isn't that the point? Shouldn't I be an oddity in a way? Huck Beck's mysterious new wife. Make people curious to meet me?"

"Yeah, I guess. But you still want to be comfortable and

appropriate to the situation."

She pulled out a few sweaters, laying them on the bed, and a couple pairs of jeans and cotton pants, and then went back to the dresser. Taking out several T-shirts and some shorts, she added them to the pile and then went back to the closet and knelt down to her shoes, all neatly stacked on a rack at the bottom of the closet.

Fingering the soft cotton of one of her shirts, Huck had an idea. "Where's your phone?" he asked.

"In my jacket pocket in the living room. Why?"

"Mine too. Stay here," he said, and then left the room. He gathered her phone from her suit jacket and his from the pocket of his sport coat, straightening it and placing it on the chair next to hers as he did.

When he came back into the bedroom, she was neatly folding the clothes she'd added into the suitcase. Most of it looked like workout gear. Huck saw a pair of sneakers and some sturdy sandals had been added, as well as a flimsy pair of flip-flops.

"Do you have any T-shirts big enough to fit me?" he asked. He wasn't of hulking height and breadth like his two older brothers, but he was wider in the shoulders than Kelsey and a few inches taller. At her questioning look, he added, "Like one you sleep in or run in or something?"

Her eyes went to the pillow at the top of her bed and Huck moved the few steps and reached out to remove the pillow. Beneath was a Harvard T-shirt and a pair of men's boxers. A second of irrational anger washed through Huck until he realized that the garments were what Kelsey slept in, not those of a boyfriend who stayed here often enough to leave his pajamas. "Yeah, this will work," he said, and cleared his throat, embarrassed by the zing of emotion that had rushed through him. But it did bring up a good point.

"Umm, is this arrangement going to cause you any difficulties with anyone?"

"What do you mean? My parents know what I do for a

living. I won't need to tell them I'm undercover or anything. They won't even need to know that I'm gone. It's not like I see them all that often."

"No, I meant like a boyfriend or…something."

"Or a girlfriend?"

He held his hands up in surrender. "None of my business."

"You're right. None of your business. But I'm straight. And uninvolved at the moment."

At the moment. Pushing that to the back of his brain, Huck picked up the Harvard shirt and held it up against his chest. Yeah, it would work. "Any others?" he asked as he set both phones on the bed and began unbuttoning his shirt.

"How many can you wear at once?" she asked, hands on her hips as she watched him. "And what's wrong with what you're wearing? Can you not arrive in the Copper Country looking like you just had a job interview? Would clean, pressed clothes raise too many questions?"

Well, yes, actually, it probably would, but Huck only gave her an eye roll and peeled off the blue shirt he wore, exposing the utilitarian white tee he wore underneath. "It's not to wear for the flight. It's to take some pictures with."

She looked at the phones on the bed and quickly caught on. Yeah, the FBI didn't usually hang on to dummies. "We can have the timestamps, the event dates, changed on our phones, so when we scroll through, it'll look like some happened when you were here in January, some in March."

"You guys can do that?"

"Of course," she said, somewhat indignant.

Huck threw his dress shirt on the chair in the room, then nodded toward the suitcase. "Got everything?"

"Just about," she said, and left the room, moving across the hall to the bathroom. She came back with assorted toiletries and a makeup bag, which she placed on the top of the folded clothes. "All set."

He was just about to close the bag when he stopped and

instead went to her closet. Rifling through her clothes, he found two dresses sandwiched between her numerous suits and her few remaining casual clothes. One was black and conservative with a high neck and long sleeves. Huck took it out and handed it to Kelsey. "My funeral dress," she said.

"Hopefully we won't be needing it, but bring it anyway," he said.

She nodded and then took a pair of black medium-heeled pumps from her shoe rack, adding both into the carry-on bag. Huck took the remaining dress from the closet: a red number with spaghetti straps and a plunging neckline. "This. This is what you were wearing the night we met."

"I forgot I even still had that," she said softly. There was something about the way she looked at the dress that made Huck want to ask her why she'd bought it. What occasion had she worn it to? With whom did she wear it, and had he slowly slid the straps down her shoulders as he…

Clearing his throat, he started to hand the dress to her, but at the last minute, slipped the silky garment off the hanger himself and placed it on the chair, partially on top of his blue shirt.

"Shoes to go with it?" he asked, and she didn't say anything as she eyed the dress on the chair, then dug to the farthest rung on her shoe rack and pulled out a pair of strappy sandals with a higher heel than anything else she had in her closet.

Still not as high as most of the girls Huck had been with wore. Certainly not Fuck Me shoes by any stretch, but he found them strangely enticing.

He zipped up the larger suitcase and the carry-on with the strappy sandals in them and then moved both bags into the hallway, out of sight. "Okay," he said, "let's make some magic."

She gave a small smile that Huck knew was anything but genuine, but at least she was trying.

He kicked off his loafers (which he'd had to find in the back of his own closet) and pulled back the comforter and sheets. Still wearing his khakis and socks, he crawled into the bed and grabbed his phone, setting hers on the bedside table. He took a picture of the chair with their strewn clothes on it, getting his legs and the bed in the foreground. "Next," he said, sitting up and stripping off his T-shirt so that he was naked from the chest up. He handed her phone to her, setting his on the table where hers had been. "Okay, get one of me sleeping," he said, plumping the pillows around so it looked like she'd been sleeping next to him and left the bed.

It was twilight in D.C., and there was just enough light streaming through the window that it could look like evening or early morning.

"Seriously?" she said, looking at him from where she stood at the side of the bed. "I'd take a picture of you sleeping?"

Huh. Wouldn't she? Girls he was sleeping with were always showing him shots they'd taken while he was asleep. "You're soooo adorable when you're sleeping," one had even said.

"Umm, well, not if that's not something you'd do normally," he said, not quite sure if Kelsey was the anomaly or the type of girls Huck hooked up with were.

From the look on her face, he was guessing that his experience was not normal. But then a look of indecision passed across her face, so odd because it looked so out of place on her. Yes, he'd only known her for a few hours, but she seemed so sure of herself that a fleeting second of "Is that what the cool kids are doing?" across her face stood out.

"It's fine," she said, and motioned with her fingers for him to lie down and pretend to sleep. It was almost like she was making the sign for a dog to roll over, and Huck wondered if the zing that again raced through his body had anything to do with the idea that maybe he liked being asked to do tricks by Kelsey Cameron.

Or maybe he just liked the feel of her bed. Burrowing his head into a pillow, he wrapped an arm up around his head as he typically did when he slept. The sheets smelled like her lemon shampoo, and he breathed deeply, taking in the scent.

"Got it," she said in a voice a little deeper than it had been. So maybe he wasn't the only one feeling the zings. That was probably bound to happen, and could be used to their benefit when they had to truly start acting like people so crazy about each other that they married after only five months and meeting in person on only three occasions.

But as helpful as mutual attraction might be, it could not fuck this up for Huck. He had too much riding on doing well and having Prescott let him back into the DEA Academy.

"Next?" she said, pulling him out of his pretend sleep and his thoughts that were just starting to turn to what the sheets might look and smell like after a night of…honeymooning.

"Got something other than an oversized tee that you could put on and join me in here?" he asked, trying to sound completely professional, with no trace of just how much he'd like to be in bed with her for real.

She studied him for a second, then gave a curt nod. Going back to the dresser, she pulled a thin cami out, then moved across the hall to the bathroom, shutting the door behind her. A few seconds later, she came back in wearing the soft pink cami, holding her shirt and bra (white, of course) in her hand. She placed them on the chair, then carefully slid in next to Huck as he held up the covers.

He tried not to notice her very noticeably hardening nipples clearly outlined against the thin cotton of her camisole top. Awkwardly, she moved into him as he held up his arm. "Okay, smile," he said, holding his phone out for a selfie of the two of them. He took the photo, then brought the phone down for them both to look at it.

Even with the lack of clothes, the photo looked too posed, too formal. Huck ran his hands through his hair a few times, messing it up. He momentarily regretted shaving around the outline of his goatee this morning, losing the four- or five-day scruff he usually sported. He'd wanted to make a good impression for Prescott, but now he wished he'd stayed with his regular look.

But mussed-up hair would have to do. He studied the photo

again. Yeah, Kelsey looked sexy as hell in her little cami, but she didn't look like she'd just spent the night in bed with him. She would have looked more…used. And he meant that in a good way. How to explain that to her, though?

He couldn't. Instead he said, "These aren't working."

"No?" she said, looking over his hand at the pictures.

"No," he said, not giving her a chance to look any longer. "It's our mouths."

"Our mouths?" she said, looking at his lips, licking her own.

Damn. That did it. "Yeah, our mouths," he said. "They need to look like we just spent the night using them. Using them a lot."

As her eyes widened and she licked her lips again, he didn't wait for her response, just bent his head down to hers and kissed her.

Yeah, he'd make those luscious lips of hers look used, even if it wasn't in all the ways he'd like to use them.

Five

―ᴥ―

HIS MOUTH WAS FIRM AGAINST HERS, BUT SHE WOULDN'T
say hard. And the whiskers of his goatee tickled her cheeks. She
tried to relax, hearing the shutter sound of the camera phone, but
she knew her jaw was tight and her eyes were closed maybe a little
too much. She probably looked like she was in pain.

"Relax," he said against her mouth. She tried to do as he
suggested, but it was difficult. She thought about the last time
she'd had a man in her bed and tensed even more.

"Kelsey," Huck said as he kissed her jaw line, the shutter still
sounding in her ears. Why had she not put her phone on silent?

"How many do we need?" she asked as she leaned her head
back, giving him access to her neck. Yeah, that felt good, she kind
of liked that, it felt like—

"Yeah, you're right. Probably only one or two good ones.
It's not like we're going to post them on Instagram or anything,"
Huck said as he pulled away from her, bringing the phone down
as he sat up against the headboard, basically dislodging Kelsey.
She rolled onto her back with not inconsiderable force. She tried
not to feel rejected, which would have been ridiculous.

"Yeah, there are a couple of good ones in here. That's good
for the bed shots. Let's take some in your living room. Cuddled
up on the couch kind of shit."

He was up off the bed and through the door before she'd fully
righted herself, grabbing his tee and blue shirt, and her Harvard

tee as he passed the chair.

"Speaking of Instagram," he said loudly from the living room as she rose from the bed and remade it. Correctly. "What do we do about social media? That could solidify our new status in a hurry, but I'm not on it."

"You're not? Not even Facebook?"

"No. Hate all that shit. But I suppose you—"

"Not on anything. It's strongly suggested we don't do any type of social media when we join the Bureau. I got rid of my Facebook account then. I'd never done much else." She didn't mention the several accounts that she had access to via the Bureau for monitoring other people. It wasn't like she wasn't on social media. She was just never on as Kelsey Cameron. Those closest to her knew it was because she was with the FBI and had hopes of being undercover one day. Those not close to her probably weren't trying to find her on Twitter anyway.

She'd been the proverbial bookworm all through school, though her parents had tried to get her to join activities as her older sisters had. But Kelsey wasn't a natural athlete (she'd prepared the hardest for the physical part of FBI training) and had much preferred reading a good book to being on the field hockey team. Still did prefer reading a good book to just about anything else.

"Okay, good. No major gaps in our online lives, then," Huck said from down the hall. She shut the bedroom door and changed out of her slacks, hung them up, and then pulled on a pair of jeans. She only owned two pairs, and had packed the other one.

She changed into a light sweater and then threw the cami in her suitcase in the hall as she made her way to the living room, where Huck was once again studying the photos on her shelves.

He'd pulled on his white tee, and when he heard her come in, he moved to the couch and sat down, lifting his arm for her to slide in just like he'd done in the bed.

"Wait," she said, "let me get one of just you first." She held out her hand and he gave her her phone, tucking his into the pocket of his khakis. Kelsey stepped back a few paces and lined up the shot. The twilight was moving quickly to dusk, and his blond hair, already with light brown streaks, seemed to turn darker before her eyes. She could only imagine the blinding, rugged beauty that he must be when the sun shone directly on him.

She tried to shove down her thoughts about how good looking (in a rough way that usually did nothing for Kelsey) Huck Beck was. But then she wondered if that wasn't perhaps a mistake—should she allow whatever physical attraction she had for him (and it had grown quite a bit in just the last hour!) to grow? Because at some point, she was going to have to conjure up some visible signs that she desired this man enough to not only marry him after only five months, but to follow him to some tiny place that she hadn't been to since she was a child and visited her grandparents.

She knew that allowing a real attraction would be fine. After all, she was the consummate professional. Real-life attraction was something altogether different from having her emotions engaged.

Yes, desperately wanting to tangle her fingers in his longish hair and desiring to lick that hard chest she'd just seen close up in her bed would not preclude her from easily packing her bags, shaking hands with Huck Beck, and leaving Houghton, the town Huck lived in, when the assignment was at an end.

"Smile like you love me," she said to him as she zoomed in on him. He gave her a steely-eyed look, parting his mouth a tiny bit and licking his lips like he might just eat her up. Oh yeah, that was good. She didn't think anybody—okay, any woman—in the Copper Country would wonder why she'd said yes to Huck Beck's hasty proposal.

Not if they didn't know the real Kelsey.

"Say 'Miranda rights,'" she said, and he laughed, which was her hope, and she got a few more pictures.

She scrolled through them as she went to the couch and finally sat in the crook of his arm.

Smoldering Huck was something to behold, and Kelsey knew she'd have no problem with allowing a real attraction to run free.

But a laughing Huck? Well, she'd need to keep a tighter rein there.

And was it her imagination, or did her body seem to fit more naturally into his arms than it had just moments ago in the bedroom? Did she notice the strength of him surrounding her a bit more intensely? Did the bristle of his beard against her cheek distract her from the clicks of the camera more than it had?

Yes, she might be a consummate professional, but that tight rein would definitely need to come into play.

They took a few more pics cuddled on the couch and then Huck changed into her Harvard tee while she went back to her room to put on a different top. They moved to the kitchen, where Huck found a mug and sat at the kitchen table, pretending to have a cup of coffee.

"A just-out-of-bed look," she said, setting up the shot with attention to detail so that it would look completely spontaneous.

"I stayed over that first night we met, grabbed your shirt from the floor when I woke up—"

"Well, it wouldn't have been on the floor, but go on."

"Yeah, I got the whole neat-freak thing. That might be a cute thing that we bicker over in front of people if we need it."

She nodded. He was good at this, thinking ahead, building an arsenal.

So why had he washed out of the DEA Academy?

Both the FBI and the DEA did their training in Quantico. Kelsey had no firsthand knowledge of what DEA agents-in-training went through, but her ego demanded that she surmise that FBI training was much harder.

"When you come into the kitchen, you find me having coffee. So maybe a candid shot, where I haven't seen you yet?" he said, tilting his head down, wrapping his hands around the coffee mug, instantly looking deep in thought.

Kelsey raised her phone and tapped, but stopped before taking the photo. "Wait, let me…" she said, taking the five steps from the doorway over to the small table and Huck.

"If we've just had a night of life-changing sex, you'd be a little bit… Here," she said as she ruffled his hair. It was surprisingly soft for how rough Huck looked.

What had she expected, straw?

He turned his head, allowing her to ruffle the other side, like a cat moving its body to be stroked.

The thought of stroking Huck Beck—anywhere and everywhere on his body—had Kelsey pulling her hand away. "Looks good," she said, turning back and returning to the doorway where she'd supposedly stumbled upon the man she fell in love with in one night.

"Okay, I come in, see the man whom I slept with on the night I met him—a first for me—and here you are, thinking deep and heavy thoughts about me."

He put his head down again, hands still on the mug, and Kelsey lined up the shot.

"And I hear the shutter from your phone, look up, and we… know it was more than just a one-night stand," he said, looking up from the mug at her and—God, how did he do that?—gave her a look that simultaneously said he wanted to eat her up and put a ring on it. Her hand trembled slightly, and she had to take a couple of pics to make sure she had the shot.

She brought the phone down and looked back at Huck. He had already transformed his expression from that of desperately-in-love suitor to uninterested coworker.

Well, he certainly wouldn't need to use any reins during this operation. The man could turn it on and off with the ease of a light switch.

"Okay, last one," he said. "Go to the counter and pretend you're making coffee or something. I'll get one of your back."

"My back?"

He shrugged. "Okay. Your ass."

"Hmmph. And I married you?" she said, but moved to the counter.

"Yeah, because I'm just that good," he said, to which she snorted.

She pretended to be turning on the coffee maker, waiting to hear the camera sound from Huck's phone, but she didn't. Maybe he'd finally put his phone on silent like she'd wished she had when they'd been in bed together.

"Umm...no," he said from behind her.

Looking over her shoulder, she said, "No? No what? It doesn't look like I'm really making coffee?"

"No. No, I wouldn't take this shot. Would you, umm, consider, umm..."

"What?" she said, tensing up. She knew going undercover demanded a high degree of realism, but she'd only been on this assignment all of four hours, and she hadn't quite worked herself up to... What? She wasn't really sure.

"Would you consider making coffee in just your panties? Or bra and panties? I'll close my eyes until you have your back to me if that—"

"No," she said before he'd even finished. There was building a believable cover, and then there was taking things too far. "We're not even sure people will ever look at our phones, see these photos and—"

"You're right. It's fine. We'll just go with what we have. I didn't mean to push."

He seemed genuinely contrite, and Kelsey took a mental step back.

Okay. Kelsey Soon-to-be-Beck just woke up from a one-night stand with someone she'd just met. A night she'd undertaken because she'd finally met a guy that she just couldn't stand *not* to sleep with on the night she met him.

They'd had a night that she'd never forget. A night so intense, passionate, and soul-stirring that she'd agreed to marry him after seeing him on only one other occasion.

Yes, that Kelsey would walk into the kitchen in just her panties and make coffee for the man who had just shattered her world...in a good way.

But she just couldn't. Not today, when she was feeling both

elated to finally be given an undercover assignment and shaken that she hadn't been given more time to properly prepare.

"I'll…just… Hang on," she said with exasperation in her voice, and left the kitchen.

"Kelsey, I didn't mean… If you're not—"

"Stay there," she shouted from the bedroom, where she did a quick change. Returning to the kitchen, she said to Huck, "This is what you get." To which he nodded, took his phone from the table, and waited for her to resume her position at the counter.

In a cami and her boy shorts, both white, she fiddled with the coffee maker, trying not to flinch at the shutter sound.

"Got it," he said, all business in his voice, her near nudity not affecting him in any way. Whereas for her, being this close to him and his…presence, in nothing but a few pieces of thin cotton, had her trying to remember the FBI credo just to bring her mind out of the gutter.

She walked out of the kitchen, trying not to pull down the hem of the cami that she knew rode up her back a little. She quickly re-dressed and was about to wheel her suitcases down the hallway when a thought struck her. She went to the tiny jewelry box that her father had given her for her sixth birthday. From the drawer under the false bottom (even at six, she had been fascinated with things like hiding places and detecting them), she pulled out a piece of paper that had been folded several times so that it would fit in the small space. She started to tuck the paper into the front zippered part of the larger suitcase, then put it back in the jewelry box and packed the whole thing. It would make sense that she'd want something so personal to her as she started her new life. She had just rolled the suitcases down the hall when her doorbell rang.

"Must be our information," Kelsey said, moving to the door, Huck joining her from the living room.

It was an agent Kelsey knew from the Bureau. Agent Evans had been in the D.C. office for just over a year and had always been polite to Kelsey, but they'd never really spoken much more than a few pleasantries when meeting in the elevator.

Which was how Kelsey was with most agents in her office. Being one of a small number of female agents in the office, Kelsey knew enough to keep the male agents at arm's length. She wanted no sniffs of impropriety attached to her name. Wanting to move up, and into undercover work, desperately, she was careful to do everything by the book, and that included little to no fraternization with her coworkers.

Yeah, that had been her plan starting out. And then it had turned to shit two years ago. Ever since then, she'd been adamant about keeping a distance from her coworkers.

After introducing Evans to Huck, the three of them went into the kitchen, where Evans handed a folder about a half-inch thick to Kelsey.

Placing it on the table, so that she and Huck could look at it simultaneously, she thanked Evans.

"Actually, I'm to also drive you to Dulles. They have you on the seven o'clock flight to Detroit. And then a midnight flight to Marquette."

"Marquette? Not Houghton?" she asked.

"I parked my truck in Marquette this morning. Early this morning. That's where I flew out of."

"Oh," she said, returning to the papers on her table.

"God," Huck said softly. "That seems like three days ago."

Kelsey had a sudden empathy for her new partner. Yes, this was all being thrown at her quickly too, but she was an agent with four years on the job. Huck, for all his instincts and knowledge, and some training four years ago, was a civilian. Kelsey would need to remember that and act as such. He was her responsibility to keep safe, in exchange for introductions. Her burden to bear for hopefully good intel.

"We need to leave now if you're going to make your flight," Evans said. "You can take that with you to study on the flight. Agent Cameron, I need to take your gun and badge."

"What?" Kelsey felt a moment of panic. She'd worked too hard for that badge to just hand it over.

"You can't take the gun on the plane without showing you're an agent. The D.C. to Detroit flight might not be a problem, but for the small flight to Marquette, you don't want to risk it. From what I understand, it's a small area, and word that an FBI agent was on a flight could get around. They don't want you flying privately for just that same reason."

"But what about once I'm there? I may need both."

Evans only nodded. "They will be returned to you once you are in place in Houghton."

Giving her gun and badge to Evans felt wrong, but Kelsey knew the protocol of being undercover, even if this was her first time doing it.

"Oh, I almost forgot," Evans said, digging into his pocket. He pulled out two gold bands. Wedding rings. Huck took the larger one and handed her the smaller one. No sliding it onto her finger as they gazed into each other's eyes. No vows. No kiss.

At least the ring fit, though already the sensation of it—the weight of it—felt foreign to her.

"Sorry, honey, couldn't afford an engagement ring," Huck said, winking at her. She didn't reply.

Evans took one of her suitcases and Huck the other as they started to leave her small apartment.

She looked around and made sure things were turned off, wondering when she'd next be in her home.

And if her life would be different when she returned.

Six

—ᴡᴡ—

"THEY STAYED PRETTY CLOSE TO THE TRUTH, WHICH is standard. Less to memorize. Less of a chance of messing up," Kelsey said from the passenger seat of Huck's beat-up Silverado. She had the light of her phone shining on the report they'd been given back at her apartment. They hadn't dared pull it out on their flights because they'd shared a row with another passenger on the Detroit flight. The flight to Marquette was on one of the puddle-jumpers and only had two seats across, but the aisle was so small, and their fellow passengers so close, that they kept the folder in Kelsey's bag until they got on the road.

The roads were bare, being the end of May, though that wasn't always a certainty in the U.P., and there wasn't much traffic this late on a Wednesday night (actually Thursday morning), so the two-hour drive from Marquette to Houghton would fly by.

Huck was thrilled as shit to be getting this second chance with Prescott, but he found as the miles flew past him that the closer he got to Houghton—and his new identity as a married man—the more concerned he became.

"Tell me again the names of your sisters," he said.

"JoAnn, Marnie, and Paula," Kelsey said.

"And that's what your sisters' real names are?"

"Yes," she said. "But remember, you haven't met them. Or my parents."

"So I married you in five months, but never met your family

in that time? Didn't ask your father for permission to marry you?"

She shot him a glance across the console of his truck that he couldn't quite read in the dark, the glow of her phone still pointed at the papers on her lap.

"No. Who would do that anyway?"

"I would," he said.

"Seriously?"

He shrugged. "Maybe not if I was eloping with his daughter and didn't think he'd approve of our marriage."

"Right. Exactly."

"And he wouldn't? Approve, that is?"

The light went out on her phone, and he drove in silence. He could tell she was silently trying out how to diplomatically tell him that no way in hell would her Westchester-residing bigwig engineer father approve of her marrying a scruffy, sporadically employed Yooper and then moving to the Copper Country.

"But that works in our favor. I came with you to Houghton in part because my family objected to our hasty marriage. That way no one's wondering why my family doesn't visit or why I'm not more in contact with them. They become a non-issue."

Which was true, but didn't exactly answer his question. But she didn't need to. Huck was surprised to find his hackles rose at the idea of her fictional father objecting to his fictional son-in-law.

File it away. Use it later. It was some of the training he'd received that had stayed with him the most: that every piece of information may play a role later. Remember everything because you never knew when you'd need any scrap of info. That went for feelings, too, especially when undercover.

It was like an Oscar-winning actor recalling a childhood tragedy to conjure up tears during a scene.

Which would be all too easy for Huck.

"And, you know," Kelsey said, pulling him from his thoughts, "if you don't remember something about my family, it can just be attributed to me not talking about them much. It's not like you've spent the last three Thanksgivings with them or anything."

"Right," he agreed, but he didn't want to have to fall back on any excuses. He'd study the file at home when they arrived and memorize everything about his new wife, before they properly hid it. Or disposed of it. Would they burn it? Would it self-destruct in ten seconds, á la *Mission: Impossible*? That would be fucking cool.

"And, of course, on your side it's easy. You're you," she said. "And I get to meet everybody as someone new, so I don't really have to memorize anything on your end."

"Right."

"Except…well, I'd ask, wouldn't I?"

"About?"

"Your family. Your mom lives in Virginia? That's how we met—you were in town visiting her, right?"

"Right."

"But you grew up in the U.P.?"

"Yeah. My mom moved out east about twelve years ago with a guy she met while he was vacationing in the Copper Country. They've since gotten married."

"Your dad still alive? They were divorced? Or…"

"Still alive. He…left the family when I was a kid. We haven't had much contact with him since."

"Oh. Sorry?"

He shrugged, his hands tightening on the wheel, trying not to give anything away in his body language, as he could tell she was looking at him. Studying him?

"It is what it is. I was seven, so I don't have a ton of memories of him being around."

"That's pretty young to lose a father, especially for a boy. Playing catch and all that male bonding."

"Yeah, well, I had two older brothers for that. One took over the father role, disciplinarian and all, one became my buddy. Kind of a good cop/bad cop thing. But they had their own lives too."

"Still. When was the last time you saw your father? Are you in touch?"

"Not anymore." He took a deep breath and let it out, telling his body to relax. Not so much because of Kelsey watching, but just so he wouldn't blow a nut thinking about it all again. "The last time I saw John Beck was four years ago. We have not stayed in touch since then."

"Four years ago?" she asked.

"Yes, why?"

"No reason," she said, but he could tell she was creating her own mental files for later recall. Color-coded with neat, tidy tabs for labeling, probably.

"And your brothers? Are they going to buy this relationship? If they're your father figures, are they going to be insinuating themselves into our lives and into this investigation?"

"We shouldn't have too much interference from my brothers as far as our...relationship."

"You show up with a wife out of nowhere and your brothers aren't going to question you about it?"

"Probably not much, no. I mean, they'll wish me well and everything, but..."

"Are you not very close with them?"

Huck had idolized his brothers when he was younger. Twain was seven years older and Sawyer eleven. After their father had left, Sawyer took over as the man of the house, even though he was headed to Tech shortly. Twain took it upon himself to keep the reins tight on Huck after that, but then Twain left for Tech too. Then he had gotten his girlfriend knocked up and had to drop out of school and marry her, all while Huck was still just in middle school.

And since then?

"They've had their own bad luck in the relationship department," he cautiously said to Kelsey. "I don't think they're going to be asking us about our first kiss, or how we *knew*, or whatever."

"Plus, they're guys," she said.

"That they are."

"And both single, I take it?"

"Yeah. Sawyer, he's the oldest, is a widower."

"Oh, I'm sorry."

"Thanks," Huck said, not looking over at his new partner. Wife. He really should start thinking of her as his wife. It would be just that much easier when they were in front of people. "Molly died about ten years ago. Car accident." It had been more than that, with Molly suffering from severe depression before her accident, but Huck felt it would be disloyal to tell Kelsey something that intimate about Sawyer.

But would he have told a real-life wife? A wife he'd only known for five months? Maybe. Probably. But he let it lie.

"Twain, he's the middle one. He and his wife Liv have been divorced for seven years. They have a son, Matty, who's fifteen. Matty's great," he added, not bothering to hide the affection that came out in his voice when speaking of his nephew.

"Proud uncle," Kelsey said.

Huck shrugged, taking a hand from the wheel and putting his elbow on the console between them. "He's a good kid. I try to spend as much time with him as I can. Which hasn't been a lot lately. I only got to one of his ski meets this year. I felt shitty about that."

"Neither of your brothers remarried?"

He chuckled. "No. Not even close. Sawyer has gone into full-on hermit mode, and Twain... Twain hasn't been a hermit, or a monk either, for that matter, but I don't think he's met anyone he's been interested in since he and Liv split up."

"And his wife, Liv, stayed in town? After the divorce?"

"Oh yeah, she's a born and bred Copper King—from Calumet—like we are. Though she lives in Houghton now too, like I do. Plus, she'd never take Matty away from Twain."

"Sawyer, Twain, and Huck?"

"Don't get me started—we've heard it all."

"Got it," she said, and stared out the window. Huck regretted saying that. He would have liked to hear Kelsey joke about the ludicrousness of his and his brothers' names. He was starting to suspect that his new wife was a little too serious and that it'd be fun to tease out her sense of humor.

But that wasn't the assignment. And he had too much at stake to risk blowing it just because he'd like to hear the sound of Kelsey Cameron's laugh.

"By the way," he said after fifteen minutes of silence, "this is Chassell, where your mother's from."

"Not much to it, is there?" she said, her face to the window, taking in the tiny town as Huck slowed down to make the thirty seconds it usually took to drive through stretch to a full minute.

"Nope, it's tiny. But it has its own charms. They host a huge Strawberry Festival every July that gets a big turnout. We'll have to go to that."

She turned to him sharply. "Do you still think we'll be on this assignment in July?"

"I have no idea. Do you?"

She looked down at the closed file folder in her lap, tracing her fingers along the top of it. "I'm not sure. It's a pretty elaborate setup, and they insisted on the marriage part of it really strongly. They must think it's worth all the trouble."

There was something she wasn't telling him. Looking behind him quickly and assuring there were no cars behind him, he swerved to the side of the road and put the truck in park. Turning to her, putting one hand on the steering wheel, and stretching one arm across the back of the bench seat, he said, "Okay, what about this whole thing aren't you telling me? If we're going to be partners, we need—"

"Nothing," she said. "At least nothing that I can pinpoint."

"Okay, what's your gut say?"

"The same thing I mentioned when we got to my apartment. That this whole thing seems off in a way."

"Right, but in what way?"

She shook her head, little wisps of her short hair catching glints of moonlight. "I don't know. I feel like I'm being tested somehow. I mean, Tarrington basically admitted that this was my chance to prove I could do undercover work. And it makes sense I'd get my first shot with a low-level case where I was just put in place as backup, and yet…"

"And yet?"

She looked at him, her brown eyes now catching the light, looking deep in thought. "It's just with Jenkins being involved, I have to wonder if I'm being set up for failure or something."

"Jenkins. The other guy with Tarrington?" he asked, although he knew exactly who Jenkins was. And he guessed he knew exactly the type of guy Jenkins was.

"Yes. We went through training together. Did our first two years together in the D.C. office. He hates me."

He was probably threatened by Kelsey. Huck could imagine his new wife showing up all the male agents in training. Some would be impressed, and some, guys like Jenkins, would be pissed. Still, it felt like more than that. Something she wasn't telling him.

"And now he's in the Midwest office? You don't have to deal with him much anymore?"

"Right. Which makes the fact that it's me doing this assignment more suspect."

"You don't buy the roots in the area angle?"

She waved her hand at the rear window and the general vicinity of Chassell behind them. "Yeah, 'cause I'm so 'invested in the area.' I didn't even know the town until you pointed it out. And it's not coming into play in our backstory at all."

He thought on that. "But it could. If people ask, we got to talking at the bar that night, you in your red dress, and it came up that your mom is from the Copper Country, same as me. And I took it from there."

"That's all you'd need?" A small smile started to form on her full mouth, but Huck wasn't sure if it wasn't meant to be a sneer.

"Hell, the red dress would have been enough for me. I'd just use the Yooper thing as a way to stay in your orbit."

That got a small chuckle from her, and he found himself mentally storing away the sound.

"Poor Huck. That's what people will say when you tell that story. Reeled in because of a slinky red dress, when it was the only thing in my closet even remotely sexy. A classic bait and switch." She turned back to the front, their discussion of their assignment possibly not being on the up-and-up apparently over.

He looked her over. Her jeans outlined her fit and toned body. The sweater wasn't exactly clingy, but it hinted at the curves underneath. Her short, spiky hair made it look like she'd been rolled around in the sheets as an active participant. That full mouth, which he had tasted ever so briefly a few hours ago in her apartment (in her bed!), glistened from her licking her lips.

He put the truck back into gear and pulled out onto US 41.

"I don't think anyone is going to be saying 'Poor Huck,'" he said very softly. He wasn't even sure he'd said it loud enough for her to hear, except he noticed her body stiffen and then her shoulders straighten.

When they pulled up to his house on the east side of Houghton, a lone light shone from a lamp in the living room. Twain had come through for him, though Huck had never imagined he wouldn't.

It was a small house built on the side of one of the numerous hills in the area. The outside looked a bit neglected, and Huck remembered he'd meant to paint it last summer but had been in Copper Harbor doing boat work so much that he hadn't gotten a chance.

He grabbed Kelsey's bags from the backseat and led her up the stairs, opening the door and standing back to allow her to enter first.

"Not locked?" she asked, turning to him in surprise. Her hand instinctively reached to the small of her back, most likely where she typically carried her gun.

"My brother came by earlier today to clean up a little. He would have left it unlocked for me." He didn't bother mentioning that he pretty much never locked his front door.

He didn't have anything worth stealing, there wasn't much

crime in the area, and Huck's house had become a kind of haven for buddies (and brothers) who didn't want to make the drive back to Copper Harbor, or even just to Calumet, after a day of working, or a night of drinking, in Houghton.

He'd have to get the word out that his place was no longer Crash Central. People would expect that of a newlywed.

But should he do that? Would it be better to have the transient workers that he befriended every summer still dropping by? Could they somehow help the case? Even though Huck still had a hard time believing that any of the hardworking, tourist-serving people that he worked with could ever be involved in something like bringing in Sudafed from Canada, he knew the FBI and DEA wouldn't join together just for the fun of it. So he had to keep an open (and suspicious) mind about everyone with whom he came in contact.

He'd talk to Kelsey in the morning about it—keeping his house open to all comers. For now, he was exhausted. His life had changed yesterday when Prescott had called him out of the blue and asked him to come to D.C. the next morning. He hadn't slept much last night thinking about what Prescott wanted, and today had been long and draining.

"Mind if we just hit the hay and get up to speed tomorrow?" he asked Kelsey, who was walking through the small rooms of his downstairs area, checking everything out.

She joined him in the kitchen. "That's fine. I'm pretty beat, too."

He started to pick up her bag again, intending to bring it up to the guest bedroom, when he saw a note on the kitchen table.

Dinner at Liv's place tomorrow at six. NO EXCUSES!! - T

"I'm taking it T is Twain?" she asked, reading over his shoulder. She would have had to stand on her tiptoes to do it.

"Yeah. Something's up with them. Liv was with him when I called, and now he's having us go to dinner at her house?"

"Maybe it's just more convenient for them all?"

"Maybe," Huck said, though he doubted it.

"Well, it will be good to get that out of the way—meeting the family and telling them we're married. Then we can concentrate on Copper Harbor."

Huck wasn't naive enough to think that one dinner with his brother and Twain's ex-wife would be all it took, but it probably was best to tackle them first. Then Huck could go find Sawyer, either at one of the houses he flipped or at the glass house he'd built past Copper Harbor, and let his older brother know that Huck was now a married man.

"Yeah," Huck said. "Let's get the Bad Luck Beck Brothers out of the way first."

Seven

—w—

"COME IN, COME IN," A PRETTY BLOND WOMAN SAID TO Kelsey as she waved her into the house on the opposite side of Houghton from Huck's.

"Thanks," Kelsey said, stepping past the woman, shorter than Kelsey and around thirty-five.

"Kelsey, Liv. Liv, Kelsey," Huck said as he entered the foyer behind her. Kelsey stuck her hand out to shake Liv's, but the other woman instead placed her arms around Kelsey and gave her a gentle squeeze.

"It's really, really nice to have you here, Kelsey," she said. She looked Kelsey up and down, not in an assessing way like Kelsey would do as an investigator, but in almost an "I can't believe it" kind of way.

Liv then moved to Huck and gave him a longer hug, which Huck returned, kissing his ex-sister-in-law on the cheek. "And you!" she exclaimed, pushing Huck on the chest once he'd let her go. "Where have you been hiding yourself? I feel like it's been months since I've seen you."

"Yeah, it probably has been. Sorry, Liv," Huck said. Kelsey was shocked to see what looked like a blush creep up rough-and-tumble Huck Beck's face. The blond—with just a hint of gray—goatee hid most of the flush, but he looked embarrassed that he hadn't been around to see Liv. He then looked at Kelsey out of the corner of his eye. "But you can see why I haven't been around much," he said, the blush now fully visible as he motioned toward Kelsey.

Wow. The man could blush on cue. Having a civilian as a partner in this undercover assignment might not be as detrimental as she'd thought. Huck Beck might be good. He'd have to be to get a second chance.

"Huck," said a large—very large—man as he came from down a long hallway. It must be Twain Beck, but he looked very different from his younger brother.

Huck was a couple of inches taller than Kelsey's five-ten and had a broad and strong physique, but his older brother was at least six-two, with probably fifty or sixty pounds on Huck, all of it muscle. His shoulders were huge, and where Huck was blond with blue/gray eyes, Twain's hair was nearly black and he had pure green eyes.

He shook hands with Huck in a clasp that turned to a half hug, which then turned to a full hug on Twain's part. "It's good to see you," Twain said when they parted. "It's been too long. You'd never know we live in the same town."

"I know. I'm sorry I've been so out of touch lately. Been a lot going on."

Again, Huck motioned to Kelsey and gave introductions to his brother Twain. Kelsey was not a small woman, but her hand was engulfed by the large man's as they shook.

"Kelsey, really great to meet you," he said, and Kelsey returned the sentiment. She'd noticed Huck hadn't mentioned her last name, her maiden name, at all during the introductions.

They hadn't discussed how Huck would tell his brother that he'd married Kelsey after only knowing her five months. After she'd woken up late that morning, she'd found Huck in the kitchen scouring the folder they'd been given yesterday by Evans, with a yellow legal pad by its side.

He'd shown Kelsey the list of people he'd worked for in Copper Harbor in the past, and a list of others that he knew about, but hadn't worked with. They'd discussed whom he should contact about possible work, and he'd made several phone calls while she sat at the kitchen table with him.

Again, she was impressed with his ability to think on his feet and how easily a lie rolled off his tongue.

She'd have to remember that.

But now, faced with this behemoth of a man and his ex-wife, both looking at Kelsey like she was a Martian, she wished she and Huck had taken some of the day to synchronize the way he planned to tell his brother that there was a new Beck in town.

"So, Kelsey, where are you from?" Twain asked at the same time that Liv motioned them into the living room.

"Originally Westchester, New York," she said, sticking with the cover given her, "but now I live in the D.C. area."

"And how did you two meet?"

Kelsey was stopped from answering by the front door opening and the entrance of a woman of about Kelsey's age and a man who could only be Twain Beck's brother, so much did they look alike. A beautiful, but older, golden retriever followed the couple in, then made for a corner in the foyer like she owned the place. She flopped down, looking up at Kelsey with disinterest, a soft bark directed at Huck.

"Hi, Lucy girl," Huck said to the dog, who thumped her tail against the floor a couple of times, then laid her head on her paws, looking tired.

So, Huck was the baby by several years, and looked totally different than his brothers. Not that those facts necessarily meant anything, but still, Kelsey filed the information away.

"Sorry to barge right in," the woman said, and Liv waved her statement away.

"No need to knock. Huck just beat you guys here. Well, Huck and Kelsey."

Another round of introductions, but this time Huck was meeting the other woman for the first time as well.

And seemed as much surprised to be meeting her as Sawyer seemed to be meeting Kelsey.

Her name was Deni Casparich, but again Huck only gave Kelsey's first name during the introductions.

Once again, Liv herded them all into the living room and took drink orders. Everyone was having a beer, and when Liv looked at Kelsey expectantly, Kelsey figured she'd just go along and have a beer, even though she hated the stuff.

"Kelsey's not a beer drinker," Huck said, rising to join Liv. "I'll find her something."

Huck and Liv moved into the kitchen, which was around a corner, but still open enough that she could hear Liv whisper to Huck, "Okay, loverboy, spill." Huck must have done something (a gesture? a face? Kelsey was dying to know) because Liv only giggled and whispered, "Oh, Huck. I've missed you."

Twain rolled his eyes and shrugged toward Kelsey, apologizing that they could all hear his ex-wife ask about Kelsey.

"You have to understand," Twain said to her, "you're kind of a novelty."

Okay. Time to slip into the role. Be the woman for whom womanizing Huck Beck would tame his wicked ways.

"Is that right? I kind of got the impression you would have met hundreds of women. Or has Huck greatly exaggerated his reputation? Yeah, that seems more likely." She smiled to let them know she was teasing, hoping it didn't seem forced.

"Oh, I don't know if it was exaggerated or not," Sawyer answered, "but I think Twain meant more of the fact that he'd never brought anyone around to meet the family before."

"Is that right?" she said, puffing up a little, as if she liked that fact. And in a way she did, until she remembered that he wouldn't have brought Kelsey to meet his family either, if it hadn't been part of an assignment.

"She lives in D.C.," Twain filled in for Sawyer and Deni, who were sitting on a large couch. "That's about as far as we got before you guys arrived."

"Yes, and that's as far as we'll get until I get some answers myself," Huck said as he and Liv came back into the room, handing out beer bottles to the others. Huck handed her a tall glass with ice and a clear liquid. "Vodka tonic," he said, naming her drink of choice. "Liv didn't have any limes, but had one of those squeezy bottles of lime juice, so I shot some in. Hope it's okay."

"I'm sure it's fine," Kelsey said, hiding her surprise that Huck knew her drink by taking a good-size sip. She nodded at him. "It's good."

"Sorry for the no limes," Liv said. "I'm kind of shocked I even had vodka and tonic in the house. We're all pretty much beer drinkers, though lately I've been able to occasionally talk Deni into having a glass of wine with me."

"Yes, let's get to that, shall we?" Huck said as he settled into the loveseat next to Kelsey. Twain sat in a large overstuffed chair, and Liv sat on the arm of it. Twain reached out and wrapped an arm around Liv's hip. The move looked natural, comfortable, and like it happened all the time.

"And that," Huck said, pointing at Twain's hand around his ex-wife. "Let's talk about that too. Seems like I've missed a lot the last few months."

"You sure did," Sawyer said, and shared a look with Deni that Kelsey tried to memorize so that she could look at Huck in such a way. "You need to keep in closer touch, bro. I know you went to visit Mom a couple of times, but…"

"I did. She's doing well. She and Gary are on a cruise for the summer right now. She was pretty geeked about that." Both of Huck's brothers nodded, either already knowing their mother was on a cruise, or agreeing with the decision to take one.

"Well, in a nutshell, I met Deni at the office and—"

"What office?" Huck interrupted.

"My office. The Summers and Beck offices. Deni's an engineer there." To Kelsey he added, "It's an engineering firm here in Houghton. I own it with my buddy Andy Summers."

"Huck mentioned something about that," she said noncommittally. Because she was quite certain that Huck had not mentioned that Sawyer owned an engineering firm.

For some reason, she had gotten the impression (incorrectly, it seemed) that the Beck brothers were more of the aimless variety. That widowerhood and divorce had made them both… Well, she didn't know what. But certainly not the men she saw before her, who both seemed really happy and very hale and hearty. No one was wasting away of a broken heart, that was for sure.

"You're back in the office?" Huck asked, and Kelsey remembered the word "hermit" being used when he'd briefly talked about Sawyer.

"Yep. Full time now. Part time when Deni and I met."

"And you're…together?" Huck said, pointing from Sawyer to Deni, even though an idiot could tell the couple was more than together. They were in love. And they weren't the only ones.

"Okay, that's great," Huck said. He shook his head a couple of times, and then a wide, genuine smile crossed his face, making Kelsey almost gasp with the rugged beauty of him. "That's great, Sawyer. So great," he said, smiling at his brother first and then at the woman who apparently had pulled Sawyer from Hermitville.

"Wow," Deni said from the couch. She looked at Liv. "I see what you meant about Huck. About all of them in the same room."

Liv nodded. "I know, right?"

Both women looked at Kelsey like she was in on their joke.

"A couple of months ago, I was telling Deni that there was nothing like it when the three Beck brothers were in a room together and all had their…wattage turned up."

Maybe it was because Kelsey had always been a woman in a very male-dominated environment. And not just any males, but alpha, take-no-prisoners sorts of guys. So she didn't think that wattage of any kind would affect her. She got that the Becks were good-looking guys, and that the sheer size of Twain, and to a lesser degree Sawyer, and the sexiness of them all, especially Huck, and the— Yeah, okay, she got it.

She nodded back to Liv and all three of the women shared a

laugh, which seemed to set the men more at ease.

Kelsey understood she'd need to get the women on her side if she was to be accepted into the Beck family. Even if it was for only the duration of this case. Liv was a local, Huck had said, and every contact could help lead to more contacts.

"Okay, great. So Sawyer is back amongst the land of the living and…with one Deni Casparich," Huck summarized.

"Crazy in love with one Deni Casparich," Sawyer clarified, and earned an adoring look from Deni. Another look that Kelsey tucked away to be stored in her arsenal.

She was a student of human nature. It had helped her become one of the top analysts in the D.C. office. But these were looks that Kelsey had only observed in others, never given or received herself.

"Crazy in love. Got it," Huck continued. He then shifted his gaze to Twain and Liv. "And what exactly is going on here?" He pointed again to Twain's hand resting possessively on Liv's hip.

Liv looked down at Twain, and a silent look passed between them. Twain cleared his throat and said, "Beck brother number two who is crazy in love with his woman."

Kelsey felt Huck stiffen next to her for just a second before he relaxed. "Yeah, is that right?" he said, but not with the same excitement he'd had when speaking with Sawyer and Deni. He then looked at Liv. "How do you feel about that?" Huck asked her.

Instinctively, Kelsey reached over and put her hand over Huck's, which rested on his knee. He turned his over to hold on to hers. The motion was not lost on the others in the room, which had been Kelsey's intention. Show concern when her husband showed concern.

"I couldn't be happier," Liv said to Huck. He studied her for a while, and Kelsey sensed that there was a bond between Huck and his former sister-in-law that had remained even after Twain and Liv's divorce. "Really, Huck, Twain and I are good. Really, really good."

Huck slowly nodded, looking from Liv to Twain and back again. Kelsey squeezed his hand, and he leaned his body into hers.

"And," Twain said, "not only are Liv and I back together. But the real reason we wanted you all here tonight—besides getting to meet you, of course, Kelsey—was to let you know…" He looked at Liv, who was gazing at him. Then they both looked at the group and said at the same time, "We're having a baby."

Sawyer and Huck were silent, causing Kelsey to look at Deni, hoping for a cue on how to react to the news. Deni seemed stunned for a second, but recovered sooner than Sawyer next to her. "That's wonderful," she said, getting up from the couch and going over to hug Liv.

"We think so," Liv said, hugging Deni back.

"What? No brotherly love?" Twain directed at Sawyer and Huck.

"I'm just…it's just…" Huck said, hanging on to Kelsey's hand.

Twain rose from the chair and sidestepped a still-hugging Deni and Liv. He stood in front of Kelsey and Huck, his huge body eclipsing them. Huck stood up and put a finger in his big— and much bigger—brother's chest. "If you hurt her again…" he whispered so that Liv couldn't hear, though Kelsey could.

"It's not like that. It's different this time. We're different," Twain said, not as quietly.

Kelsey watched as the brothers had a staring match, wondering if her first official act in this assignment would be to break up a fight. After a long, tense moment, Liv broke away from Deni and placed a hand on Huck's arm. "It's okay, Huck. He's right. We were trying for this baby. We wanted it. Desperately."

Twain held up his arm and Liv slid in underneath, reminding Kelsey of the movement Huck had made yesterday in her bedroom and living room so that they could take pictures together.

Pictures of a false relationship. Which was all part of the job. But when placed into a situation with all of this real emotion, real-life stuff happening with hermits coming out of their caves for love, divorced couples getting a second chance, and a new baby... Kelsey felt a little crappy for the next bombshell that would be dropped in Liv's living room.

Huck apparently finally saw what was obvious to Kelsey—that Twain and Liv were deeply in love and ecstatic about having a baby. He hugged Liv, Liv putting her arms around Huck in a motherly, protective way that warmed Kelsey. So, Liv had looked after Huck after the mom had moved out east with her boyfriend. She seemed a warm and nurturing sort. Her home was soft and lived in, with lots of homemade things around and great knit throws on every piece of furniture.

Sawyer and Deni joined in with the hugs, and Kelsey stood too, not wanting to be the only one sitting. Lots of back slapping between the brothers, but Kelsey could see the strong emotion that they tried to hide in front of their women.

"Well, I'm not sure I can top Sawyer being in love and at work, and Twain and Liv getting back together with a baby on the way," Huck said, "but I'll give it a try."

Sawyer and Twain exchanged glances, and Kelsey thought she read a "How did the kid fuck up this time?" look, which Huck thankfully didn't see because he was looking at Kelsey. Slipping an arm around her shoulder, he said, "You all met Kelsey, but I didn't properly introduce her."

"Yeah, I don't think I even caught your last name," Deni said to Kelsey.

"Then let me remedy that right now," Huck said. He squeezed Kelsey's shoulder, and she put on her best "I'm in love with this man, and am soooo happy to be by his side" adoring gaze. "I'm happy to say that I'm Beck brother number three in love with his woman. And in my case, not only my woman, but...my wife. May I introduce you to Kelsey Beck."

Eight

—m—

"SO, YOU'RE GOING TO BE A BIG BROTHER, EH?" HUCK said to his nephew Matty later that evening.

They were in Matty's room, Huck lying on the bed, his arms behind his head, staring up at the ceiling, his nephew straddling the chair at his desk, facing Huck.

"Yeah, I guess," Matty said.

Matt. He'd informed Huck that he went by Matt now. Sheesh, you go to D.C. a few times to fall in love and get married and your nephew grows up behind your back.

"I always wanted to be a big brother," Huck said.

"Yeah?"

"Yeah. I thought I could do it so much better than those assholes who were mine," he said, eliciting the laugh from Matt that he was going for.

The room hadn't changed much since Huck had been in it last, right around Christmastime. But it seemed that his nephew had. Seemed like he'd grown two inches, too, looking more and more like his father.

Like a Beck.

"But seriously," Huck said, careful to keep his eyes looking up and not at Matt. "How are you feeling about it all?"

He felt, more than saw, Matt's shrug of feigned indifference. "It's fine. Whatever."

"It'll be good to have your dad back in the house, right?"

"I guess. Although he's never lived here before, so it's kind of weird. I have to show him where stuff is…things like that."

"Yeah, that would be weird."

"But my mom's really happy, so…"

"Right."

"When they told me they were getting back together, for a second I felt, I don't know, like a little kid or something. Like I'd gotten everything I'd wished for on every birthday cake candle, you know?" He spun around in his chair, facing his desk. Huck knew it was hard for any fifteen-year-old boy to talk about his feelings. When you threw in the Beck genes…even harder.

But Huck had always had a strong bond with Matt. Since Huck was only thirteen when Matt had been born, Matt almost felt more like a younger brother than a nephew.

"You know, I was only a year older than you when your Grandma Cathy met Gary and moved to Virginia."

"Really?"

"Yeah. She wanted me to go with her, but I wanted to stay here and finish high school at Calumet."

"Yeah, I would too."

"But it was weird for me, to see my mom, being so happy about a guy. It'd been a long time since my dad had left and I just… I was the only kid still at home…"

"It wasn't so much that Mom was…with a guy. I mean, she dated Kevin for a long time. It was that it was my dad."

"But that should be better, right?" Huck knew that there were the usual father/son fights between Twain and Matt, even more so as Matt became a teen and started to become his own person. But he'd seen them together, especially in the woods, and there was no denying the love they felt for each other. There was a serious case of hero worship on Matt's part toward Twain.

"I guess." The chair twirled as Matt's feet padded along the floor in a circle. "I mean, I just knew Kevin would never break her heart. That even if they broke up, she'd be okay. But with my dad…"

"I get it," Huck said. And he did. "Granted, I've only shared one dinner with them—you missed a great lasagna, by the way—but they seem pretty solid." He didn't want to say to Twain's son that it seemed to Huck that Twain was finally deeply in love with his wife.

"They are, I'm pretty sure," Matt said.

"And the baby?"

"Yeah, it's okay, I guess. My mom's pretty excited about it. So's my dad."

"When my mom left with Gary, things were kind of weird. I got to stay in the house until I graduated. Your Aunt Molly was still alive. Do you remember her much?"

"A little bit."

"Well, she and your mom took turns bringing food and stuff to the house, making sure I had what I needed, that I got to school."

"I don't remember that."

"You would have been around three or four. You guys were in that apartment in Houghton. Sawyer and Molly were in Houghton too. Molly started...not feeling well; didn't go out as much. But your mom? Even with a three-year-old, she'd come up to Calumet at least three or four times a week and bring me dinners and lunches, do my laundry, clean the house. Lots of time she'd bring me stuff from your grandparents' restaurant."

Nothing from Matt, so Huck continued. "I guess what I'm saying is...I don't know any woman alive who was born to be a mother more than Liv. It's been in her since I've known her. And that she wants another child, even when she's got the world's greatest kid already, does not surprise me. That woman's got so much love to give. There is plenty to go around."

"I'm not worried about that. Is that what you think? That I'm jealous of a little baby that isn't even born yet? Is that why they sent you in here to talk to me?"

Huck sat up on the bed, swinging his legs over to the side and resting his elbows on them. "Nobody sent me in here. Shit,

Matt, how many times have I hung out in here with you after your mother fed me?"

"A lot," Matt conceded.

"Exactly. I'm just following habit here. Thought you might want to talk about all the changes happening."

"Like you getting married?"

"Yeah, that's one of 'em, for sure."

Matt nodded at that, looking away, and Huck wondered if it wasn't Huck and Kelsey's whirlwind romance that he was thinking about.

"How about you? Anybody special?" he asked his nephew, dreading the answer. Hell, Huck had lost his virginity at fourteen, but it was different with Matty. Wasn't it?

"There's this girl. But she's got me in the friend zone."

"Ouch. That's a tough zone to get out of," said the man who'd never in his life been put in the friend zone by a girl.

"Yeah. Plus she's kind of hanging out with this other guy."

"Double ouch."

"Yeah. Sucks to be me right now."

"Maybe," Huck said. "But the operative words are 'right now.' You never know what can happen. Look at your parents. Look at me."

"So you're saying five months from now I could be married to someone I just met, or having a baby?" Matt said, giving Huck a grin.

"Bite your tongue," Huck said, laughing with his nephew.

"You got that right."

"You've had the safe sex talk with your dad, I'm assuming?"

"Yeah. Not that I've needed it. Yet."

"Well, you know you can always talk to me about that shit too, right? If you ever need condoms but don't want to be seen buying them, stuff like that."

"I know. Thanks, Uncle Huck."

"Anytime, buddy."

"Matt? Huck? Are you guys down here?" Kelsey called from

the hallway.

"In here," Matt said. The door opened, and Kelsey stepped in.

"I was sent to collect you both for dessert."

"What are we having?" Matt said as Huck rose from sitting on the bed behind him.

"I think your mom said it was Stormy Sunday or something like that?"

"Rainy Day Sundae," both Huck and Matt said, and then fist-bumped each other.

"A good one, I take it?" she asked as she backed out of the doorway and walked down the hallway.

"The best," Matt said, walking past her, his long legs eating up the yardage. Just as she approached the opening into the living room, Huck caught up to her and clasped her hand in his.

KELSEY TURNED TO HIM, caught by surprise, and he smiled at her in a way that said he would be happy to skip dessert—fabulous or not—and hustle her home for a sweet treat of their own.

She knew it was for his family's benefit. Her peripheral vision (tops in her training class!) let her know that at least one of those giant brothers was in the living room facing in their direction.

"Eat fast," he said to her in a fake whisper that could surely be heard by his brother.

"I don't know," she said, trying to put a flirting tease in her voice that had never come naturally to her, "this sundae thing sounds pretty good. Sure you can compete with it?"

He released her hand and slid it along her waist, pulling her into his chest. "Oh, Kels, you *know* I not only can compete, but can win."

She giggled. It sounded foreign to her, but was actually natural. She just didn't get all that many chances to giggle in her line of work.

And pretty much all she did was work.

"Uh, I'd say get a room, but I'm fresh in love myself, so I'm a bit more sympathetic," Twain said to them.

They pretended like they had just noticed Twain, and she looked embarrassed while Huck looked cocky. Following the big man into the kitchen, they joined the rest of the group at the large wooden table, leaves in for what Kelsey guessed was full expansion.

"Kelsey, no allergy to peanuts, I hope," Liv asked as she dished out pieces of an ice-cream-cake-looking thing from a pan.

"No. No food allergies at all."

"And certainly none to ice cream. She loves the stuff," Huck said, sitting down next to her and taking his own dish from Liv.

"I do," she admitted, trying to remember if she'd mentioned that to Huck when they'd talked about their likes and dislikes on the flight yesterday. She was pretty sure she hadn't.

The dessert had an Oreo crust, vanilla ice cream, and a topping of a hard caramel-chocolate mixture with Spanish peanuts embedded in it. "Oh my God," she said after the first bite. "This is amazing."

Liv beamed. "I'll get you the recipe. It's really easy."

"Kelsey's not much of a kitchen person," Huck said. "At least that's not why I married her," he added with a wink to his brothers, who rolled their eyes at him but shared smiles as well.

"I might spend more time in the kitchen if this was the result," Kelsey said, taking another bite of the cold, dreamy confection.

"What will you be looking for as far as work up here?" Deni asked.

They had been asked the basic questions over dinner. How they had met. Where Kelsey was from, her family, what she did for a living. She'd given them the facts from the dossier they'd been provided, with Huck throwing in a few answers to show he knew oh so much about his new bride.

"I can't think of too many places up here large enough that they'd need a dedicated office manager with your background."

They'd told them that Kelsey had been an office manager for one of the political consulting firms in D.C. That they'd given her a year off so that she could join her husband in his hometown until they figured out where they wanted to settle down.

"Maybe the mill," Twain said. "I can ask if you want."

"That would be great," she said, though she had no intention of working in a mill, unless said mill was in Copper Harbor, where she'd be focusing her efforts.

Assuming she was ever actively used on this case and not just left in the wings as backup.

"We're going to head up to the Harbor in a day or two," Huck said to Twain. "See if I can't get on with a boat. Maybe Kelsey will find something up there, too."

"You don't think it's time to find something a bit more permanent?" Sawyer asked. A fair question posed to a twenty-eight-year-old man who had just acquired a new wife, but Kelsey felt Huck tense at her side. "Something with year-round stability?" Sawyer added.

"It might be a good idea," Twain added, cautiously.

Twain, the middle son, the peacemaker, Kelsey surmised.

She smoothed a hand down Huck's arm. "We gave ourselves the summer to just have fun, work a little in this Copper Harbor that Huck's always talking about. Call it our honeymoon. In the fall, we'll start looking for real jobs—isn't that right, babe?" Her hand moved up his arm, feeling the tightness of his muscles underneath his sweatshirt, to the back of his neck, where she weaved her fingers in his longish hair, tucked back behind his ears.

She didn't have to, she knew. They could have been a couple that kept their hands to themselves around family. Kelsey didn't allow herself to examine too closely why Kelsey Beck was the type of person who wanted to touch her husband in front of others.

A lot.

"So, thanks for the offer, Twain. Can you hold off on talking with anyone at the mill until fall?" she said, sending her brother-in-law a grateful smile.

"Of course," he said, smiling back. A small, silent pact was made between them. She would help him keep the peace amongst the brothers if needed.

But she wouldn't be around for long. And Twain, and all of these really nice people at the table with her, would either hate her for breaking their Huck's heart or blame him for messing up badly enough to marry a woman he barely knew only to lose her months later.

"I think that sounds wonderful—spending the summer in the Harbor," Liv said.

"I'm looking forward to it," Kelsey said, giving Huck's hair a playful tug before returning her hand to hold the bowl so she could scoop every melted drop of the dessert onto her spoon.

There was some murmuring at the end of the table where Deni and Sawyer sat, with Sawyer eventually saying "Fine" to Deni a little louder than he'd probably intended.

"Huck, you know Sawyer's place up past Copper Harbor, right? I'm assuming you helped build it with him?" Deni asked.

"Yes, I know it. It's been a while since I've been there."

"Well, why don't you and Kelsey stay there for a couple of weeks until you figure out where you'll be working and if you want to commute back to Houghton or not?"

Huck studied Sawyer, who gave a reluctant nod.

"That's okay. We can just make the drive."

Sawyer and Huck seemed happy with that outcome and returned to their desserts.

"That's crazy," Deni said, more to Kelsey than to Huck. "It's pretty much roughing it—outside john and all, no refrigerator, which in the winter isn't a problem. So you'd have to eat most of your meals in the Harbor. But the sauna is amazing."

"They're not going to want to do that every day," Sawyer said to Deni. "I can't see Kelsey wanting to use an outside john."

Which was totally true, but Kelsey wondered if she should be offended.

"But the view...the view is worth going to the biffy," Deni said.

"Thanks for the offer," Huck said, "But I really think that

we'll make the drive until we figure out what we're doing."

Sawyer nodded, like that was the logical thing to do, which it was. But it was probably what made Huck perversely say, "But you know, it might be fun for a couple of nights. You're sure you guys don't want to use it?"

The look that Sawyer gave Deni told Kelsey just exactly what the couple had used the cottage for. The sly smile from Sawyer, the dreamy look from Deni.

"Yeah, we don't want to be there if you guys would use it," Kelsey said.

"We won't be," Deni said. "We can't get up there this week or weekend because we're heading to Munising on Thursday for a job. And when we're done next week, we're going on to Farmington Hills so Sawyer can meet my mom and brothers."

"Ooh, meeting the family," Twain teased Sawyer, who took it good-naturedly. "Moving pretty fast."

"Not fast enough," Sawyer said to Deni, who gave him a warning look, but then softened. "Besides, nobody moves as fast as Huck," Sawyer added. "Have you told Mom yet?" he asked Huck.

"Not yet. She's on that cruise with Gary, and I really wanted to tell her in person. Have her meet Kelsey. We'll head to D.C. as soon as they're back. So I'd appreciate you guys not mentioning it if she emails or calls you from the cruise or anything."

"No problem," Twain said. Sawyer looked at Huck for a few seconds and then nodded his agreement.

"So, anyway, the Ice Cube—that's what we call Sawyer's place," Deni said, with an aside to Kelsey, "is available for at least the next two weeks. Probably more."

"Okay. Thanks," Kelsey said.

"Oh," Liv said, causing them all to look at her, even Matt, who had barely lifted his head from his second helping of dessert. "We should have a reception for you. So that all of your friends can meet Kelsey. And to celebrate your marriage."

"No," Huck said at the same time Kelsey said, "Thanks, but

that's not necessary."

Acting like a married couple in the confines of a dinner with family or working on boats together was one thing. But to be the center of attention, having your love on display for an entire party? Kelsey wasn't sure she was up for that—no matter how badly she'd wanted to get into undercover work.

"Oh, please," Liv said. "I'd so love to do this for you. It would be small, just family and close friends. Huck, you could invite all your friends from Copper Harbor."

"Liv, you shouldn't go to that trouble. Especially in your condition."

She waved a hand at the objection. "Oh, please. I'm pregnant, not an invalid. I can put together a small party. Besides, it would give Twain and me the perfect opportunity to let people know we're back together and expecting a baby."

"You gonna put a ring on her finger before that baby makes its appearance?" Huck asked his brother.

"Oh yeah, that's already been decided and agreed upon. We've just got to nail down the date." Twain stood up and started stacking his bowl into Liv's, then stopped and put his hands on her shoulders. "We've got the whole shotgun wedding thing down, don't we, Liv?"

Liv laughed, her hands going to rest on top of Twain's. Leaning back, she looked up at her giant and said, "That we do. That we do." Twain leaned down and kissed his ex-wife. Kelsey stole a look at Matt, who was stealing a look at his parents as they kissed. Most teenagers would surely have an expression of exasperation, maybe even an accompanying eye roll, but Matt watched his parents with fascination, a quiet appreciation. Finally, he put his head down, but Kelsey swore the kid had a smile on his face.

"Yep," Twain said, straightening again and continuing around the table, stacking empty bowls. "Shotgun weddings are our thing. Why, we're so—" He stopped abruptly and looked at Kelsey and Huck, then at Liv with a "Did I fuck up?" look.

Kelsey realized that Twain was thinking what everybody in the room was wondering, or possibly assuming.

"I'm not pregnant," Kelsey said. "No shotgun. Just a quickie wedding."

It seemed like relief went through the big bodies of the older Beck brothers.

"Not that it's any of your business," Huck added. Twain held his hands up in surrender and then took the stack of bowls from the table to the kitchen sink. Sawyer sighed and shook his head at Huck.

"Anyway," Liv said, "I insist about having a reception."

"Even less reason you should do this if you're going to be planning your own wedding soon," Kelsey said, although without as much steam as her previous refusal. The truth was, a social gathering of Huck's crew from Copper Harbor would be an excellent opportunity for Kelsey to be able to gather information. It would seem perfectly natural for a new bride to ask her guests questions about themselves. All under the guise of wanting to know her new husband's circle of friends better.

"I insist," Liv said.

"Well, thank you. I would like to meet all of Huck's friends," Kelsey said before Huck could object.

She looked at him, and he nodded to her. "Thanks, Liv," he said. "It's very nice of you. And I have to admit, I like the idea of showing off my new bride."

"Of course you do," Liv said, her happiness on her face.

The woman really did glow, and Kelsey wasn't sure whether it was pregnancy or the fact that Liv and her ex had reunited. Nor did it matter.

The party broke up after dessert, with Twain, being a logger, needing to get up at some ungodly hour to get into the woods.

On the short drive back to Huck's place, Kelsey played the day over in her mind. They had some appointments to see people the next day in Copper Harbor. They had successfully presented their cover to Huck's family and had seemed to pass muster.

"Will it bother you?" she asked as they entered Huck's home.

"What's that?" he asked, but she guessed he knew what she meant.

"Lying to your family like we are? Most undercover assignments you go in cold, to an area not your own. You usually wouldn't directly involve your family. Have to lie to them so blatantly."

Huck shrugged, pulling his sweatshirt over his head. "All families have their lies."

He went to the kitchen, opened the fridge, and pulled out a beer. He motioned the bottle to her in a "Want one?" gesture, and Kelsey shook her head.

"I'll stop and get some vodka tomorrow," Huck said.

"About that," she said. "And the ice cream. How'd you know that about me? I don't remember talking about it."

He shrugged again, tossing the cap from his bottle into the trash and then leaning against the counter. "You had very little in your refrigerator at your apartment. Some condiments, a shriveled lime, and a half-liter of tonic water. In your freezer was a bottle of Stoli and pints of ice cream. I figured you didn't cook much—either did takeout or"—he crooked his head to the side, like he was summing her up—"more likely, ate dinner at your desk most nights. But…the ice cream and vodka, those were there, and plentiful, so they must rank right up there for you."

She moved to the counter across the small room from him and leaned against it herself, placing her hands on the laminate behind her. She tilted her own head, returning the summation. "You're going to be good at this, aren't you?"

"What? Detective work? Crime fighting? Saving America from Sudafed-smuggling Canadians?" He was teasing, being casual, but Kelsey sensed a deeper need. He wanted this. Badly. And he wanted her to believe in him.

"Yeah. All of it," she said, not willing to commit to more. So he'd been observant while in her apartment. She hadn't seen him in action with anyone other than his family. How he'd be with people who were potential suspects was something else altogether.

"So, what's with the undertow between you and Sawyer?" she asked.

He quirked a brow at her and crossed his arms across his chest but didn't say a word.

"You're not the only one who can observe things," she said.

He sighed, dropping his hands, and then ran one through his hair, letting it fall to the sides instead of being pushed back.

"I love my brother. Brothers. But Sawyer is just that, my brother. He's not my father, even though he may think it at times."

"Surely you realize he just cares about you."

"Yeah, I know, but sometimes it bugs the shit out of me, that's all."

Having had her share of issues with her three older sisters, all incredible overachievers, Kelsey understood Huck's bristling at any perception of disapproval—imagined or real—from his oldest brother.

"I think it went well overall," Kelsey said, bringing the subject back to safer ground.

"Yeah. It was okay. But we weren't good enough. Not convincing enough. I thought we'd be able to skate since it'd been so long since my family had been around people in love, but Christ, the room was rife with it tonight."

"There were quite a few…stolen looks going around. I can only imagine what's going on now at their respective homes."

"Exactly." He took a step away from the counter, and Kelsey's body went on alert. Which was crazy. She'd spent the last forty-eight hours practically joined at the hip with Huck Beck, so there was no reason that being so close in his kitchen should— Okay, he took another step toward her with a definite…*look* in his eye. "They're all at home, most likely burning up the sheets. And do you think they're wondering what we're up to?"

"Ummm…"

"Probably not. Even though we're the newlyweds of the group." Another step closer. Damn, it was a small kitchen. "Oh sure, you put a hand on my knee and put your hand in my hair during dessert… I liked that, by the way."

He was in front of her now, placing his hands on the counter next to hers, sliding his feet between hers, leaning into her, yet not touching her. "But there was something missing. Something I wouldn't have even noticed if it hadn't been so obvious in Sawyer and Deni and Twain and Liv."

"What's that?" she said softly. Because with Huck so close, there was really no need for anything above a whisper.

"Their…ease with each other's bodies. They were in each other's space so easily, so naturally. It wasn't that they were all over each other or anything. It's just, I don't know." His eyes dragged down her body and then back up, landing on her mouth. "It's hard to name, but do you know what I mean?"

She did. She nodded once. "What do we do about that?" she whispered, looking into his blue eyes. Eyes that seemed to turn darker as they looked down into hers.

"I think you know," he said. There was questioning in his eyes, and he held his body away from hers even though she could feel the heat of him. Heat she desperately wanted to envelop her.

Wanted Huck to envelop her.

"I do," she said, the words swallowed by Huck's mouth coming down on hers.

Nine

SHE TASTED LIKE OREOS AND CHOCOLATE. JUST ONE more reason to love that dessert Liv made—it made Kelsey taste even more delicious.

Yeah, he'd kissed her yesterday at her apartment, but that was just to make her mouth look kissed for the camera. But it had given him the smallest taste, and for the past twenty-four hours he'd wanted nothing more than to kiss her again.

Kiss her for real.

Except none of it was real.

But it felt real to his body, which leaned into Kelsey's as he slanted his mouth over her full lips. She opened to him, and he tangled his tongue with hers before sliding deep into her mouth, wishing he were sliding in deep elsewhere too.

"Kels," he whispered as he nipped her bottom lip, then wished he hadn't when he felt her body tense. It didn't last long. She relaxed and moved her hands to the side, sliding over his, which were still on the countertop. Turning his over, he slid them against her palms, then to her hips, the rough denim of her jeans feeling like heaven as he grasped her.

A whisper of a sigh left her lips, and Huck needed to capture them again, kissing her deeply, sliding one hand up her back, pushing into her, her firm ass backed into the counter.

Finally, her hands left the counter and she wrapped her arms around his neck. Huck felt like singing *Hallelujah*, it felt so good to have Kelsey Cameron's body smashed up tight against his.

"Like this?" she said, breaking her mouth from his and kissing his neck, which, holy shit, felt even better than having her arms around him.

"Like this, what?" he asked, returning the favor and kissing her neck, nudging the material of her sweater and tee away, wanting—needing—to get to the soft, pale skin beneath.

"Like being in each other's space like this?" she asked. "Is this what you were thinking?" There was a teasing in her voice that Huck hadn't heard before, hadn't been convinced that Kelsey was capable of, and he found he liked it. A lot.

"Yeah, I was thinking of this," he said honestly.

"I like how you think," she said in that teasing voice again, pulling Huck from his thoughts and making him all the more hard.

He sucked on the skin just beneath her ear, and heard her sigh turn into a soft moan.

He could make her moan even more, he knew that. He could make her come apart, and he'd enjoy doing it.

But how would she feel about it tomorrow? And how would they work together? She already thought he was a liability, being a civilian. Oh, she hid it well and seemed to listen to his thoughts as they'd discussed the case this morning at the very kitchen table he was now contemplating laying her across so he could get those jeans off her.

And let's face it, his history with "the morning after" was not exactly stellar. He didn't do it well, he knew. Sometimes he didn't even do it, leaving before the woman he was with woke up. Around the Copper Country, it was no big deal. Women knew what they were getting into when they hooked up with Huck. No attachments and usually no repeat performances.

And never did he wake up and have to work side by side with the woman, like he'd have to with Kelsey.

Instead of that thought freaking him out, it kind of made it all the hotter. He moved his hands up inside her sweater, but still outside of her tee.

"Huck," she whispered on a moan when his hand grazed the underside of her small, but perfect breasts, even through the soft cotton of her shirt.

His name being said through a moan was not new to him, but damn if it had ever sounded quite as sexy as it did coming from Kelsey Cameron.

Agent Kelsey Cameron.

Flashes from four years ago zipped through his quickly blissing-out brain. He knew he only had a couple of seconds of rational thought left before his brain fried and his dick took over completely. Which was usually great, but right now, he concentrated hard on what his memory was dredging up.

The phone call to Prescott that he wasn't coming back to training.

The months and months afterward of drinking and not giving a shit about his life.

The months after *that* of pulling himself out of the bottle and starting over.

The call two days ago from Prescott saying he was needed.

His hands eased back down Kelsey's trim body, to her waist, where he carefully disengaged himself and took a small step back.

He just couldn't risk it. He didn't trust that he could be better with Kelsey than he usually was with women, even though he knew Kelsey could possibly be the only woman for which he'd want to try.

Not even for one night with her would he risk his entire future. Shit.

"We have to stop," he said, finding the words hard to get out over his labored breath. And judging by her movement to follow him as he moved back, she hadn't even heard him.

"Kelsey, we can't," he said a bit more firmly.

This time she heard, and if the stunned look on her face was any indication, she didn't necessarily agree with his statement.

But then something changed, and her look vanished, replaced

by a blank look that Huck couldn't read. He doubted that anyone could read that look, completely devoid of any emotion as it was. Total Agent Cameron.

"I just think… I mean, I shouldn't have even started—"

Her hand shot up, cutting him off. "No need. You're right," she said. She turned and left the kitchen, Huck watching her straight back as she went down the hallway. He listened to her quietly tread up the stairs and heard as she closed the door to the guestroom. Not stomping up the stairs, not slamming the door. Cool, controlled, totally professional.

And Huck wished he had shut his thoughts out quicker because, dear God, it would be sweet to see her lose all that control.

Ten

—⚊—

"SHOULD WE TALK ABOUT LAST NIGHT?" KELSEY ASKED once they'd had several sips of strong coffee that they'd purchased at a Holiday gas station on their drive to Copper Harbor.

"What's there to talk about?" Huck said with a shrug.

"Well, you're certainly acting like a husband this morning," Kelsey said, taking a drink of coffee and turning to look out the window.

The sign at the side of the highway told her they were entering Calumet. "This is where you're from, right? Calumet?"

A grunt from her partner's side of the truck. They entered the village (as the sign called it), and Kelsey realized it was larger than Chassell, which they'd driven through the other night on their way into town. It was probably the size of Houghton or Hancock.

Huck let out a huge sigh and slowed the truck down. For a second, Kelsey thought he was going to pull to the side of the road like he'd done the other night, but no, he was just turning off the main highway.

"Calumet was on our left. Now I'm going to take you through Laurium. I want to show you the houses."

The houses? From what Kelsey could see, they weren't much to brag about. Or was that Huck's point? Did the socioeconomic situation of parts of the area create a window for people to turn to easy passage of some Canadian drugs to help make ends meet?

Desperate people did desperate things.

The houses were small, close to the streets, and old, some well kept up, some not.

"Why are they so close to the streets? With hardly any driveways?" she asked Huck.

"Less snow to shovel in the winters. Practicality rules over landscape every time in da Yoop. These are all mining houses. Where the workers lived." He took a few more turns, and Kelsey's jaw dropped at the difference. "And these are where the owners of the mines and the bigwigs in the companies lived."

Five or six mansions, most looking vacant or abandoned, ran the length of the block. "Do people live there?"

"Some. Some refurbished. Some are vacant. My brother Sawyer dabbles in house flipping, and I wish he'd do one of these. But he says he could never make any profit because it would take so much to modernize them, and nobody up here has the kind of money to buy the finished version. The ones who do put the money into refurbishing try to get their money back by renting. Way below what they're worth, of course."

"So they sit," she said.

"Yep." He took a turn at the end of the block, then another, and soon they were back on the highway and headed out of town toward Copper Harbor.

"You're right," he said after a few minutes of silence.

"About what?"

"We should talk about last night. I sounded like a real husband—a guy—before. But you're my partner and we need to keep this professional, even though we need to bring the physical into it at times."

Professional. The heat that had gone through her body last night as Huck approached her had felt anything but professional. The way her body ached as he finally pinned her against the counter was not typically covered in the FBI handbook.

And when he'd stopped, making her feel cold and adrift. Not only had that been deeply unprofessional, it had Kelsey feeling something she had never felt for a guy—yearning.

"We're partners, and we need to be able to talk to each other about this as if it were just another aspect of the case, another piece of our cover," he said, but it sounded like he was trying to convince himself of the words.

"That's right," she said, trying to convince herself that she could separate the physical from the emotional. "You had the right idea. We did need to be more comfortable around each other physically."

"Yeah, but…"

He was going to cop out, she knew it. Say something stupid and guy-like. When they both knew exactly why he'd stopped.

"But then it became too real, and I guess I hadn't anticipated that and needed to step away. It's my fault for not realizing the endgame before I snapped the ball. That's something that can blow a whole case, or get you killed—not thinking ahead. So, I apologize that I didn't think it through. And I regret that I didn't discuss it more with you, my partner, first."

Huh. So…not some variation on a "Listen, baby, I think you're totally hot, but I just wasn't feeling it" deflection.

"And now," he continued before Kelsey could pull her thoughts together on his completely non-emotional analysis of their kiss, "if I'm reading the vibe in the truck correctly, there is a fair amount of sexual tension at play here, and that was the last thing that I wanted to happen."

"No?"

"No. Newlyweds don't have sexual tension, they have, you know…sex. All the time. Like rabbits."

Sex like rabbits with Huck Beck. Huck, with his hair and beard and piercing blue eyes. What was he saying…oh yeah, sexual tension.

He looked over at her and must have seen her thoughts through her foggy, disheveled brain.

He ran his hand through that sexy blond hair and sighed, looking back to the road. "Listen, if you were just a girl, and we'd made out last night, I'd completely know how to handle this situation—and it wouldn't be with the honesty I'm trying to muster up right now."

Kelsey nodded, but stayed silent. Honestly, if she spoke, she wasn't sure if she'd burst into giggles, tears, or an oration on the rules and regulations of an FBI agent undercover.

"But you're not just a girl, you're my partner. Though you had to have noticed that my body seemed to forget that fact last night."

Yes, his erection pressing into her had been a clear indication that he'd *really* become more at ease with her body.

But if he was being candid, so could she. "You weren't exactly the only one responding," she said.

He didn't look at her, but she could see a small smile on his lips. The lips that had burned a trail down her neck last night. Lips that had come so close to going further.

"Yeah, it was good. No denying that," he said, the smile a little bigger, though he kept his eyes on the road.

"You know," she said, then stopped. She'd wanted to say that there was really no harm in them pursuing the physical a little bit more. It would help cement their…*physicalness* around each other when out in public, and as long as they kept their emotions out of it…

"Yeah," he said, as if reading her mind, "but would we be able to keep our heads about us?"

She couldn't stop herself from saying, "Surely you've had just physical relationships before. No emotional ties, just a few months of…finding the ease in each other's bodies."

What was she saying? It was as if she was challenging him to be her fuck buddy for the duration of the assignment.

Was she?

She knew she was a good enough agent to keep her wits about her while on the case. Why shouldn't she enjoy the time she spent in bed each night? It had been a woefully long dry spell for her. She shuddered thinking about her last sexual experience and its fallout.

Wouldn't a couple of months spent underneath Huck Beck do wonders?

He wasn't an official agent or a suspect, so no rules would be broken. Yes, it would be frowned upon that she slept with someone she worked with, but Kelsey knew it happened all the time in undercover operations.

Suddenly the idea took on a life of its own. A tingly, aching, images-of-body-parts life, and she found she really wanted to hear Huck Beck say he was on board.

Basically, she just really wanted Huck Beck.

"Yeah, of course I've had those kinds of relationships," he said. "Not that I'd even call them relationships. More like multiple hookups."

"And you kept your emotions out of it?"

He snorted. "Believe me, keeping my emotions out of sex has never been a problem for me."

Great. Her body started firing, but she didn't show any outward signs. They were on the clock, so to speak. They could discuss it all they wanted, but they had people—possible suspects or informants—to meet today.

"But here's the thing," he said, and she felt her body cooling off. Why did there always have to be a "thing"? "Can we guarantee that it could be just sex at night and the case during the day with us? I mean, look at us today, and all we did was kiss last night."

"That's because we hadn't had this talk. Hadn't set the ground rules." What the hell was she doing? Now it sounded like she was begging him.

Kelsey liked sex, liked the feel of it, loved the release. And sadly, she knew from experience that she could have sex with someone she wasn't emotionally attached to, though she'd never had a one-night stand with someone she'd just met, like the cover story they'd come up with.

And she missed sex. But damned if she was going to beg Huck—

"And it's not like I don't want to. I do." He glanced over at her, but she didn't look back. "A lot, Kelsey. A whole lot."

"Okay," she said.

"And maybe it's because I want to so badly with you that I know it's not a good idea. This assignment, like I said, is really important to me."

"More important than a couple of months of no-strings sex," she said. "I get it." She really did. And she was glad he was reminding her just how important this first undercover assignment was to her, too.

She had no doubts she could keep the case front and center, even if she was enjoying the fringe benefits of their cover. But maybe Huck couldn't. Maybe he was realizing that it might be too much for him to handle. And if he couldn't handle it, that was surely a bad thing for their combined efforts.

She stifled her sigh of resignation. Really, she was in no different place than she'd been in yesterday evening before they got home and Huck had kissed her.

Sex with Huck hadn't even been on her radar. (Yeah, okay, she thought he was sexy as hell, but that was about it.)

But now, she couldn't help but feel that she'd somehow lost something that she'd desperately wanted.

"So, we're good?" Huck said. "We tried to experiment with getting closer on our own and decided not to pursue it, right?" He summed it up, putting it in its compartment, which was exactly how Kelsey liked to work—take a piece of information, examine it, come to a conclusion, and then put it in its own compartment.

"Right. We're good. And the bonus is we know that if we need to show some touches and feels in front of people, that we can do it without it looking too fake."

He glanced at her again. This time she met his gaze until he turned his eyes back to the road. "Not fake. Right."

Kelsey turned her head to the window so Huck couldn't see her smile.

And why did she suddenly hope that the opportunity would

come up for them to display their can't-keep-their-hands-off-each-other newlywed bliss?

Eleven

—⚶—

HE INTRODUCED HER TO A LOT OF PEOPLE, AND IT WAS a testament to Kelsey's training, memory, and desire to succeed with this assignment that she quickly memorized all the names, physical traits, and other information that she would analyze later.

There wasn't much charter action going on yet, it being too cold for tourists to come to the U.P., but there was quite a bit of maintenance going on. Huck made the stops with each boat and let the captain know he was available.

And that his new wife was with him.

Kelsey got a kick out of the men's reactions at learning Huck Beck had taken a bride—and one he'd only known for five months. There were some knowing "You got hit hard, boy!" slaps on the back, some "Are you some kind of idiot?" puzzlement, and some genuine well wishes.

But the women.

There weren't a lot of them, and many seemed to be either married or with someone, but Kelsey could feel the curiosity—and in a couple of cases, animosity—emanating from each of them.

"Just how many hearts will be broken today when news of Huck Beck being married makes the rounds?" she asked him when they went to the Seafarer, a place in Copper Harbor, for a late lunch.

He didn't pretend not to know what she was talking about.

He'd have had to be blind not to notice the reactions of the women who worked on the boats.

And in the restaurant.

And the cute little shops down by the water to which he'd taken her.

"Fewer than you're thinking," he said, and took a drink of his Coke.

"I don't know," she teased. Then she thought about it a little more. And looked around to see no tables occupied nearby and their waitress (another among the shocked and visibly disappointed when Huck introduced Kelsey) at the other end of the large room. "I probably played that wrong, didn't I. I mean, I found it kind of funny how the men were aghast that you'd even gotten married. And the women all seemed to accept it as some kind of challenge. It was amusing, but I probably should have played offended, right? More territorial in front of the women?"

It wasn't like her to doubt herself, particularly when working, but this was new territory for her. Not only the going undercover part, which she felt immensely prepared for. But also, maybe mainly, how it would feel to really be married to Huck and have women react like it was a barrier, but not an insurmountable one, to being with Huck.

"Yeah," she said, "I should have—"

"You played it right," he said.

"I don't know," she said, thinking on it. She took a bite of her grilled lake trout and had to stifle a moan of delight. "My God, that's good."

"Probably caught yesterday," Huck said.

She took another bite, savoring the fresh fillet and the subtle sauce that it had been baked in.

"Here's the thing," Huck said, watching her as she ate. "I wouldn't marry someone who was the jealous type. All of that territorial shit that some women play at? That would drive me up a tree. Just be yourself. The more people get to know you, the more they'll realize you're nothing like the girls I usually..."

She raised a brow, waiting for his next choice of words, but just continued to eat her fish. And the fries. God, the fries were delicious too.

"Umm…you're just different from them, that's all. Which will seem like the reason we got married so quickly—because to me, you're different from all the others."

She nodded, wiped her mouth with the napkin, and took a drink of her Diet Coke. "But how do you know that? I met you three days ago. How do you know I'm different than the girls you usually…you know."

He shrugged. "Well, the outward stuff, of course. Raised on the East Coast. Come from a well-off family. A city girl. A bit more…hmm…a bit *less* laid-back than the folks around here."

"Uptight, you mean."

He shook his head. "No. Not uptight, or at least I've seen no signs of that. Driven? Yes. Ambitious? Yes. Focused? Absolutely."

"And what? Everyone in the Copper Country floats around aimlessly, never achieving anything? I've seen too many signs to the contrary. Two universities. A tourist industry that seems to be doing okay, even though it's early in the season. A—"

"Yes, of course there are driven, focused people here. I'm just saying the Copper Country as a whole is not as fast-paced as a city, the East Coast especially."

She knew that was what he'd meant, but she found that she kind of liked baiting him.

"And Copper Harbor even more so. It's a tourist area, so the people work hard and customer service is key. But people are also up here because they love it. So much so, they leave other jobs, more lucrative jobs, just to live up here."

She sat back in her chair, her plate demolished and the beginnings of a food baby forming in her belly. But she was also very satisfied.

"Like that waiter over there," Huck said, pointing with his chin at a man in his thirties who was sitting at the end of the bar, apparently clocked out, and going through his orders for the day.

"He got an engineering degree from Tech. Got a great offer from Ford to work in Detroit. Did for a couple of years and hated it, wanted to be back up here. So, he left his great job and moved back up. He wanted to spend the summers in the Harbor, didn't want an eight-to-five gig. So he's a waiter. Probably making a quarter of what he was, but loving his life."

Kelsey studied the man while Huck continued. "You see a lot of that up here. People with graduate degrees working in the shops or on the boats, just because they love the life."

"A life that I am very much different from," Kelsey summed up for him.

"Right. Which was alluring and fascinating to a guy like me, who had spent his whole life in the Copper Country and almost every summer since I was sixteen in the Harbor."

"Ah, but when my exotic allure wears off, and you realize that I'm just a woman after all, big-city-raised or no, then where will I be?" The teasing in her voice was plain, but she found she didn't quite feel as playful as she had a minute ago.

"Well, I'm guessing that allure will wear off right around the time that we get the word we're done." He laughed at his own joke and smiled at her. She smiled back, but both their smiles faded quickly.

As they left the Seafarer, the late afternoon sun was high in the sky, though the day was still chilly.

"Where to now?" she asked.

"We've hit all the spots here that might have work for us. So, we head back to Houghton and see if anybody gives us a call in the next couple of days. If not, we come back up and try again."

"Shouldn't we come back up tomorrow, whether we hear anything or not?"

He shrugged. "We could. But that would be seen as being pushy."

She laughed. "Let me guess. You don't do 'pushy' in Copper Harbor."

"That's right."

As he led the way to his truck, another pickup, this one dark blue, pulled up alongside them. The driver rolled down his window, and Kelsey recognized him from earlier in the morning.

Frank Belson, owner of a smaller boat that could be chartered for trips to Isle Royale for smaller groups of people.

"Glad I caught ya," he said to Huck and Kelsey. "I thought you might be eating here."

Since Kelsey had only seen a handful of restaurants in Copper Harbor, and Huck's beat-up red truck was in the parking lot, Frank's odds of finding them had been pretty good.

"I forgot to mention earlier that a new boat was docking in the marina now."

"I didn't see any I didn't recognize," Huck said. Kelsey thought about how integral Huck's knowledge of the community would be to this investigation.

Tarrington had been right about that; Huck was a shortcut to fact-finding, in a big way. And people had spoken very freely around her this morning just based on the fact that she was Huck's wife and thus part of the gang.

"He was out this morning. Probably went over to the island. Might be staying over; he's done that a few times."

"This early in the season? Does he have charters?"

"I'm not sure. He mostly keeps to himself. Nice enough guy, though. I take it he's doing this as sort of sideline business. Anyway, his name is Jim Peterson. Boat is the *Mina*. It's a thirty-eight-footer. He might be looking for help, if you didn't find anything after we spoke."

"Nothing definite," Huck said. "Thanks, I'll look for his boat. You know if he has any crew?"

Frank shook his head. "Nobody regular that I could see, but his slip is at the other end of the marina from me and he keeps to himself, so I'm not really certain."

"Thanks a lot, Frank," Huck said, and Kelsey nodded her thanks as well.

"I'll let you two get back to it—newlyweds and all," Frank

said with a playful chuckle, rolled up his window, and drove off.

Huck drove them through the marina again on their way out of Copper Harbor, but the *Mina* was still out.

He got back on the main road and headed to Houghton, taking the drive through Eagle Harbor and Eagle River, which wound its way around the shores of Lake Superior.

While she admired the breathtaking scenery, Kelsey's mind was at work. "How often do new boats show up here? I mean, boats that aren't just tourists passing through?"

"Not very often," he said, with the same suspicion in his voice that Kelsey was feeling.

"I think we should come back tomorrow after all," he said.

"You can blame us being pushy on your city girl, different-from-anyone-I've-ever-banged wife," she said, the teasing now back.

"Banged? What are we, fifteen?" But he laughed, and she wasn't sure what was more beautiful—the wild, untamed waves of Lake Superior crashing against the shore, or Huck Beck's wild, untamed face when he smiled.

Twelve

WHEN THEY GOT HOME, THERE WAS A SMALL CASE ON Huck's kitchen table, which Kelsey went to immediately.

Huck watched as she opened it up, revealing her Glock and her FBI identification. He'd had hunting rifles and shotguns in the house before, though Twain kept those at his house now. And he had done some shooting with a pistol during the DEA training, but he'd never had a handgun in his house.

"We need a secure place to hide these," she said, carefully handling the gun and checking the ammunition in the case.

"Yeah, guess I'll have to start locking the door," he said, then chuckled at her shocked expression.

"You mean you don't lock your doors?"

"No. How do you think they got in so easily to leave this for you? Whoever 'they' are."

"*They* are the FBI and a locked door is not much of a deterrent."

"Even less so when it's not locked."

"Is crime here really that low that you could just never lock up?"

He shrugged, went to the refrigerator, and pulled out a beer. He hadn't had a chance to pick up any vodka for Kelsey. When he motioned to her with his beer, this time, she reluctantly nodded that she'd join him.

He pulled out a bottle for her and opened it, and they both

sat at the table, the case holding the gun between them.

"It's not so much lack of crime—though yeah, it's pretty low here—as it is a) I don't have much to steal, and b) I let people crash here all the time, and it's just easier to leave it unlocked than to have to have people track me down for a key or to let them in."

"What do you mean, let people crash here?" She took a small drink and barely hid her distaste of the beer, though she took another sip before placing the bottle down on the table.

"Mostly Harbor people who are in town. Don't want to drive back up due to partying or need to be back down here the next day or something."

"And they just show up, these people?"

"Sometimes. Sometimes I get a text asking if it's okay. As you saw today, there's no cell service in the Harbor, so it's not like they can call ahead. So, they either just show up at my door or text once they're in town."

"It might have been good to mention this before."

His mind was going to where hers had already jumped. If someone showed up unannounced, would their cover be blown?

Shit, there'd been times Huck would wake up to find a buddy sleeping down the hall in the guestroom.

The room Kelsey slept in.

Plus, now there was a gun in the house.

"And are some of these people who crash here women?" she asked.

"Sometimes," he admitted. Yeah, okay, he wasn't above being on the receiving end of an impromptu booty call. Rather liked it, actually.

Her mind was working, and he found he liked watching her think. Wanted to know exactly what she was thinking, the conclusions she'd come to. Wished he could climb into her mind and play around.

Playing around with her body would be fun, too.

But no, he'd laid down the law today, after throwing a wrench into it all last night by kissing her. He couldn't be the one to backtrack now, just because he thought she was sexy as hell with a gun in her hand and a thought in her head.

"Do you think making the rounds today would be enough to stop this barrage of freeloaders? Or do we need to get the message out?"

He sighed and took a swig of beer. "They're not freeloaders. Just pals who need somewhere to crash. I've done it plenty up at the Harbor."

She was thinking again, and this time shared her thoughts. "On one hand, the more people we have access to, the better. For observation and investigation, of course, but also to solidify in others' minds that we're a couple."

"Right, but—"

"But there's always the chance that our cover couldn't hold up to that kind of scrutiny. Are our toothbrushes near each other? Can you make my coffee the way I like it in the morning? Not to mention someone crawling into the guest bed with me."

A flash of fury shot through Huck from thinking about anybody crawling into bed with Kelsey. Anybody but him. Even though he'd had the same thought a second ago. But hearing her voice it and say it in a way that sounded like her only concern of a stranger in her bed would be a blown cover? No.

"I'll put the word out that Hotel Beck is closed for the duration. Newlyweds wanting to do it all over the house and all."

She took another small sip of beer, her face not scrunching up at the taste this time, as she studied him. Finally, one small nod.

"That's probably the safest route."

"Okay."

"In the meantime, do you have a safe hiding place?"

"There's a trunk in the attic. Nobody ever goes into the attic, let alone the trunk that's tucked in a corner."

"That'll work," she said, and took another drink. Her bottle was nearly half gone, and Huck took a couple big swigs of his own just to keep up. She stood up, placing the gun safely in the case with her badge and shutting it up. "Let's go put this away now and then talk about the people we met today. I want your take on them, then I'll give you mine as an outsider."

Huck felt his chest puff up with pride and excitement that an experienced FBI agent like Kelsey wasn't pulling rank and refusing to involve Huck in the case other than as an introduction to the area.

After he showed her to the attic and they'd hidden her gun and badge, they returned to the kitchen and spent the next two hours going over everyone they'd come into contact with that day, plus a few others that Huck told her about.

And they drank more beer, Kelsey even seeming fond of the golden brew after a while.

Huck becoming fonder of her and her analytical abilities.

She remembered everyone. Had obviously noticed everything, too. From the boats that needed major overhauls—and therefore owners that needed money to afford said overhauls—to cars in parking lots that seemed too expensive to belong to the working-class crews.

When they were done, they had three names Kelsey was going to have financial reports run on from the D.C. office the next day. He asked if she was going to give those three names to Jenkins, and she said not until after she'd seen the financials. He wasn't sure that was the way to go, but kept quiet, deferring to an agent who had four years on the job to his…well, none.

Just as they had concluded their talk and Huck was trying not to think about sleeping just down the hall from Kelsey for another night, his phone rang.

"It's Twain," he said to Kelsey as he answered.

"Just seeing how the day went at the Harbor," Twain said.

"Pretty good. We're heading back up tomorrow. Got a few good leads." At Kelsey's widened eyes, he added for good measure, "On possible jobs for the summer." She let out an exaggerated sigh of relief, and he rolled his eyes at her.

"That's good. So you're home now?"

"Yep. Got back a couple of hours ago. Just having a beer."

"Yeah? Having that beer with clothes on?"

Huck chuckled. "Yeah. Unfortunately for me."

"Or fortunately for us. Liv and I are outside. Grab your bride and come on out with us for a drink."

"What, now?" Huck said, surprised. He didn't go out with Twain all that much anymore, his brother keeping such long hours in the woods. Especially during the week, though Twain often logged on the weekends, depending on his workload and the weather conditions.

"Yeah, now."

Huck looked at Kelsey. She'd obviously heard Twain's invitation. She raised a brow, then shrugged. Huck could see she was quickly thinking out the pros and cons. The pros being they would be seen in public as a couple. The cons would be…having to act as a couple in public.

"Well, we've already had a few…" he said to Twain, still not sure what the best option would be.

"Excellent. And we have a designated driver in Liv, so get your asses out here." The call ended before Huck could say more.

"Do I have time to change or anything?" Kelsey asked, looking down at her jeans and T-shirt.

"Probably not. You look fine. This is the Copper Country, after all," he said, rising from the table, looking around. Thoughts of one of his cronies from the Harbor ending up in bed with Kelsey—before Huck got the chance to get the word out—had him reaching for his keys.

This time he'd lock the door.

Thirteen

THE CAT'S MEOW, KELSEY FOUND OUT, WAS A TYPICAL
neighborhood bar. One long room with a beautiful wood bar
taking up the whole length on one side. Pool table at the back,
tables along the side and in the front by the large window, looking
out onto the main drag of Houghton.

And it was very crowded.

"Oh, crap, I forgot about the Tech students," Liv said as they
entered and pushed their way through the throng of people to the
one empty table near the end of the room.

"It's not usually this crowded?" Kelsey asked as she sat next to
Liv at the table while Huck and Twain went to the bar.

"No. Well, honestly, I haven't been here in a while. But
Tech just had finals last week, and summer track doesn't start for
another two weeks. So these are all the kids who stayed up here for
summer school, but haven't started yet."

"Thus, spending a Thursday evening in the bar."

"Exactly. Tech students aren't immune to partying, of course,
but the academics are so tough that you wouldn't see this kind of
crowd in here on a weeknight when classes are in session."

"Did you go to Tech?" Kelsey asked.

Liv ducked her head, then brought it up as she tucked her
long blond hair behind her ears. "No. I didn't go to college. Twain
went to Tech for a year and a half. But then…we had Matty."

"Who seems like a great kid, from the little I spoke with him last night."

The pride on Liv's face when speaking of her son was apparent. "He is a great kid. Well, he can be most of the time. The other part of the time, he's a teenager."

"'Nuff said."

"But I work at Tech," Liv added. "That's why I know the schedule of classes."

"What department?"

"The Psychology Department."

"I'll bet that's interesting."

Liv shrugged. "It can be. It's not that large of a department, given that Tech is mainly an engineering school, but it can be challenging to keep all the plates spinning."

"I'll bet," Kelsey said, taking the drink that Huck handed her as he and Twain came back to the table.

"Vodka tonic," he said, motioning to her drink with his chin. He had a bottle of beer for himself. Twain handed Liv what looked like a soda and sat down next to her, taking a drink from his own beer.

"What're we talking about?" Twain asked, placing a big hand along the back of Liv's chair.

"Liv's job," Kelsey said, noticing the casual way Twain had of twirling a strand of Liv's hair around a finger.

"Which we don't have to talk about anymore," Liv said. "It's boring, really."

"Hey, it's not boring," Twain said to her, and she looked up at him with a smile on her face.

"It's pretty boring."

"Well, maybe it is to you. Did you tell her about your knitting business?" Twain asked. Kelsey and Liv both shook their heads.

Twain pointed to Liv, a look of pride on his face. "She makes really cool shit. Knits it. Has her own business that's doing great. Gets orders from all over the world."

"Wow," Kelsey said. "I noticed some of the knit pieces in your home. They were amazing."

"Yeah, and we just get to keep the rejects. The really good stuff goes to buyers."

"That's really cool," Kelsey said.

Liv waved her off, but Kelsey could tell she was pleased not only with Kelsey's appreciation of it, but the pride in Twain's voice as he boasted about her.

"Pashminas and shit all over the word sure ain't boring," Twain added. "Besides, nothing's more boring than being in a forest all day," he said to Liv. She rolled her eyes, and they shared a laugh. Kelsey was captivated by them, studied them, wished she and Huck seemed as natural and easy together as they did.

Of course, Twain and Liv had known each other for over fifteen years, and Kelsey had supposedly only known Huck for the five months they'd told everybody. Three days in reality.

Still, she prided herself on being a good agent, and she wanted to do as well in the field as she had behind her desk.

She took a sip of her drink, then placed a hand on Huck's knee. It was under the table, but it was obvious where her hand was to Liv and Twain, who both watched the movement.

Not missing a beat, Huck put an arm around the back of her chair, while taking a gulp from his bottle of beer.

"So, any luck today in the Harbor?" Twain asked them.

She and Huck recapped their day of job hunting. It sounded much different than the debriefing they'd done earlier with each other. No talk of suspects or motives or opportunity. The only opportunity mentioned was that of possible employment.

Huck asked Twain and Liv if either of them knew of a new charter boat named the *Mina*, but neither of them did.

"It's actually been a while since I've been up there," Liv said. To Kelsey, she added, "My whole family is in Calumet, but as you've seen today, the Harbor is quite a drive past that."

"It is," Kelsey agreed, remembering Calumet as across the highway from Laurium, which held the old mining mansions Huck had shown her.

"Oh, I don't want to forget," Liv said, "I have a date for your reception."

"Liv, you really don't have to do that," Huck said before Kelsey could.

"I know. But I want to. We can't have the town not knowing the newest Mrs. Beck, can we?"

Huck stayed silent, so Kelsey just gave Liv a smile of what she hoped looked like gratitude.

"It's three weeks from now. The third Saturday in June. So, when you get on with a boat, make sure you have that night off."

"If you're sure…"

Liv nodded. "I am. I wanted to wait until Sawyer and Deni were back, of course, and the first weekend after that, we're busy. So…put it in your calendars."

She motioned for them to do it, so Kelsey and Huck both pulled their phones out of their pockets and entered in the date.

"Do you have pictures from your wedding on your phone?" she asked Kelsey, leaning forward.

Crap. They'd thought of candid, in-love photos, but not wedding ones. Though there wouldn't have been time to find a fake dress and go to City Hall.

"Not of the wedding, no," Huck said quickly, calling up the photos on his phone. "We agreed not to take our phones to City Hall. Didn't want any distractions. When we saw everybody taking photos with theirs, we knew we'd messed up. They took a few of them there and are supposed to email them to us." He turned to Kelsey while holding his phone out for Liv to take. "Which reminds me, I haven't received anything from them, have you?"

He was good on his feet, she'd give him that. "No. Not the last time I looked at my email. But with the cell reception in Copper Harbor, who knows. I haven't checked since we got back to Houghton."

"We paid enough for them, they better deliver," Huck muttered like an average disgruntled customer.

"Is this at your place, Kelsey?" Liv asked as she thumbed

through Huck's photos.

"Yes."

"It looks really cute. It's in D.C.?"

"Yes. Dupont Circle. Do you know the area?"

Liv laughed. "God, no. Born and bred here in the Copper Country. Never lived anywhere else. We didn't do a lot of traveling when Matty was young, either. And since then, the only trips I take are to see my folks in Florida during the winter. Though I didn't get there this year, just Matty went for his spring break." Something she said at the last made her look up at Twain with a twinkle in her eye. He returned the look with a devilish grin. A grin that was similar to the one Huck had given Kelsey four years ago right before the panel snapped shut.

"Maybe with this one it'll be different," Twain said to his wife (ex-wife? Kelsey was pretty sure), putting his hand gently on her nonexistent stomach.

"Probably not," Liv said, chuckling. "With Matty, we were both so young and broke. Now we're old and tired." It didn't sound like a complaint to Kelsey, and given the look that passed between them, she knew it wasn't meant as such.

Liv's and Twain's eyebrows raised at whatever they were looking at on Huck's phone, and Kelsey looked over the top of it to see the photo of her back in a cami and boy shorts making something at the kitchen counter.

"Huck, why did you take that?" she said, reaching for the phone as she swatted Huck in the gut. Twain grabbed the phone out of her reach and Liv playfully swatted him.

"Babe, do you know how good you look in the picture? At the time, I wasn't sure when I was going to see you again. I… needed to have that image with me," Huck said.

Typically, Kelsey Cameron would not put up with a man calling her "babe." But she found that Kelsey Beck liked it just fine. At least when it came from Huck Beck. "Is there anything else on there that I'd rather your brother not see?" She had a playful tone in her voice. Easy to achieve when she knew full well that there was no way in hell he had anything more provocative on his phone.

"Nah, that's the worst of them," he said, then chuckled. "Or the best of them, as the case may be."

Twain handed the phone back to Huck, who placed it in his pocket, took a drink of beer, and then leaned forward, his forearms on the table, hands cradling his beer bottle.

"So, Liv, this reception thing. It's going to be small, right? We don't want anything too big."

Liv nodded. "Not too big, check. I need you to get me a list of names and contacts from the Harbor group that you want invited. I think I know most of the people in Calumet, Hancock, and Houghton that you'd want there."

Huck nodded, taking another drink of beer. The way he was leaning, the cotton of his sweatshirt pulled taut across his back, and Kelsey found it perfectly natural to reach out and place her hand there, rubbing in small circles.

Both Liv's and Twain's eyes went to Kelsey's movement and then to Huck's face, seemingly to watch his reaction.

Right. Huck Beck didn't like territorial women. Did that include any PDA? Because what Kelsey's movement felt like to her was much more wanting desperately to feel the heat and strength of him than to mark him as hers. The rings on their fingers alone should do that quite nicely.

Huck didn't flinch under her hand or show any other outward sign that her touching him in a public bar bothered him in any way. And, as if to show his approval, he slipped a hand down under the table and wrapped it around her thigh. High up on her thigh.

"Your mom is on that cruise with Gary, but should we invite your dad? We'd give him enough notice that he could travel—"

"No," Huck said low, but firmly.

"He might not be able to make it, but we should still—"

"No," he said to Liv again, this time with a little bit of bite in his voice.

"Huck…" Twain said with warning in his voice.

Kelsey smoothed her hand up and down Huck's back, feeling the tension that hadn't been there a second ago.

To Liv, Huck said, "I'm sorry. You're great to want to do this for us. But I want to keep it local, okay? If Mom can't be there, then I don't want to invite…John. I think that would hurt her feelings if she found out."

Liv studied him while Kelsey took a sip of her vodka tonic with her free hand. If they were really married, she'd understand his obvious negative feelings about his father, and so she pretended that she did and was supportive of her man.

Kelsey came from an overachieving family that valued money and status. Two things Kelsey couldn't care less about. Her sisters were doctors and a lawyer, her father a prominent engineer with an aerospace firm. Most of the time, Kelsey felt she had nothing in common with them, and she was aware that they disapproved of her choice of vocation. But at the end of the day, she knew her parents loved her.

Feeling the abandonment of a father at seven, as Huck had, could seriously mess with you, and she didn't begrudge Huck his feelings for his father. But it seemed to go deeper than that. Twain didn't seem nearly as jumpy or bitter when John Beck's name came up.

Mentally placing that tidbit in her Huck Beck folder, Kelsey was just about to thank Liv again for all her trouble on their behalf, when she was jostled from behind by a couple of students who had started dancing to the song on the jukebox.

They apologized to her and moved deeper into the crowd, which now had several other couples dancing as well.

"Is there a dance floor here I'm not seeing?" she asked. Huck, Liv, and Twain all smiled and shook their heads.

"No, but this happens every now and then. People want to dance, they dance," Twain said. "Wherever there's room." He turned to Liv. "I think they're onto something. What do you say?"

Liv looked a little startled to be asked to dance by Twain, but quickly recovered and nodded. Twain rose, pulled out Liv's chair for her, and the two of them melded with the group of couples dancing. Though, with Twain's height, they didn't completely disappear.

"Huck Beck. Long time," said a young woman who planted herself in front of their table, in the empty spot left by Twain and Liv.

"Janie," Huck said by way of greeting.

Janie was short and curvy, and the two best words Kelsey could think of to describe her were "hair" and "makeup."

If this was Huck's usual type, no wonder Kelsey had gotten all the strange looks when introduced in Copper Harbor as the new Mrs. Beck.

"Hi, I'm Kelsey," she said, holding her hand out to Janie, who seemed shocked by the action.

"Janie Kuurtu, meet Kelsey Beck, my wife."

Janie shook Kelsey's hand quickly, letting it drop like she'd catch something. Funny, Kelsey was thinking the same thing about her, though she managed to hide it better.

"I'd heard," Janie said, "but didn't believe it."

"Believe it," Huck said with as much force as he'd told Liv about his father not getting an invitation.

Janie's eyes traveled to Huck's left hand, wrapped around his beer bottle, though his wedding band was still visible. Then she looked at Kelsey's left hand, which was out of sight because it was still resting on Huck's back.

"Would you like to join us?" Kelsey said, indicating Liv's empty chair. "Liv and Twain will be back, but we can—"

"She can sit at the table, but she won't be joining us," Huck said as he started to rise from his chair. "Because I intend to dance with my wife." He placed a warm hand on Kelsey's shoulder and gave a visible squeeze. And it didn't feel too shabby, either. "Come on, baby," he said, placing his hand at her back to help her rise.

"It was nice to meet you, Janie," Kelsey said as she got up from the seat, took Huck's hand, and followed him a few steps away to join the other dancing couples.

The song on the jukebox was ending, and Kelsey thought their exit might have been for naught. Then the next song started up, a slow ballad, and Huck wrapped his arms around her middle, pulling her close to him.

Wrapping her arms around his neck, she pressed herself to him, feeling Janie's eyes on her back.

Huck slid his hands down low on her hips, nearly to her ass, and bent his head to her ear in a nuzzling motion.

"Janie can be a bitch, but she's a hell of a gossip, so whatever we do here will make the rounds quicker than introducing you around to a bunch of boat people," he whispered in her ear, audible to no one but her.

"Basically she can cement our cover in just one evening," Kelsey whispered back, and she rested her head on Huck's shoulder.

"Yep," he said, one hand sliding up and down her back, the other gripping her hip tightly. "So, we may be playing with fire given the other night in my kitchen, and us both deciding to not do anything about that. But…"

"But?" She sank a hand into his hair, the ends well below his collar. She felt his goatee tickling the side of her face and had to admit she liked the feeling.

"But how about we act like the newlyweds we're supposed to be and can't keep our hands off each other?"

She raised her head, looking at him. His blue eyes seemed grayer in the dim light of the bar. Out of the corner of her eye, she could see Janie still staring at them. But she knew what she was going to say and do next had very little to do with that fact.

"Deal," she said, leaning forward and kissing Huck as she swayed in his arms.

Fourteen

~~~

THEY HAD DEFINITELY PLAYED WITH FIRE. HUCK TURNED the previous night over in his mind as he poured his first cup of coffee and sat down at his kitchen table.

Gone running. A note left for him by Kelsey. His respect for her went up another notch. Yeah, he should be thinking about getting into prime shape himself if this thing worked out and Prescott came through. Maybe he'd start running with her in the mornings. Though if they got on full time at the Harbor, they'd need to leave Houghton at the ass-crack of dawn every day.

Plus working on the boats had its share of hard physical labor, so that might be enough.

But he had a sneaking suspicion that early hours and backbreaking work during the day wouldn't deter Agent Cameron from taking her daily run.

It was probably odd that she'd refrained from it the first few days they'd been here.

A vision of running alongside Kelsey flashed through his brain. She would be in the tight running clothes he'd seen her pack, challenging him, setting the pace. He would be trying to keep up, enjoying the view of her backside and long, toned legs and loving every minute of it.

So, yeah, running. With Kelsey.

Another flash slammed through his brain, but it wasn't just his imagination this time. This was an actual physical memory of her wrapping herself around him on the dance floor and planting a big, wet kiss on him.

He'd been the one to bring up making a public display, but he'd been taken aback by how easily, and quickly, she'd jumped in.

On some level, Huck had known it was all for show for mainly Janie, but also Twain and Liv and the other people that Huck recognized in the Cat's Meow. But at some point, something shifted and it was, to him, as if they were the only two people in the room. It wasn't a show anymore, but him wanting Kelsey as close as possible, her body pressed deeply into his as slow song after slow song played on the jukebox.

He *thought* she felt the same way, that there was no way she was that good of an actress and that the pull, the attraction, was real on her part too.

It sure had been the other night in this very kitchen.

But he wasn't as sure about last night. Twain had eventually tugged on his arm and said, "Let's get out of here. We both need to get a room with our women." Huck hadn't even looked back at their table to see if Janie was still there. He'd only nodded, grabbed Kelsey's hand, and followed Twain and Liv out of the bar and into Liv's car.

There had been minimal talking on the short drive to Huck's place, but Twain's hands wandered over to Liv and Huck couldn't help but do the same to Kelsey, who unbuckled her seatbelt and slid over next to him, burrowing her body into his as he slung an arm around her shoulder.

She'd held his hand the whole way up his walkway into his house, waving over her shoulder to a retreating Liv and Twain. But as soon as the door had shut, she'd dropped his hand and gone to the living room, where she pulled out her laptop.

He'd gone to the kitchen to get a beer. Before he could even offer her one, she'd taken her laptop and gone upstairs to her room, closing the door behind her.

And now, here he was alone again, holding the note she'd left him.

He couldn't blame anyone but himself. He'd been the one to say yesterday that they shouldn't take the physical any further in real life, that he didn't need the distraction when this assignment was so important to him.

And it was to her, too, he knew, but she'd seemed semi-open to the idea of exploring where their kiss could lead.

Huck already knew where it would lead. Straight to his bed. Or maybe it would not even get that far and instead test out the strength of the very kitchen table at which he now sat.

And it would be good. He knew it. Possibly better than he'd ever had, because not only was he hot for Kelsey, but he also liked and admired her. Which he didn't often say about the girls he took to bed.

And that was the crux of it all. She was too different from what he was used to for the normal short-term, but oh-so-enjoyable hookups.

And no way did they have any kind of future. She was FBI; he was a civilian living hundreds of miles away. Even if he did get on with the DEA, chances were he wouldn't be able to pick and choose where they sent him.

And let's face it, though she treated him with respect and seemed to value his opinion, there was a little bit of "What the hell happened to you, anyway?" that crossed her face when she would remind him that she was the agent and he was just support.

He wished he could clue her in, tell her what had happened to him. He felt he could trust her, but something held him back.

Let her think he'd just washed out from DEA training, hadn't been up to it. It would probably work in his favor if she underestimated him.

He was going for his third cup, and making a new pot, when Kelsey came in, winded a little bit, but her face fresh and glowing. She was wearing running leggings and a running bra; he could see the straps peeking out of the Harvard sweatshirt she also wore. Her shoes were expensive running shoes but a bright pink, which seemed out of place and almost frilly on the most non-frilly woman he'd met.

She went to the fridge and got a bottle of water as Huck resumed his seat at the table. "New pot will be ready in a minute," he said, watching as she held on to the back of one of the chairs and pulled her foot up behind her, stretching out her hamstring.

"Thanks," she said, and he realized she was more winded than he'd originally thought.

"Pushed hard today?" he said, though he didn't know her regular running routine. She just seemed…different.

"Yeah, I guess," she said.

Maybe her body needed the release that neither of them had gotten last night. He knew he sure needed something.

"Mind if I join you tomorrow morning?" he asked, surprising her as she took a deep drag of the water.

"You run?"

"Not in a while. Was never regular with it. But…I liked it when I did it."

"I run nearly every day," she said. The underlying message was: "I do not want to be held back by you."

He shrugged. "If I can't keep up, leave me in your dust."

She studied him for a second, and he willed himself not to squirm under her scrutiny. Not for the first time did he think that he wouldn't want to be a suspect interrogated by Agent Cameron.

"Fine," she finally said. "But I absolutely will leave you in my dust if you can't keep up."

"Fair enough," he said, raising his coffee mug in a toast to her.

And silently praying that he wouldn't be left on the side of the road puking up his guts the next morning.

LATER THAT MORNING, after they were both showered (separately) and dressed, they drove back up to the Harbor, intending to meet with the owner of the *Mina*.

Huck kept silent, not wanting to repeat the conversation of yesterday about how nothing should happen between them.

He still felt that way, even though he'd wanted nothing more last night than to take her to bed after an evening of holding her in his arms as they danced. And the dance-floor kissing didn't help, though he'd certainly enjoyed it.

Kelsey didn't bring it up either. Nor did she mention the bar last night. Or the dancing, near grinding, they'd done.

They rode in silence, Huck choosing Covered Drive instead of getting to Copper Harbor via the lake route and Eagle River and Eagle Harbor.

"This is pretty," Kelsey said while they drove through the twisty, hilly terrain.

"It's spectacular during the fall, with the colors on the trees hanging over the highway."

"I'll bet."

It was pretty now, too. A canopy of green hung over them as they drove, enveloping them in a natural cocoon.

"Which way do you usually take?" she asked. "This route or the one we did yesterday?"

He shrugged, his wrist slung over the top of the steering wheel. "Depends on the mood. This way is a little faster. The other way is a better view, though this is nice too."

He didn't mention that his sister-in-law Molly had died in an accident on this stretch of road. Huck knew Sawyer avoided Covered Drive if he could, but Huck didn't, though he always thought of poor Molly.

The *Mina* was in port at the marina and Huck and Kelsey made their way over to it. Huck took inventory in his mind as they approached the docked boat.

Thirty-eight-foot Fairline. A few outriggers attached to the port side for fishing. The boat wasn't brand new, but probably only three or four years old. It was well maintained and definitely had room in its below-deck area for a boatload (pun intended) of pseudoephedrine and other shit coming over from Canada.

But then, so did every boat in this marina. If it was big enough to take on the rough waters of Lake Superior, it was large enough to mule drugs across international waters.

After asking permission to come aboard, they introduced themselves to Jim Peterson, the owner and captain of the *Mina*.

He was in his early to mid-fifties, Huck guessed, with black hair and brown eyes, handsome in a classical way, with deep tan lines around his eyes, which suggested he'd been boating for a while. And that he either laughed a lot or squinted into the horizon a lot. Or both.

His handshake was firm, and he met Huck's eyes when they shook, but that didn't say much. No one was ever prosecuted on the basis of a dead-fish handshake, though in Huck's personal opinion, that should change.

He was fit and was wearing expensive clothing, which was unusual for the area, but then, so was Jim Peterson.

"Frank Belson told me you might be stopping by today," he said as he waved them to take a seat in the deck area. Nice seats, and Huck noticed that the fishing chairs were also top of the line. There was some money here, for sure.

"I hope we didn't keep you at dock because of it," Huck said as he settled into a comfy chair next to Kelsey.

Jim shook his head. "Not at all. I didn't have any groups scheduled today. Frank said you were newlyweds? Congratulations."

"Thank you," they both said. "So you can see why we're trying to pick up extra work anywhere we can," Huck added.

"Ah, yes, wives don't come cheap. Just ask my two ex-wives." He said it with no bitterness, just amusement.

"Husbands don't come cheap either. I mean, look at this boat," Kelsey said, but in a teasing, non-challenging way.

"I'm sure that's true," Jim agreed. He studied Kelsey for a few seconds and then smiled at her. She smiled back, and Huck felt a weird flash of emotion skitter through him.

Certainly not jealousy, right? He should be happy that Jim liked Kelsey—more chance of him hiring them. So why did Huck suddenly feel like telling Jim Peterson to fuck off and throwing Kelsey over his shoulder and getting off the boat?

Yeah, real caveman shit, but he couldn't deny he was feeling it.

"Frank also sang your praises, Huck. Said you were a great deckhand and he'd trust you behind the wheel of his boat any day."

Huck stuffed down his feelings and nodded at Jim. "That's nice of him to say. I've worked for Frank a lot during busy times, high season. He's a good captain."

"And I'm pretty new at this. I took early retirement, sold my firm to fulfill a lifelong dream of owning my own boat. And I love it, I really do, but it's a hell of a lot harder than sitting at a desk all day."

"That it is," Huck said.

"And trying to break in up here is hard." He waved his hand out toward the other boats docked in the marina. "All these other boats are well established, with returning charters."

"That's true," Huck said, a picture forming in his head of a man who overextended himself to fulfill a dream and then realized the dream was a bust.

What would that man do to save his dream? Take on muling?

"But, little by little, I've managed to build a small but loyal clientele. I have a few fishing charters that say they'll come back. Small groups that want to go to Isle Royale for a few days and don't want to either be roped into the schedule of the *Ranger* or the other boats that make timed trips. Or want more privacy for their trip than those larger boats would offer.

"So, it's starting to come along. Enough so that I could use some help, on a part-time basis."

"That's great," Huck said, mentally rearranging the picture in his mind. Of course, if Jim was muling, his workload might be such that he needed the help.

But then, why risk witnesses?

"We understand it would be part time, as needed," Kelsey said. "There may be times that we're on other jobs, but if you have enough notice of your charters, we would definitely make ourselves available."

Jim nodded at her. "Back to the expensive prospect of marriage, right?"

Kelsey shrugged. "Have you seen Huck's house?" Huck bristled next to her, and she put a hand on his arm. "No offense, honey. It was perfect when it was just you and the people who crashed there. But it needs a lot of work to be a house we can make a home."

She was setting up the fact that they needed money. He knew that, yet still his pride took a swan dive at the fact that his wife was disappointed in her new home.

But that played in perfectly too, and she'd known that.

Smart cookie, Kelsey Cameron.

"I told you, I'm working on that," he said, embarrassment seeping through his words.

"I know, honey," she said, smoothing her hand down his arm, her gold band reflecting the sun. "But we need the money to make that happen. Let's just take it everywhere we can find it." To Jim, she said, "We're not afraid of hard work, and lots of it. We've got a bunch of things we want to do on the house, and every little bit helps."

"It does, indeed," Jim said, giving her a warm smile with something that Huck took as pity in his eyes.

Yeah, it would work. Jim would want to help Kelsey and not mind throwing Huck under the bus to do it. It could play out in their favor.

"I have a fishing charter scheduled for Sunday. I'd love to have extra hands." He looked at Kelsey. "Can you cook at all?" he asked her.

Given the state of her fridge and cupboards at her place in D.C., Huck knew the answer to that. "I've done my fair share of cooking on boats," he said. "I'm no chef, but can do a good, hearty lunch for fishermen, or cocktails and appetizers for a sunset cruise."

Jim nodded. "Good. Because I have a few of those scheduled,

too. Let me go get the dates of those, as well as other charters planned."

He rose and went below, coming back up with an iPad on which he was bringing up his calendar.

They spent the next half-hour coordinating dates, pay, and menus for charters. Jim paid the going rate for work, so he was neither throwing money away nor trying to undercut them and save a buck just because he knew they needed the money.

After another half-hour of touring the boat, they all shook hands, and Kelsey and Huck headed to his truck.

"Can you really cook?" she asked once they were buckled in and driving out of the marina.

"Yep," he said, pulling on to the main highway, taking a right away from Copper Harbor and toward Eagle Harbor. He'd decided to take the scenic route home. Maybe they'd even stop at Fitzpatrick's in Eagle River and have a drink or food while watching the sunset.

"Good to know," she said. "Marriage to you may have its perks."

"Yep," was all he said in reply.

They drove in silence for a while, then Huck said, "Now that we've got employment, sporadic as it is, maybe we should think about getting a cheap place up in Copper Harbor or Eagle Harbor or somewhere."

She turned to him, taking her eyes from Lake Superior. "Is that what you normally do?"

He nodded. "Most summers. I get a tiny, cheap cabin for the season. Making this drive every day can suck."

She again looked out the window and gave her head a tiny shake. "I don't know how this view could ever suck."

"Yeah that's great, but…"

"You do realize that most of the people I work with have a daily commute longer than this? At least in time, if not miles."

"Do you?"

"No. But that's why I got the apartment I did—so I could be

close to the office."

"That's why I rent a shitty cabin."

"Why does it have to be shitty?"

"Because all the good ones they use for tourist rentals. They keep the shitty ones for cheap housing for seasonal workers."

"But renting a cabin, even a shitty one, goes against what we're putting out there, that we're desperate for money."

"Case could be made we'd spend as much in gas going back and forth as we would on a cabin."

She thought on that and gave a small nod. "I'll run the numbers on that, see if it's feasible."

"It'd probably be close," Huck said.

"Maybe we should think about using your brother's place. The one Deni offered up."

"We could, but…"

"Why, is it even shittier than the shitty cabins?"

"No. Not shitty at all. The thing is an engineering masterpiece, with downright breathtaking views."

"Better than this?" Kelsey said, pointing out the window as they neared Fitzpatrick's on the shore of Lake Superior.

"Better. Hard to believe, but yeah."

"So, why aren't we staying there?"

"The shitty cabins would be roughing it, but they'd have running water and electricity, not to mention an inside, working john. Sawyer's place is *roughing* it."

She looked over to him as he parked the car. "I'm not exactly ultra prissy, you know."

An uncontrollable laugh bubbled out of Huck, and Kelsey smiled back at him. "I got that, yeah," he said.

"So?"

He shrugged. "You say that now, and God knows I'm not someone who needs a luxury shower—"

"Oh, right, a shower," Kelsey said. "I was just thinking of that outhouse. But yeah, a shower."

"There is a sauna, so you'd be able to shower, in a sense. Ever had a sauna?"

"Of course."

He raised his eyebrows while cutting the ignition. "Really?"

"The last gym I was a member of had one, and I took them all the time after running. The gym I'm with now has a steam room, not a sauna."

"So, electric."

"Yes."

"There's a difference," he said, and got out of the truck. By the time he'd made it to her side, she was already out of the door.

"Wait for me to help you out, would ya?" he said.

She stopped in her tracks. "I can get out of a truck just fine. Seriously, you're a smart guy, but your image of me is way off, if you—"

"As a *gentleman*, I'd like to help a *lady* out of the truck. That's all. I know you can handle yourself. Never have I doubted that. Shit, I'm just hoping I can keep up with you."

She looked at him. "Oh."

"Yeah, oh."

She started walking again, and he took her hand in his and walked with her.

"Oh, do you think we're being watched? That's why the helping me out, taking my hand?" She looked at the building, with few windows on the parking lot side. The place was nearly all windows on the side facing Lake Superior.

He wasn't about to start lying to her now.

"No, I don't think we're being watched." He squeezed her hand.

Fifteen

—✺—

THE NEXT DAY, SATURDAY, THEY DID GROCERY SHOPPING and ran errands.

Just like your typical married couple would.

At the grocery store, they took two carts. One for their place, one for the *Mina*'s menu, paid for by the money Jim Peterson had given them to do the shopping.

They passed the liquor aisle and Huck went straight for the beer, putting a couple of cases in the cart he was steering and a six-pack, a bottle of vodka, and a liter of tonic in the cart she commandeered.

Saturday night, Huck grilled steaks for them, and Kelsey thought she'd never tasted anything so good. She usually avoided red meat in favor of fish or chicken as her protein, but she was seriously considering taking that back when she tasted Huck's tender and juicy rib eye.

They discussed the case some more. It seemed that Huck was pinning a lot on Jim Peterson. Kelsey got that Huck wanted to believe that none of the locals that he'd lived and worked with for years could have turned to illegal carrying of drugs.

Finally, Kelsey said, "You do realize that with him being the only new person we've come into contact with, the chances he's the other agent on this case are better than the chances that he's our target."

He'd known that; she saw by his quick acceptance of the idea.

She found herself glad that he'd already thought of something she found quite obvious. He just hadn't wanted to believe it.

He was smart. And he would learn to keep his personal feelings out of it, Kelsey was sure. She still didn't know the specifics of why he'd washed out of DEA training four years ago, but it wasn't because he didn't have the brain for it.

"Yeah, I know. Is there a way we can find that out? So we're not spinning our wheels or spending all our time on someone who in turn is spending all his time investigating us?"

"Probably not. I'll throw his name to Jenkins and see if there's any reaction. If they weren't able—or willing—to give us this agent's name at the beginning, they're not likely to now. But you never know. Jenkins may just say to move on from Peterson or something, and we'd know."

He studied her over the kitchen table, their empty plates between them, only steak juice remaining on either of them. "It really kills you to report to him, doesn't it?"

She didn't like that he saw her so clearly, and she tried to replay in her mind the tone she'd just used when speaking of Jenkins.

"You didn't give anything away," he said, reading her mind. "In fact, he gave it away during our briefing. The smirk. He was loving putting you in a lesser position as backup only, not letting you in on the whole case, that you had to report to him. That fucking smirk." Huck shrugged. "I figured it was probably mutual, though you're too professional, and too good of an agent, to let it show."

"That fucking smirk," she whispered, looking down at her plate. She wanted to tell Huck more, wanted to tell him something she'd never told anyone, but she stopped herself. Not because she didn't think she could trust Huck. Even though she'd only known him five days, she instinctively knew Huck Beck could keep a secret.

No, she didn't tell him because she didn't want his opinion of her to be tarnished. His obvious respect he had for her as an agent was apparent, and she found she didn't want to lose it.

And that fact alone scared the crap out of her.

Why should she care what Huck Beck thought of her? He was just a civilian local helping her get close to an investigation. In a few weeks, or months, she'd never see him again.

And yet she still cared.

THEY WORKED THE SUNDAY fishing charter for Jim Peterson, and it went well. Huck made the most heavenly sandwiches for them all, and Kelsey savored every morsel.

She worked the lines while they left the dock, and helped Huck a little in the kitchen. She set up the meal for the fishermen to come into the cabin and eat, which they did in shifts, always a couple manning the fishing lines.

They were serious fishermen, but Huck told her those charters were sometimes just a big party, with hardly any lines cast into the water.

He was telling her this while Jim was in the galley with them, seeming to glean as much information from Huck on what to expect from various charters as Kelsey did.

"A lot of times," he said as he put the sandwich meats back in the refrigerator, "these guys tell their wives they're going fishing, but it's really just an excuse to get drunk with the boys."

"Nobody says anything when they come back with no fish?" Kelsey asked.

"Even serious fishermen strike out."

"They can't just say 'Honey, I'm having a boys' weekend. We're going to get drunk on a boat. See you Monday' or something like that?"

She knew it was for Jim's benefit, but still she liked it when Huck rounded the counter, came to stand in front of her, and leaned down to her face. "Are you telling me that's all I'll need to do with you, darlin'?"

"Yeah, that's all you'd need to do," she answered, not quite able to keep the breathiness out of her voice.

He planted a big kiss on her and then returned to his task. Over his shoulder to Jim, he said, "Do I have the best wife ever, or what?"

Jim laughed and nodded, but studied Kelsey.

"Just don't say it to me too often," she added, which made both Jim and Huck laugh, her husband flashing her that devastating smile.

And even though the winds were brisk on Lake Superior, she suddenly felt very warm inside.

"I'M ASSUMING THAT since you were able to receive this call you're not up at the Harbor," Twain said when he called Huck three days after their first charter with Jim Peterson.

"Nope. We don't have another job until Friday. An early morning fishing gig, then a sunset cruise later."

"Nice, a two-fer."

"Yep," Huck said to his brother.

The days they were up in the Harbor had been good. They pretty much had the run of Jim's boat while he was captaining and the charters were fishing trips.

Much to Huck's chagrin, they hadn't been able to find anything even slightly suspicious. He badly wanted the culprit to be Jim Peterson, rather than a local that Huck knew, but he knew that it did him no favors to focus on only one suspect, lest he miss anything from anyone else.

He'd also gotten up and run with Kelsey the last three mornings. The first one, he'd been heavily winded, and she had indeed left him in her dust. But this morning he felt pretty good, and though she was definitely ahead of him the entire way, he was able to see her the whole time.

And what a sight it had been.

"Need a favor, then, if you can swing it," Twain said now, pulling Huck away from his thoughts of Kelsey in her long, skintight running leggings.

"Sure thing."

"Liv and I drove to Escanaba today. I had to meet with a prospective landowner, and Liv thought she'd get some shopping done in Marquette."

"Sounds like a good day," Huck said, though both Twain's and Liv's parts of the day sounded sucky to him.

"It was. It is. That's the thing. We'd like to stay in Marquette tonight. Do dinner. Liv wants to shop a little bit more. Take our time. Have breakfast in the morning and then head back."

"Liv doesn't have to work?"

"She's got the break off until summer track starts up next week."

"And Matty?" Huck said, realizing as he did the reason for Twain's call.

"Yeah, that's the thing. Can he crash with you and Kelsey tonight? You'd just need to pick him up at our house a half-hour or so after school gets out, take him to your place, feed him, throw him in your guestroom, and get him to school tomorrow morning. We'll be home before he gets out of school."

Matt never got to stay with Huck, and he'd always felt bad about that, because he loved his nephew. But with Matt's parents being divorced and Liv having a ton of family in the area, there was always someone to take Matt if Twain wasn't available.

"Of course, no problem. We'd love to have him," Huck said. As soon as he did, he remembered that the guestroom was currently occupied. By his wife.

"Or Kelsey and I could just go stay at your place. That way Matt doesn't have to pack up or anything."

"But then you guys would have to. We don't want you to go to any trouble. Besides, it'll be a little adventure for Matty too. He'd love it. And I know you always keep your guestroom made up for strays."

"Yeah, I kind of put the word out that strays no longer need apply. Can't have people walking in here any time of the day or night anymore."

"Good call," Twain said. "Listen, if it's a hassle—"

"No. No hassle at all. Matty's no stray, and he always has a place to stay with us."

"Thanks, brother," Twain said.

Something caught in Huck's throat, and he cleared it before answering, "Anytime."

"I'll call Matty and give him the details. He'll have a bag packed and be at our place by four thirty."

"Got it," Huck said, and was just about to hang up when Twain caught him.

"And just so you know, he got busted a couple of months back sneaking out of his buddy's house during a sleepover. Went to see some girl. So don't let him pull anything."

"Got it," Huck said again, smiling while thinking of his nephew's antics. Like father, like son.

"And he's only legally allowed to drive with Liv or me in the car. He'll probably tell you it's okay with any family member, but that is not the truth. Don't let him behind the wheel."

"Got it," Huck said. "Jesus, I can't believe he's old enough for his permit."

"It flies by, Huck, just completely flies by."

"I guess."

Twain chuckled. "And we're doing it all over again," he said, disbelief and yet wonderment in his voice.

"Yeah, about that..." Huck hadn't been alone with Twain since he and Liv dropped their bombshell, and he wanted to make sure his brother was okay with what was happening.

As if he knew where Huck was headed, Twain cut him off. "I know, it's crazy. But I gotta tell you, Huck. I am nuts about my wife. Can't wait to get a ring back on her finger and see her belly grow with my child."

Wow. Huck knew that Twain had always cared for Liv, but he'd never heard his big brother gush about his feelings. Come to think of it, he'd never heard Twain mention the L-word when it came to Liv, except for the other night.

"That's great, man," Huck said, the awe in his voice surely

coming through.

Twain laughed. "I know. Like I said, crazy. Thirty-five years old and deeply in love for the first time in my life. And with my ex-wife, no less."

"Yeah, crazy," Huck agreed.

"Says the man who fell so fast he married the woman after five months of knowing her. You know crazy, I'm guessing."

Huck chuckled at that. "You got that right."

They made some more arrangements about Matt, and Huck hung up just as Kelsey walked into the living room, her notebook in hand.

She jotted down notes during all their discussions, then put the notebook in the trunk in the attic with her gun and badge each night.

"I know nothing new has happened since the last time we went through it, but I thought maybe we could just go over everything again. See if anything different jumps out at us."

The first round of financials had come back from D.C., and nothing had seemed out of place. They weren't ruling anyone out, but continued to put their focus on Jim Peterson. Jenkins hadn't let anything slip when Kelsey had brought up his name the last time she'd checked in.

"I'd like that," he said. "But first, we need to move you out of the guestroom and into my bedroom."

Her startled look had Huck quickly explaining Twain's request and their current situation. And that he'd be leaving in a couple of hours to go fetch Matt from Liv's house.

"Right. Let's get my stuff moved first, then talk about the case," she said.

As they were hauling her clothes out of the tiny closet in the guestroom, Huck apologized for the hassle.

"Hey, he's your nephew. And your brother was asking. What were you going to say? No?" Kelsey said in a tone that made Huck believe her words. She wasn't pissed at all about how the night was going to play out.

Or, he realized when he walked behind her with an armful of her clothes and saw her stopped in his doorway, staring at his bed, she hadn't thought it all the way through yet.

"No, I couldn't say no," he said, squeezing past her into the room and taking her clothes to his dresser. "But I could have said I needed to ask you first."

"And then say no? So he hates his new sister-in-law?" she said, pulling her eyes away from the bed and moving her hanging clothes into his closet, which was much larger than the guest bedroom one, and, because of Huck's limited wardrobe, had more empty space.

"No, that's not what I meant. We probably would have still said yes. I mean, a married man would probably have said something like that, right?"

She hung the clothes up and turned to him, thinking. "Maybe. But also, a *very* single man like yourself, just newly married, probably wouldn't think of that straight off."

She was probably right, and Huck felt marginally better.

"That's something I'd train you at over time," she said with a smile, and went to get another load of clothes. "If we hadn't been thrown into this so fast."

A short time later, they had all of Kelsey's things moved. While she moved her toiletries from the guest bath to the en suite off his room, Huck made up the bed Matt would sleep in.

The sheets he removed smelled of Kelsey, and Huck had a flash of being in her bed in her apartment. How good he'd felt in it. How right.

Would Kelsey feel the same in his bed tonight?

After getting the bed done, Huck was leaving with the used sheets balled in his arms when he noticed Kelsey's jewelry box on top of the dresser. Since there wasn't anything else of hers on top, it had been easy to overlook. Huck grabbed it and balanced it on top of the sheets.

He loved his old house. It had been a steal when he'd bought it six years ago. A steal in an already low-cost area. It was small and placed precariously at the top end of one of Houghton's many hills, which made getting to or from it a bit hazardous on icy days. But it had a lot of charm, which he had unearthed in the past four years as he slowly fixed it up. Creating a master suite and using one of the three bedrooms as a storage area.

But one of the best features was the laundry chute that dropped straight to the basement from the second floor.

Sure, he had to carry the laundry back up when it was done, but down was one short drop away.

He opened the chute with his elbow and just as he was about to deposit the whole ball, he remembered the jewelry box and grabbed for it.

He got it by the lid, and the sheets fell to the basement with a thud. The jewelry box dangled from his fingers, and he quickly righted it. But as he did so, something popped from its mooring, revealing a sheet of paper. Taking a closer look, he pulled the paper out to reveal a false bottom in the jewelry box. Clever. And kind of convenient for someone in Kelsey's line of work.

He started to stuff the piece of paper back in, but in doing so, one of the many folds came undone, and Huck realized the paper contained a drawing of some kind.

Was Kelsey an artist? It didn't seem to fit with her personality, but one thing Huck now knew was not to underestimate Kelsey Cameron.

Carefully he unfolded the paper, feeling a little shitty about doing it, but his curiosity overrode his morals.

When he had it fully opened, he stared at a sketch of himself. And not just a drawing that resembled Huck or even closely resembled him.

No, this was Huck completely. It was like someone had taken a photo of him and Photoshopped a pencil-drawing filter onto it or something, it was so accurate.

He instantly knew where it was from.

If Kelsey had ever looked at this sketch tucked deep inside her jewelry box, she was sure to have remembered him.

So why hadn't she said anything?

But the better question wasn't why didn't she mention remembering him, but rather...why did she still have his sketch?

Sixteen

HUCK SAID HE DIDN'T FEEL LIKE COOKING, WHICH Kelsey understood. After all, he'd cooked on the boat the day before pretty much the entire charter.

And since Kelsey didn't cook, they took Matt out for dinner at a place called the Commodore, where Kelsey promptly fell in love with a taco pizza called a Tostada.

She didn't know how long she would be in the Copper Country, but she was definitely coming back to the Commodore again before she left.

Maybe a few times.

Matt was a good kid, and they talked about skiing. Her family had taken an annual trip to Vail, as well as a few weekend trips to Vermont, to ski.

From the lake-view room at the Commodore and its huge window, Matt pointed out Mont Ripley across the Portage Canal and told Kelsey that was where he skied. It was green now, but not lush quite yet, the spring coming so late to the Copper Country, Huck explained to her.

She enjoyed talking with Matt, and again felt a twinge of crappiness that she and Huck were lying to the Beck family. The adults would understand why Huck had done what he'd done, if he was indeed taken on by the DEA. If not, Huck made it seem that his brothers would not be surprised that a rash decision he'd made had gone bad.

But what about Matt? Would a kid understand? He seemed pretty mature for a fifteen-year-old. Certainly more so than a couple of Kelsey's nieces, though she didn't see them all that much.

And he obviously adored his Uncle Huck. Would Matt understand when the newly met Aunt Kelsey left for good?

At least his parents were back together, and he'd soon have a baby sister or brother to distract him.

Beyond chatting with Matt, she didn't say a lot to Huck over dinner. Something seemed to be up with him. Ever since they'd gotten the house ready for Matt's visit, he'd seem preoccupied.

He was probably just thinking about the case. Kelsey took a drink of her cola and thought about that.

Had Huck had a thought pertaining to the case that was bothering him? Something he should be discussing with her?

She knew he was hanging a lot on the suspect being Jim Peterson and not a local that he'd known for years, but Kelsey wasn't so sure.

Would Huck keep something from her that pointed to a local?

Would he outright lie if she called him on it?

She studied him as she ate more of her pizza, and he talked with Matt about some kind of wood that Matt and Twain had harvested earlier in the spring. Kelsey knew squat about types of wood and logging, and had never even heard the term "burl" before, but both of the guys seemed pretty excited by it.

She tried to mentally retrace their steps yesterday at Copper Harbor and what Huck might have seen or heard that Kelsey hadn't.

But no, he'd only started being preoccupied this afternoon, when they hadn't seen or talked to anybody.

At least, she thought Huck hadn't seen or talked to anybody. For all Kelsey knew, he could have been texting away all afternoon in the other room as she got herself settled into Huck's room.

Did she have to point her radar in his direction too? Would he withhold something not only because he didn't want to believe someone he knew could be involved in this? Or, and this was a worse thought to Kelsey, was he holding out on her so that he could make headway on his own, show Prescott that he was worthy of the DEA? Just as she wanted to prove to Tarrington and her boss that she was good enough to do undercover work on a regular basis.

But she wouldn't throw Huck under the bus to do it. Would she?

When they got back home, Kelsey's mood matched Huck's, and they both seemed relieved when Matt said he needed to go to his room and study for his finals, which were this week.

They didn't risk Matt overhearing and talk about the case. Besides, in theory, there was nothing new since the night before when they'd gotten home from Copper Harbor.

She worked on her laptop, answering emails to her sisters, pretending she was still in D.C. and at her apartment. Huck prepared something in the kitchen that they'd freeze and take with them to Jim's boat on Friday.

If it wasn't completely fictional, Kelsey could easily get used to a husband so handy in the kitchen.

After a couple of hours, Huck told her he was going to go make sure that Matt didn't need anything, and went upstairs. Kelsey waited a while and then decided to turn in herself.

Not knowing if Huck was coming back down or not, she turned off all the lights and locked the front door. Years of doing it at her own home had her going to the back door too, as well as all the windows, making sure the perimeter was completely secure.

Perimeter. More like small, but cozy, bachelor pad.

She made her way upstairs and quietly walked down the hall, intending to pop her head into Matt's room and say goodnight to both him and Huck.

But their voices carried down the hallway, and she stopped in her tracks.

"You and Aunt Kelsey seem pretty solid."

"Yeah, we're good," Huck said.

"And you got married after only knowing each other for five months? Holy wah," Matt said.

"The thing is, Kelsey only *thinks* we met in January," Huck said to Matt.

"You didn't?"

"No. We actually met, very briefly, four years ago."

"How?"

"We didn't exchange names or anything, and it was only for a minute or two." One minute exactly, Kelsey remembered, stopwatch and all. "But we were in a room with a bunch of people and I just…couldn't take my eyes off her." Yeah, because it was the assignment. Still…

He remembered her? Remembered the observation exercise of four years ago? Why hadn't he said anything?

Why hadn't she?

She backed away from Matt's bedroom door, which had been open just enough for Kelsey to hear the tail end of Huck's admission.

She knew he'd been embellishing for Matt's benefit, but still. Unfamiliar feelings flooded Kelsey. Could she have made the same impression on Huck Beck four years ago that he'd made on her?

And what exactly was that impression?

After clearing her throat, and loudly walking the few steps she'd just backtracked, she said, "Huck, Matt, you guys okay?" Then she walked down the hall to Matt's room (her room until a few hours ago) and stood at the door.

"You can come in, babe," Huck said, and Kelsey pushed the door open and stood in the doorway.

Huck was sitting up on the bed, his back on the headboard, arms behind his head, his black tee pulled tight across his chest. His legs were up on the bed, feet crossed at the ankles, shoes still on, the denim of his jeans showing just how well they fit his muscular legs. Matt was also on the bed, but on his stomach lying cross-wise at the foot, his long, skinny legs hanging over the side at his ankles, his arms draped off the other side. He was looking down at the floor, his hand nonchalantly smoothing against the grain of the carpet.

"I didn't mean to interrupt. I just wanted to say goodnight and see if you guys needed anything before I turned in," she said.

"I'm good, but thanks," Huck said.

"No thanks, Aunt Kelsey," Matt said.

Kelsey found she had to steady herself mentally so she didn't flinch at his words.

She'd been called Aunt Kelsey for years, her eldest niece being almost seventeen. But Matt had not called her Aunt Kelsey until just then, and she found it… Hmmm, not as off-putting as she'd first thought.

Kind of nice, actually.

"Okay. Huck, let Matt know what all's in the fridge or pantry that he could grab if he gets hungry later." To Matt she added, "Huck is the master of the kitchen."

"That ain't the only room I'm master of," Huck said with a tease in his voice.

Kelsey rolled her eyes while Matt laughed. Then she said to the boy, "Matt, make sure you get all your information about girls from your father and your *other* uncle. Don't listen to this one."

Matt laughed and Huck chuckled, and Kelsey waved goodnight to them and left.

"I'll be there soon," Huck called after her. Then he mumbled something low that only Matt could hear. Probably more on the riff of master of the bedroom, if Matt's laugh was any indication.

Kelsey moved down to the room she would share with Huck tonight, still thinking about the fact that Huck had remembered her from four years ago.

Why hadn't he said anything?

She spied her jewelry box on the top of Huck's dresser and again wondered why *she* hadn't said anything.

She took a quick shower, brushed her teeth, and changed into the boxers and oversized tee she wore to sleep in, thankful for the en suite bathroom so Huck couldn't walk in on her in the act of changing.

He'd offered his bedroom to her the first night they'd arrived, saying he'd take the guestroom, but that had seemed foolish to her given that all his stuff was in the master.

But now, enjoying the large shower and bathroom, she almost wished she'd taken him up on it.

And the bed was a king, and incredibly comfy, she noted when she slid in. A king, yeah, so lots of room for them to have their own side.

There wouldn't even be any need for them to touch if they didn't want to.

So why did Kelsey desperately want to all of a sudden?

Seventeen

———

HUCK TOOK A LONG SHOWER, GRATEFUL THAT KELSEY
had seemed asleep when he'd come into the bedroom.

He sat in the shower and thought about telling Matt about
meeting Kelsey four years ago.

Meeting? Yeah, more like seeing for exactly one minute.

And yet four years later, he knew. He hadn't at first, not in
the FBI offices, though he had felt that strange sense of familiarity.

But the minute he saw that picture in her apartment of her
with her family, and the ponytail she'd had then, it had become
crystal clear.

He'd of course noticed her in that one minute, but that was
kind of the point. The DEA training class was, in theory, helping
out with an FBI training exercise, but Huck knew that somehow
they would circle around and use what they saw later in training.
And after only a minute of looking into her big brown eyes, he
knew he was going to hunt all over Quantico to find her.

But his whole world had fallen apart a few days later, and
he'd left Virginia behind, as well as his memories of the cute,
ponytailed girl who had stared at him with fierce determination,
which, over the course of the minute, had turned into interest.

But she had kept the sketch of him. And obviously had a
great talent for description for the sketch artist to nail him so
completely.

He put a towel around his waist as he left the shower, and ran another towel through his hair. Used the john, brushed his teeth, and found an old pair of sweats he'd cut off to sleep in. Usually he slept naked, but that probably wasn't a good idea tonight.

Thank God he had a king-sized bed. He'd just stay on his side, get some good sleep, and forget he'd seen that stupid sketch.

But when he got in the bed, he smelled her. The lemony scent of her shampoo. Or lotion. Or maybe it was just the scent of Kelsey. His intention to sleep on his side, facing away from her, was soon forgotten, and he rolled over to face her.

To find her staring back at him.

"Hey," she whispered.

"Hey," he softly said back. "Sorry if I woke you."

A tiny shake of her head. "You didn't. Or I don't think you did. I might have dozed off for a minute or two."

They stared at each other for a few minutes, Huck silently willing her to close her eyes. 'Cause he sure as hell wasn't going to.

He moved his hand down from the pillow and slid it to the center of the bed. Still not touching, not even all that close. But close enough that she could reach out and touch him.

If she wanted to.

Please God, want to.

She slid her hand down from her own pillow and moved it slowly—so fucking slowly—toward his. But stopped inches away. He looked up from their hands to her big brown eyes.

"You said there was too much at stake," she said.

"There is."

"But then…"

"I find," he began, trying to be as honest as he could, with both her and himself, "that in this moment, right here, right now, that I want you more than I care about what's at stake."

She smiled, and it literally took his breath away. Somewhere in the back of his head, a voice told him to breathe again, and he tried, but he knew his breathing was heavier and quicker than just a second ago.

"Are you sure about that?"

"Yes," he said without having to think about it. She raised one brow at him, questioning. "Well, I wouldn't want to lose you as a partner," he added. "I'm learning from you, I like the way we bounce ideas off each other, and I think we work well together."

"We do," she said, and he felt his body relax. He knew he hadn't imagined the last several days and how well they worked together. He'd never gotten as far as having a partner of any kind, and he knew Prescott worried that maybe he wouldn't play well with others.

And maybe he wouldn't, but he sure played well with Kelsey Cameron.

Could their partnership there, in his bed, be just as good? Yes, instinctively he knew it would be, and he kept his hand in the middle of the bed, not reaching further, but not pulling it back, either.

"Do you think if we…you know," she said, eyeing their hands, "that we can just go back to being regular partners? That it won't spill over?"

"I want to say yes," he said, "But I also don't want to blow smoke up your ass, just to get what I want. It can't help but spill over a little, but we can control the spill."

"How do we do that?"

"Well, for one thing, it will only help strengthen our physical reactions to each other in public, which plays out in our favor."

"So…take one for the case?" she said with a smile, which he returned.

"Sure, we can tell ourselves that. We're true patriots."

She gave a tiny snort of laughter, so spontaneous, so natural. And a sound Huck had not heard out of her before.

A sound he very much liked.

But it was the sound she made when he reached over and finally took her hand that he liked best. A breathy sigh of surprise and desire, which rocketed through him, making him instantly hard.

"You won't lose me as a partner," she said softly, her hand

turning to better clasp his.

"I won't?" he asked.

A tiny shake of her head. "No. We can deal with the spillover. Who knows how long I'll even be here, anyway."

He didn't like that thought, so quickly pushed it away and said, "This is gonna sound like a chick in a bad melodrama, but… will you still respect me in the morning?"

Another laugh, and Huck knew he could spend a lifetime trying to elicit that sound from her.

"Seriously?" she asked, and he shrugged.

"It's just, I want to be taken seriously at this, prove I'm good enough to be with the Agency."

"You are," she said with no hesitation, and Huck found his chest swelling at almost the same rate as his cock. Almost.

"Besides," she added, "you're the civilian here. I'm the agent. I should be above this professionally."

"But technically we're not breaking rules or anything, right? We're supposed to be a married couple."

"Right. And I know from hearing the talk that in undercover situations this sometimes happens. The…spillover, as it were."

"I'm sure it does." He couldn't stop himself asking, "Has it for you? Before?"

Her eyes clouded over, and he regretted saying anything.

He was just about to take it back when she said, "This is my first undercover assignment, remember?"

"Right. Yeah, of course. Plus, it's none of my business anyway."

"No, it's not," she said, with no venom behind the words.

"So…"

She rubbed her thumb along the outside of his and then squeezed his hand. "Even if we can justify it, and we are stretching to do that, it's still probably a pretty stupid thing to do."

He smiled. "Haven't you ever done something pretty stupid?" He knew he had. Pretty much weekly since he'd been fourteen. And it almost always involved a girl.

She looked down at their entwined hands, then further down the sheets, and Huck regretted asking her the question. It was obvious whatever she was thinking about pained her.

"Only once," she whispered, and although Huck desperately wanted to know what could bring that haunted look to her pretty face, he didn't ask her to elaborate.

"Listen, Kelsey, we don't have to do—"

"You were right, though," she said.

"About what?"

"About wanting something—someone—badly enough that you stop thinking about what's right or wrong, or stupid."

"Me and you?" he said, hope in his voice.

"Yeah. Me and you. You. I want you, Huck Beck, very badly."

"I want you too. For a long time," he added.

A soft smile crossed her face, parting those full, sumptuous lips. "A whole week?"

He took a deep breath and let it out. "Longer," he said.

He knew the second she got it. And it didn't take her long. She knew that he knew. Still, she didn't call him on it, so he didn't push further.

"Huck?"

"Yeah?"

"Done talking?"

"Yeah."

"Start kissing?"

"Oh yeah," he said, then moved across the bed toward her.

Eighteen

HE HAD WANTED HER FOUR YEARS AGO. HE DIDN'T SAY it, but she knew. Knew because she'd felt the same way, even after seeing him for only a minute.

So, yeah, this might be stupid, even more stupid than the biggest mistake she'd made in her life two years ago. But she didn't care. She wanted to be with Huck tonight. The rest would have to work itself out so that she wasn't making a colossal mistake with her career.

Or her heart.

"We'll have to be quiet," she said as Huck inched his way across the great expanse of bed between them. "Matt," she clarified when he looked puzzled.

"He's a teenager; he'll sleep through anything. Probably has his earbuds in anyway." He took her face gently in his hands, framing her, then leaned in and gave her a small kiss. He pulled back, a smile on his gorgeous face. "See, it's like we're really married, worried we're going to wake the kids."

She laughed, and then her breath was gone as Huck leaned back in and took her mouth in his, like he was trying to capture her laughter. Instead, she captured his tongue in her mouth, twirling hers with his, wanting to taste him. Bringing her hands up to his forearms, she held him as he continued to frame her face with his hands. She loved the hold he had on her, and she dug her hands into his arms, trying to convey that.

Looking at him, he reminded her of how he'd looked at her four years ago. Studying her, memorizing her. But then it had been for training purposes, and now it was a look of, well…like he treasured her. Like he was trying to memorize every feature, not to call them up later, but so that he'd never forget.

And God, she liked the way he looked at her. She liked being treasured.

How many times had she pulled out that sketch over the past four years? A dozen? More? Wondering about the man she had so accurately described to the sketch artist.

She still wondered about that man, even though she was now staring back into his eyes as he ran his thumb along her jaw line.

"Okay?" he whispered.

He was giving her an out, but no way was she going to take it. She nodded, then moved into him, dropping her hands from his arms and sliding them up his strong back, turning to her back as she did.

Sliding his body over, he nestled on top of her, placing his hands back on her face, and she ran hers up and down his back, opening her legs for him to fit on top of her, which he easily did.

Easy. Yes, it all seemed easy with Huck. Even this type of intimacy, which she'd never really been good at.

"Kels," he whispered, nipping at her lips, pulling out her bottom one with his teeth.

"God," she said, sliding her legs up, resting her feet on the back of his calves.

"No, it's only Huck," he said, and they both laughed. Then he stared down at her and the amusement fled out of both of them as the exquisite heat rose and rose.

He kissed her again, deeply, and she squirmed under him. "Don't worry, baby, I'll take care of you," he said, kissing down her neck.

She didn't even want to think about how many women he'd said that to, or how cheesy it probably sounded. All she wanted was to believe that Huck Beck would give her exactly what she needed. That he'd take care of her. At least in bed.

"Yes," she answered, moving her neck to the side, giving him all the access he wanted. All the access she had to give, she'd gladly give to him.

He rose up, and she slid her hands around to his bare chest, reveling in the light hair and defined muscles. The heat emanating from him rivaled what she was feeling inside. Reaching down, he pulled at her Harvard tee, and she lifted from the bed enough for him to pull it over her head, holding her arms up while he peeled it away from her and tossed it to the floor.

When she was younger, she'd regretted not having bigger boobs. But as she aged, began running, and joined a predominantly male workplace, she came to terms with having smaller breasts. Was quite fond of them, actually.

But she was extremely happy with them as she watched Huck's expression as he stared down at her. Especially after seeing the buxom women that had been in his past.

"Perfect," he whispered. "Fucking perfect, Kels," he added, then dipped his head to kiss her on her "perfect" breasts.

Her hands left his chest and smoothed up his back, lodging in his soft hair to hold him to her. To never let him go. His hands sculpted her breasts while his tongue laved her nipple, causing her to arch up from the bed.

"Shhh, easy, baby. Let me play," he said, and then bent his mouth back to her breast, taking the nipple into his mouth and sucking. And causing a bolt of lightning to skitter through Kelsey's body. She gasped as she held his head ever closer to her. A gentle bite from him had her writhing underneath him.

"Huck," she said. Pleaded. Whatever. She just knew she needed more from him, though she never wanted him to stop doing what he was currently doing. He switched to her other nipple, drawing it deep into his mouth, swirling his tongue around the tip. She felt her breasts swell and pebble up, a delicious heat running through her, settling right between her legs, where Huck was starting to move against her. When he took her wet nipple between his thumb and finger and rolled it, she bucked beneath him. Then he gave it a pinch, and she nearly came undone.

"Wait for me," he said to her, giving her breasts a few more kisses before rolling off her.

"I don't know if I can," she admitted, but she was wrong. Because the moment that Huck's body left hers, she felt bereft and cold, wanting the heat to continue. Desperate for it to continue.

He looked over his shoulder at her as he moved to his side of the bed and the nightstand there. "Then I'll hurry," he said, and opened the drawer of the nightstand and pulled several (several!) condoms out and put them on the bed. One he kept in his hand and returned to her with it. "Where was I?" he said softly, settling back into the cradle of her spread legs.

"Right here," she said, moving her hips beneath him, making him smile.

"Oh, yeah, that's right," he said, and bent down to again suck on her breasts. Her hands flew to his hair; she knew she would never get tired of sifting through the blond silk. He rocked into her, and she grew wet feeling the weight of him. All of that would soon be hers. Inside her.

She took her hands from his hair, roamed down his defined back, and came to the waistband of his shorts. Made of soft sweats material, the waistband easily allowed her hands to slide beneath and down to his hard ass, which she wrapped her hands around, pulling him into her, wanting more.

He chuckled. "Okay, babe, I got the hint. My wife wants it hard and fast." She looked up at him, his eyes twinkling in amusement, and she smiled and nodded. The smile faded away as he added, "At least the first time."

There would be more than one time? *Thank you, God.* And Huck Beck.

He rose back onto his haunches and moved far enough away to peel her boxers down and off her. He looked them over and smiled as he stuck his hand into the fly. "Dang, this would have been convenient. Next time," he said, throwing them to the floor to join her shirt.

She was trying not to fixate on his using the words "next time" when all thoughts turned to mush as he peeled his own shorts off and tossed them aside.

God, he was beautiful. Golden and strong, but too rugged looking to be a pretty-boy Greek god. A treasure trail of light hair led down six-pack abs to his hard cock, standing at attention for her.

She reached out and circled a hand around his hard shaft, stroking lightly. He looked down, watching her hand on him, his nostrils flaring, his breathing becoming heavier, as was her own. He put a hand at the base of her throat, running it down her middle and into her curls, their forearms rubbing against each other as they felt each other's passion.

"Christ, so wet," he said as he slipped a finger down.

"So hard," she countered, stroking him with a tiny bit more force.

A wicked smile crossed his handsome face. "All the better to fuck you with, my dear."

She smiled back. "Prove it," she said just as he put a finger inside her, making her gasp.

"Oh, I intend to," he said, swirling his finger up and adding another one.

"Huck," she said, and she knew he could tell what she needed. Him.

He removed his fingers, creating a mewling sound from her that she'd never heard before, a sound she didn't even know she was capable of making. But his fingers were back as soon as he'd put the condom on. He took her hand and returned it to his cock, too.

Their eyes locked as their hands moved on, and in, each other. A look so intense Kelsey desperately wanted to look away, afraid that Huck saw too much. But she kept his gaze, held it close to her heart, knowing she'd want to pull it out later and think about it. Kind of like she did with his sketch.

He easily worked her to the fever pitch he'd had her at before he broke away for the condom. "Huck," she said.

"I know, babe, I know. Just hold it for a few seconds. Wait for me."

Again she told him the truth. "I'm not sure I can."

He smiled down at her. "You can. You're tough."

She tried not to laugh, afraid to move any internal muscles lest she lose it completely. Finally—*finally*—Huck took his fingers out of her and brushed her hand off his cock, taking it in his own and positioning himself right where they both wanted him. He lowered himself so he rested on his elbows and again framed her face with his hands.

"Look at me," he ordered, and she did, not even aware that her gaze had slid down to their nearly joined bodies. He pushed inside her as his blue eyes pierced hers, and she felt like molten lava was oozing all through her bloodstream.

Slowly he began moving, still looking at her. She wrapped her legs around his hips and her arms around his neck, resting her hands on his shoulders, picking up his rhythm, which she quickly matched.

"Fuck," he said as she clenched her muscles around him. "Yes," she said to him, not sure what she was agreeing to or with, just knowing how good it all felt.

He moved faster, keeping his eyes on hers. She raised her knees against his sides, pulling him deeper, and they both gasped at the sweetness of it. "Sorry, baby, it's not gonna last long this time," he said, and all she could do was nod her okay. Fast and dirty was more than okay with her. As was the promise of a next time.

Taking a hand from her face, he raked it down her body and around her front, placing his thumb against her clit. He made a slow circle around it, and she twitched, her breath coming quicker. Another circle, and her hips bucked up. One more circle, then his thumb rested directly on her and she arched back, exploding into shards of nerve endings. And happiness. Definite shards of happiness.

"God," she called out, her hand fisting in Huck's hair as her body was racked with tremors. Huck's thumb was still active, and his hips pounded into her body as he stroked harder. She was just starting to come down, had not really even left the peak, when his body tensed, he moaned, and came as he stared down into her eyes.

She wasn't sure if the glaze was in her eyes or his, but it felt like a filter had been placed across her vision and all she could see—all she could *feel*—was Huck Beck staring at her as his body shuddered into hers.

She wrapped her arms around him more tightly, burying her head in his shoulder, afraid of the intensity of his gaze. Afraid of what hers might give away.

He rested for a minute, and she held him. Then he made to move off her, out of her, and she knew she had to let him go, even though she would have gladly held him against her all night.

Maybe every night.

She looked away as he got settled to her side, not trusting quite yet what her face would show.

As if letting her have her privacy, he just kissed the top of her head, not forcing her to look at him.

She felt the rumble of a chuckle in his chest as she laid her head there. "What?" she asked, enjoying the sound he made.

"Well, it was a little delayed. But it was a hell of a wedding night."

She laughed too, relaxed and happy. And very, very tingly.

It was only much later in the night that she allowed herself to think about what tomorrow would bring. But Huck turned his body toward hers and made her forget all over again.

Nineteen

HUCK WOKE UP ALONE, WHICH WAS REGRETTABLE. IF they were going to do this only once, he would have liked to go one more time.

Though the three times they'd gone at it had left him so dead to the world that he hadn't even lifted a lid as Kelsey left the bedroom.

He looked at the clock and remembered he needed to get Matt off to school. Shit. His one morning to be Mr. Responsible and he'd blown even that. And Matt was going to be late during his finals week.

Rising from the bed, he quickly made a trip to the john, brushed his teeth, and then threw on a pair of jeans and a tee. He shoved his feet in some shoes and rushed down the hallway to Matt's room.

But when he got there, the bed was empty (made, even), and Matt's stuff was gone.

Then he heard them downstairs. Laughing. A flash of Kelsey laughing as she came the fourth time last night played in his mind.

She hadn't been laughing for the first one. It was too intense. The second, ditto. The third was when she'd been riding him, and she'd smiled down at him. The fourth a freebie for her, and she was shocked, he thought, when she realized that Huck still wanted more.

His efforts with his head between her legs had made her gasp and moan, and then, as the last burst ripped through her, she threw her head back and the most joyous laughter came out. He was afraid they'd wake up a soundly sleeping Matt, but found he didn't care.

It was Matt who was making Kelsey laugh now, Huck saw as he entered the kitchen to find Kelsey at the counter with her back to the room and Matt at the kitchen table, watching her back.

Watching it like a fifteen-year-old boy would. Which was to say, staring at her ass.

"Seriously, I'm happy to just buy lunch, Aunt Kelsey," he said. Huck walked past him and swatted the back of Matt's head.

"Eyes elsewhere, my favorite nephew," he said, and Matt looked arrogant and embarrassed all at the same time.

Though he couldn't blame the hormone-filled kid. Kelsey had on her running outfit, and even though her tee was baggy and overly long, it didn't quite cover her spectacular ass. And it certainly didn't hide her exceptionally long and toned legs.

Legs that had wrapped around his hips and clung to him with brute force the night before.

She was a sight to behold at the counter, and he was reminded of the fake photos they'd taken at her place. She had looked sexy as hell, as she did now in her running gear.

"Sorry," Matt said under his breath so only Huck could hear. Huck made his way over to the coffee maker, shooting his nephew a forgiving smile, which was returned.

"Morning, babe," he said to Kelsey, then ran a hand down her back, giving her waist a squeeze. He was eternally grateful that Matt was there and he could still use the "cover" umbrella to touch Kelsey the morning after. Because, honestly, he had no idea what her reaction would be otherwise.

"Morning, Huck," she said, and leaned over to give him a quick kiss. Too quick. But he liked when she called him by name. Liked it a lot. Especially like last night, when she'd cried it out as she was coming.

Pulling out of his memory haze of lust, he realized that Kelsey was making lunch for Matt. Or trying to. Some poor tomato had just bloodily given its life to be sacrificed onto what Huck thought was supposed to be a sandwich.

"Um, want me to help out here?"

"No, I've got it," she said, completely oblivious to how hard she was making the simple act of a ham and Swiss. "But if you could fix Matt something for breakfast, that would be great. Something kind of fast, though."

"On it," he said, and began getting stuff from the fridge to feed his nephew.

Something big and hearty, 'cause Huck didn't think the kid was going to be eating that lunch.

Huck talked Kelsey into going with him to drop off Matt so they could then drive on to the Tech trails and do their run there. She agreed, and Huck quickly changed into his running gear and the three headed out.

As they drove to Houghton High, Huck felt good. After last night, that was no big surprise, but it was more than that.

Kelsey getting Matt up, making him lunch while Huck made breakfast. Them bringing Matt to school, waving goodbye as he exited Huck's truck…it all felt good. Right. Like a little family, it was so domestic.

Which typically would scare the shit out of him, but he found that it didn't. Not at all. In fact, while he and Kelsey ran through the forest, he felt a weird pang that maybe he'd missed out on something by never having gotten serious with any girl.

Not that he was ancient. He was only twenty-eight. Still, Twain had married at twenty, Sawyer at twenty-three, and Huck had never even remotely thought about settling down.

Until this morning.

Was it Kelsey, or was he just at a point in his life where he could think about a wife and kids without breaking out in hives?

His timing, as always, sucked. Here he was thinking about his future as a family man when hopefully he'd soon be working for the DEA and going to God knew where.

Not that you couldn't be married while being in the DEA. Or the FBI.

On the trail ahead of him, Kelsey rounded a curve, taking them to a denser part of the woods, and it was like a dimmer switch had been turned on, the bright sun hidden, the cover of trees reminding him of Covered Drive.

And suddenly thoughts of marriage, of kids, of if the FBI and DEA would frown on an inter-agency relationship all flew from his mind, and the only thing left was to touch Kelsey again.

Now.

With a burst of speed that surprised him given the strenuousness of the night before, Huck closed the distance between them and looped an arm around her waist, pulling her from the ground, her long legs swinging as he pulled her close to his body.

"What? What's the matter?" she said, her eyes already sweeping the area for any unknown danger.

He laughed and continued to twirl her until the momentum from her running finally wore down. "Nothing. Nothing's wrong. I just wanted to hold you. Touch you."

They were completely stopped now, his arms around her waist, one of her arms around his neck, the other resting on his chest, finding her balance. Both of them were breathing hard, but Huck wasn't convinced it was all from running.

"Is there someone here?" she whispered as she smiled at him. "Someone watching us?"

He shook his head. "No. This isn't for show. This is just for me." He moved a hand down from her waist to her succulent ass, encased to perfection by Lycra.

"But...nobody's watching," she said, though she kept her hands on him, even sliding the hand around his shoulder up his neck and lodging in his hair.

"Nobody was watching last night," he said, staring into her brown eyes, watching them glass over as memories, the same memories that had taunted him all morning, flooded through her.

"Do we want to push our luck? Last night might have been stupid, but we survived and are still okay this morning."

"Oh, I'm more than okay," he said, pushing his fast-growing erection into her.

"But to continue on, to not quit while we're ahead…"

"Makes us not quitters. Yay us," he said, and she smiled while giving his hair a playful tug. Which made his hard-on harder.

"You were the one who made the statement that you had too much to lose. That first day driving to the Harbor. It was very important for you not to get sidetracked."

"Baby, I'm already sidetracked. I'm pretty sure I'll always be sidetracked around you."

Her face softened, and he pushed his luck. "So, in a way, this would be great training for me. How to keep my focus when I'm constantly"—he ground into her and she gasped—"sidetracked."

"Well, if it's for the benefit of your training…" Her smile turned wicked, and Huck was thankful that just a few steps off the trail the forest was dense enough to hide their extracurricular activities.

"Consider it your duty, Agent Cameron, to further the training of your subordinate."

"Is a subordinate kind of like a submissive?" she teased.

"Not even close," he said. He broke their embrace, took her hand, and led her off the path and into the woods. "But baby, if you're into those types of games, it's going to take all your training skills to keep me on task."

She giggled. "Challenge accepted."

Hand in hand, they walked deeper into the woods, looking for a soft place to land.

Twenty

THE NEXT WEEK WAS A BLUR FOR KELSEY. THEY PICKED up a couple of charters from other boats in the marina, and Jim Peterson had three for them. They were fully into June, and the weather was starting to turn warm, though there were a couple of days when the black flies made being docked unbearable, and Kelsey was ecstatic when they'd pulled away and headed out onto Lake Superior, where the wind kept the flies at bay.

She and Huck had complete freedom in Jim's boat. Jim was happy to hand the deck and cabin reins over to Huck and her, happy to just spend his time at the wheel.

The background check on Jim bore out exactly what he'd told them. Sold his tech company for big—though not gargantuan—bucks, retired early, and was fulfilling his passion.

A second divorce a few years ago—prompted by the desire to follow his dream? Or was the boat a cure to his divorce? One grown daughter who was married with one child and lived in Chicago.

All on the up-and-up, and yet Kelsey sensed a...sadness in Jim that kept her on her toes. There was something in his life he didn't want to either think about or deal with, and Kelsey sensed a melancholy about Jim. A man with demons, perhaps. And that could be dangerous. A nothing-to-lose mentality might have someone taking chances that they might not normally take.

She was pretty sure he was exactly what he seemed, that

Jenkins wasn't playing games for once, but Huck was so hopeful that a local wouldn't be involved in smuggling meth ingredients that she stayed in there, looking through the cabins when she was below deck and Huck was talking with Jim at the bridge.

No empty Sudafed boxes incriminatingly lying around. Not that she expected there would be. He might be having a midlife crisis, but Jim was no dummy.

They didn't work for him every day, so he could be doing anything with his boat on the days he didn't have charters. But she and Huck were now going to the Harbor every day, whether they had something scheduled or not, and the *Mina* was docked when they weren't scheduled to work on it.

They hadn't done any night surveillance yet, and that would be their next step, if something didn't break in the next few days. A night in the woods with Huck didn't sound too bad, seeing as their one adventure running the Tech trails had ended with her back against a large tree and her legs wrapped around Huck as he'd pounded into her.

When they'd returned from their run that morning, they had both hovered in the upstairs hallway, waiting for the other to say something about moving her stuff back to the guestroom now that Matt was gone.

Neither of them did. Finally, Kelsey moved to Huck's room, peeled off her running clothes, and headed for the shower.

She'd never returned to the guestroom.

As far as she could tell, them sleeping together hadn't affected their focus in any way while on the job. Of course, she could have been so blissed out on hormones and orgasms that she missed any lost focus.

And it sure made the smoldering looks and stolen touches in front of people (and when no one was around) look all the more real.

Because they were.

Somewhere in the past week, Kelsey had gone from being Huck's partner on this case, with a lovely fringe benefit thrown in, to a partner in every sense of the word.

Having spent her whole life devoid of any serious relationship—by her own choice—she was shocked at how easy and comfortable it felt.

Was it because Huck was so laid-back and a good foil to her hyper-analytical mind?

Four or five days after the morning in the woods, she decided to keep all her analysis for the case and just take a breather on thinking when it came to Huck and her.

The sex was outstanding, they worked well together on a boat, and worked even better when discussing suspects and other aspects of the case. She was going to just ride the wave until she was called back to the D.C. office.

And continue riding Huck Beck.

The night before, they'd had a call with Jenkins to discuss the case. Kelsey had quickly put him on speakerphone and let him know Huck was listening too. She'd done this for a couple of reasons. One, so Jenkins wouldn't be a complete ass, like he probably would be if he were speaking to Kelsey alone. And two, she wanted Huck to know that she truly felt they were partners on this case, even though she was the agent and he was a civilian.

The way he looked at her as she did it proved he got it. And appreciated it.

Jenkins still wouldn't reveal who was the primary agent on the case, or if they were even working out of Copper Harbor or the Copper Country as a whole, but listened as they reported on their findings. Or non-findings, as the case may be.

He told them he'd call them in a week, but to report in sooner than that if they saw anything suspicious. Neither Kelsey nor Huck asked for an ETA on when the case might wrap up.

The fact was, Kelsey was enjoying herself immensely, and not just because she was having great sex on a regular basis.

She loved working on the boats, and the drive back and forth didn't bother her much because it was so beautiful. They had put the idea of renting a shitty cabin on the back burner for the moment. Most days they had a drink at the Seafarer or maybe dinner at Fitzpatrick's in Eagle River before heading back to Houghton.

Without exception, every time they drank or ate somewhere, somebody Huck knew would stop by the table and want to be introduced to the new Mrs. Beck.

Word had spread. Fast. Kelsey wasn't sure if that was because it was a small-town area, or because of Huck's reputation with the ladies. Probably both in equal measure.

They all seemed shocked, some hiding it better than others, to meet the woman who had tamed Huck Beck enough to get him to the altar.

The shock became more understandable whenever a woman who was obviously a former lover of Huck's would saunter up to them at the bar or their table.

All blond, all small and curvy. All had a likeness to Janie Kuurtu, who had approached them at the Cat's Meow.

All total opposites from Kelsey.

Which made her feel both pride and trepidation. Was Huck bedding her because it was just so damn convenient? Or had he truly become a part of the backstory they'd created and wanted Kelsey *because* she was so different from the other women he'd been with?

Yeah, so maybe she hadn't *completely* put away her analytical mind.

On Saturday, they worked a fishing charter early in the morning, and then restocked and cleaned for a sunset cruise later that evening.

Jim had gone into Calumet with a list Huck gave him while she and Huck cleaned, moved the fishing gear off the deck, and put out comfy chairs and loungers.

And they also gave the cabins and every hidey-hole a thorough search.

Nothing. Again.

Jim took them out for an early dinner, which was enjoyable

in both food and the company. Jim told stories of his early days with his company that had them all laughing.

Yet another curvy blonde came up to express her shock upon hearing that Huck had actually—gasp!—married someone.

Kelsey draped her arm across Huck's lap—very high up on his lap—and assured the interloper that Huck Beck was now most assuredly off the market.

Huck grinned the whole time and then gave her a kiss to prove Kelsey's point.

They returned to the *Mina* in good spirits and did a few last-minute things (Huck making his amazing sangria among them) until the group for the sunset cruise arrived.

They were up on deck, all three of them, when two cars full of people pulled in the marina not far from the *Mina*'s slip.

There were at least three couples getting out of the car, and just before Kelsey recognized Liv and Twain, Huck said under his breath, "Oh, shit."

Twenty-One

HUCK WATCHED HIS BROTHER AND LIV, AMONG OTHERS, walk toward the *Mina*.

Hands on hips, he stood at the stern and looked down the dock to them. "Are you shitting me? When did you guys come up with this?"

Twain laughed and pointed to a large man behind him who was holding hands with a very petite woman. "Not me. This was all on Petey."

Petey Ryan. Of course. This was exactly something that the big joker would pull.

Shrugging, Petey confirmed, "I saw Twain last week. He mentioned you had a gig on a new boat and a new wife." His eyes cut to Kelsey, who was standing at the bow with Jim. "So I said we had to come and check it out. Al loved the idea of a sunset cruise, even begged me to book it."

The little woman put an elbow to Petey's stomach. Not with much force, but Petey still made a big show of being hurt. "Not true," the woman said. "He had it all booked before he even told me about it. But it'll be fun."

As they approached the side of the *Mina*, Huck walked the length of the boat with their guests, him on the deck, them on the dock. He noticed they all had their eyes on Kelsey at the bow, and Huck irrationally wished that he hadn't left her side when he first spotted his brother and posse in the parking lot.

She looked adorable. The other day, Jim had given Huck and Kelsey several navy polo shirts each with *Mina* embroidered small and tastefully on the chest. They were both wearing them now. Kelsey also wore khaki shorts and a pair of Sperry Top-Siders, which had arrived from Amazon yesterday. He'd teased her about becoming a true boat person, and she said she just wanted to look the part.

But Huck figured that came more from female vanity than wanting to blend in undercover. Her long, toned legs had gotten tan in the two weeks working on the boats, even though they had to wear long pants on most of the morning fishing charters, bundling up on Lake Superior. But the afternoon work of cleaning and stocking afforded them time in the sun, and it showed on both of them.

Jim was helping the three women on the boat, the four men following.

"Welcome to the *Mina*," Jim said when they'd all settled on the deck. "It appears you know my crew."

"This is my brother Twain," Huck said to Jim. "And his much better half, Liv," he added, gaining a smile from Liv. Handshakes, and then the introductions continued, coming from Huck, Twain, and even Petey.

There were Twain and Liv, Petey Ryan and his girlfriend Alison Jukuri, Lizzie and Finn Robbins, and Zeke Hampton.

Huck knew Petey and Zeke pretty well. Had met Lizzie a couple of times when she'd been with her twin, Zeke. He remembered Alison as the therapist whom Sawyer had seen after losing Molly, though Huck didn't know her well. Finn Robbins he'd never met.

"So, Huckleberry, you up and eloped without a word to your family? Not even Liv, who has treated you like one of her own? What do you have to say for yourself?" Petey said good-naturedly.

Huck walked the few paces to Kelsey and slung an arm around her shoulder, speaking in language Petey would understand. "Saw her. Boom. Got her to the altar before she could wise up. Didn't mean to leave anyone out"—he pointedly looked at Liv—"but I wasn't taking any chances she'd change her mind."

Petey studied Huck for a second and then burst out laughing. "Well, shit. Fair enough, son. Fair enough."

Huck almost bristled at Petey calling him son, but with his arm around Kelsey, her warm body tucked neatly into his, he didn't have it in him to get riled about anything. Even Twain and his buddies booking a charter to check out Huck and Kelsey and, presumably, give him shit.

Petey and Zeke had been Twain's best friends at Tech, and a twelve-year-old Huck had idolized the hard-bruising hockey hero Petey Ryan. Twain would bring them to the house a lot for their mother's home cooking, back when she was still around and cooking for her sons.

Zeke had gone on to become a pilot for the Navy, another hero-worship-inducing profession. They'd both always kept an eye on Huck, even after Twain had to drop out of Tech and become a full-time father, husband, and logger. Huck saw Petey most summers when the NHL player would be home in his off-season. He saw less of Zeke, the Navy not having an off-season.

Liv stepped forward and squeezed Huck's arm. "Don't listen to him, Huck. It's your life. You don't need to let your family in on the decisions you make." Then she turned back to Petey, fully standing by Huck's side. "Besides, I told you about the reception we're having so everyone gets to meet Kelsey. You've RSVP'd already, Petey."

Petey waved a hand in the air. "Yeah, yeah, I know. I just know that when *we* do it"—he squeezed Alison's body closer to him—"we're going to have everyone we love nearby."

"Whoa, tiger, slow down there," Alison said, with a little bit of edge in her voice. Petey looked down at her with a smile, which promptly died when he saw her warning look. "Sorry," he said. "I know I said no pressure. I'll be good." Alison raised a brow at him, and Huck realized that Petey had finally met his match in Alison Jukuri.

"Let's get the party barge on its way," Twain said, smoothing over the weird silence.

Kelsey took drink orders while Jim welcomed his guests once more and moved to the bridge. Huck went to the side of the *Mina* and started working the ropes as the engine roared to life.

They were off. And Huck wasn't sure if this would be a fun little sunset cruise or if his brother, Zeke, and Petey would spend the entire time riding Huck's ass.

It turned out it was both.

KELSEY GOT A KICK OUT of Twain's friends. The big guy, Petey, was apparently a recently retired hockey player. When he found this out, Jim invited him to come to the bridge with him and talk hockey. Apparently Jim was a lifelong Blackhawks fan and had seen Petey play many times.

It was obvious that Lizzie and Alison were BFFs, apparently had been since grade school. They had a third, they'd told Kelsey, a Katie who was currently out on the PGA Tour with her husband. Kelsey didn't follow golf or hockey, so she hadn't recognized Petey Ryan's name or that of Katie's husband, Darío Luna. And certainly none of them had any airs about being, or being with, professional athletes. No, they were just like any of the other Yoopers Kelsey had met, and she quickly came to like them all.

She also liked how Alison and Lizzie included Liv in their girl talk, even though it was obvious that Liv had not been part of their group originally. Kelsey liked Alison and Lizzie even more for that. Then she realized how protective she felt about Liv, and the feelings took her aback. It wasn't a good realization for her to know that she cared—really cared—about Liv Beck's feelings.

Because Kelsey herself was bound to hurt them the most. Again, she felt guilty about the reception Liv was throwing for Kelsey and Huck. Because it was more than just cost and effort to Liv, but truly a labor of love for her brother-in-law and his new wife.

Kelsey had been doing a great job of keeping her growing

feelings for Huck compartmentalized and out of their work. But now she had to add her very real feelings for her in-laws.

And she felt like shit about it.

No wonder so many agents who came back in after years of undercover work seemed so messed up. Kelsey had always assumed that they didn't have the mental toughness, the ability to compartmentalize like she had in spades. Now she knew it wasn't that. It was the guilt of lying to people you genuinely came to like.

To love.

Shaking those thoughts, she enjoyed the sunset, as she always did on these outings. The couples had all found each other, with Zeke, the only one without a date, going to the bridge to chat with Jim. Even Huck came out of the galley with another tray of snacks, and then came to Kelsey's side and slipped an arm around her waist as they watched the horizon. All four couples lined the length of the side of the boat facing the sunset, each with their arms around each other, watching in silence as the sun, a brilliant orange with shades of pink, slipped beneath the lake.

It was like they were all holding their breath, watching something so precious, in the arms of the one they loved. Too special to even say a word.

Kelsey could feel the love emanating from the other couples, and she leaned her head into Huck's shoulder and neck, his arm wrapping more tightly around her.

And for just now, for just this sunset, she let herself think that she was just Kelsey Beck, loving her job in the outdoors, loving the beauty around her, and…loving her husband.

She felt as calm and peaceful as the unusually still Lake Superior.

After a few more minutes, Jim turned the boat back toward Copper Harbor, the couples broke apart, back to their snacking, drinking, and chatting, and Kelsey came back to reality.

Not Kelsey Beck in the arms of the man she loved.

Agent Kelsey Cameron working on her first big break.

She smiled at Huck as he moved to the pail of drinks and got another beer for Petey. He gave her a soft smile back, and Kelsey swore he knew exactly what she was thinking.

And more, that he felt the same way.

Which made her both happy and sad.

Twenty-Two

PETEY SUGGESTED THEY ALL GO TO THE SEAFARER FOR a nightcap, and Twain coaxed Huck into agreeing that he and Kelsey would meet them all there after they were done working.

Then the men also invited Jim. Huck was glad, hoping his boss would say yes. To date, they'd had a lot of interaction with Jim, but it was mostly on the *Mina*, and Huck would like to get him off the boat, get a couple of drinks in him, and see if he maybe revealed some of the things that shadowed his eyes most of the time.

Kind eyes, Kelsey called them, which made Huck silently grind his teeth, though he didn't disagree. His wife had made a different kind of bond with Jim, a caring that guys just didn't show, or show often. And Jim seemed to return it, though more in a fatherly way, which Huck was okay with.

They quickly cleaned up from the cruise and did the switch over to the fishing charter they'd do the next day, though thankfully it wasn't one that started at six a.m., as some of them did. This one would be an early afternoon start.

"Okay, meet you at the Seafarer?" Jim said as the three of them left the *Mina*. "Oh, wait, I meant to give you something." He disappeared below deck, and Huck stood waiting with Kelsey until Jim came back with a very large, and very expensive, bottle of champagne in his hand.

"I got this for you two today. A belated wedding gift."

"You didn't have to do that," Kelsey said. She looked at the label and then at Huck to see if he knew exactly what Jim was giving them. Huck didn't have money, but he'd been around enough moneyed tourists and their expensive tastes to know ballpark what Jim had spent on their present.

His raised eyebrows to Kelsey let her know that he got it. "Jim, this is too much. Really," he said, his hands up.

"Nonsense. You can't drink while working a charter, but you can certainly have a toast on me on your own time. I insist," he said, handing the bottle to Kelsey, who reluctantly took it. "You two have been lifesavers for me. I didn't know what I didn't know, and I thank you for helping me with that."

"Of course," Huck said. Nodding at the bottle, he added, "Thank you. The first toast will be to you, who gave us our first jobs together. It means a lot that we can be together every day."

They started walking down the dock to their vehicles, and Jim laughed. "God, I remember a time when I wanted to be by my wife's side all day long." The laughter died when he added, "That seems like a lifetime ago." He was at his Lexus SUV and turned to them, his face serious. "Treasure this time together. Try not to let real life interfere."

At the term *real life*, Huck looked at Kelsey and saw the minute movement of her jaw. No one else would notice, but Huck now knew her every expression. But she quickly recovered, knowing that Jim just meant everyday life and its problems, not *real* life as they knew it.

Kelsey was silent on the short drive from the marina to the Seafarer, so Huck kept quiet as well. Finally, she put her hand over the console of the truck and on his arm.

"That was fun," she said.

He took his hand from the steering wheel and clasped her hand, resting them both on the console. "It was. At first I thought Twain and Petey might have been up to some kind of bullshit, but

I think they just wanted to show their ladies a nice night."

"Yeah, and if ordering you around a little bit was just a fortunate by-product, so be it."

He looked over and smiled at her. "Yeah, I felt like I was twelve years old again a couple of times. Fetching my big bro and his buds beers."

"I really liked the women, too."

He nodded. "Yeah, they seem cool. I remember them a little bit, have seen them around, but I didn't really know them well."

"And, of course, I adore Liv."

"Yeah, me too," he said, smiling as he thought of his sister-in-law.

"And I hate lying to them. I can only imagine how you feel about it."

She squeezed his hand, and he realized he'd tensed up. "Yeah, I do. But this is what I tell myself…I'm this close to being able to do something that I've always wanted to do. Something that I believe I'd be really good at."

"You would. You *will* be," she said, and Huck found he had to clear his throat to go on.

"So, even though it's shitty how I went about it, I think ultimately they'll be really happy for me that I'm realizing my dream, you know?"

"Yes, of course they will," she said, maybe a bit too enthusiastically, but Huck appreciated it nonetheless.

He shrugged, loving that she clasped his hand so tightly. "I mean, they'll give me shit about it, no doubt, but hopefully they'll come around quickly."

"They will. They love you. You're their brother."

Huck pulled his hand away, ostensibly to run it through his hair, but more because he was uncomfortable. "Yeah, well, at least Sawyer will get off my ass about full-time employment. The man who basically checked out on life for ten years."

He could feel her eyes on him, but he didn't look her way.

Finally, she reached out and took back his hand, which he'd rested on the steering wheel. She held it tightly again, like she wouldn't put up with him trying to pull it away.

"Sawyer obviously went through a hard time, but from what Liv says, you and Twain were there for him whenever he'd let you in, and sometimes even when he didn't."

"Yeah," he admitted. Dark days right after Molly died that he didn't want to think about. Then Huck had left that next fall for Northern, only able to see Sawyer on weekends, which he did pretty much his whole freshman year before Sawyer told him that Huck had to embrace being a college student, weekends and all, and not to come home all the time.

A year after that, his mother, already gone for three years, sold the house in Calumet and gave the money to her three sons. Twain and Sawyer promptly gave their shares to Huck to buy his small home in Houghton so he'd have a place to come home to.

He loved his brothers and knew he'd have to come clean with them soon.

And not just about being undercover.

The guests from the *Mina* had commandeered a large round table in the corner of the Seafarer's bar area, and Jim, Huck, and Kelsey joined them, leaving their bottle of champagne in the truck. No way in hell was Huck sharing something that good with the likes of Petey Ryan and Twain. Liv, yeah, he'd share with Liv, but she couldn't even drink.

He went to the bar and got beers for himself and Jim and a vodka tonic for Kelsey. Jim took exception to Huck buying for him and said he'd get the next round.

It was a good night. Stories of Zeke, Twain, and Petey at Tech were shared, with Lizzie and Alison adding in other Petey and Zeke adventures. Finn seemed a little like the odd man out of the group, but he didn't seem to mind. He sat back and listened, his eyes mostly on his wife, Lizzie, a small grin on his face as she would get animated telling a story or outright laughing when she'd imitate Petey, using every swear word known to man.

Through the conversation, Huck learned they'd been married a little over a year and had a baby named Sam and sole custody of a girl and boy from Finn's first marriage.

Petey and Alison mentioned that they'd been a couple since January, and Huck found that hard to believe, since they were so easy with each other and obviously had a ton of history.

But then, sitting next to his "wife" that he'd married after only five months, he was not about to start closely questioning other people's relationships.

He was pulled out of this thought when Zeke said something that had both Lizzie and Petey loudly saying, "You did what?"

Zeke shrugged as the table quieted down. "I gave my papers. When my due date comes, I'm getting out of the Navy."

Petey and Lizzie turned to each other and said simultaneously, "Did you know about this?" Then they both shook their heads, and everyone around them laughed like they were some comedy team.

"Nobody knows. I'm telling you now. Telling Mom and Dad tomorrow. I have one more six-month cruise to do that leaves in a week. When that's done, I'm done."

"I'm...speechless," Petey said.

"And that's saying something," Alison added, getting a sheepish grin from her boyfriend.

Lizzie reached her hand around her husband to touch her twin's hand, which was on the table. "Zeke, promise me you'll be very, very careful for the next six months. We are not going to get this close to you coming back to us to have it snatched away in your last six months."

He rolled his eyes but then looked at his sister with compassion. "I promise, Lizard. We'll have a drink just like this in six months, with me growing out my hair and looking for a job."

Huck saw tears start to form in Lizzie's eyes as she swallowed and nodded at Zeke. Then she pulled her hand away and buried herself in her husband's chest. Finn quickly put his arm around her and patted her back.

"Well, hot damn, it'll be good to have you home," Petey said, and they all toasted Zeke's next phase in his life. Conversations broke out in different areas of the large table, and Huck was trying to follow along with one Twain was having with Zeke when he felt a nudge at his elbow.

"Hey, Huck," he heard, and looked to his side to see Janie Kuurtu standing there looking down at him.

She was done up to the nines, with lots of cleavage, lots of leg, and lots of makeup. "Hey, Janie," he said. No questions that would lead her to keep talking, no asking her to join them.

He'd been over it with Janie many times. They'd have a hookup, with Huck being clear that was all it would be, and then Janie would spend the next three months trying to make it more.

It was Huck's own fault for ever having repeat performances with her, but it almost kind of felt like a summer tradition. Like the season hadn't arrived until he'd banged Janie Kuurtu and then regretted it.

"Wanna have a drink with me?" she said softly, but not so softly that Kelsey couldn't hear. Which had been the point.

"I'm good here, thanks, Janie," Huck said, aware that the various conversations around the table were dying off and eyes were turning his way.

"Are you sure? I know what you like…in drinks, that is." She bent down, ostensibly to say this to him, but mostly to put her impressive tits in his face.

"Excuse me," Kelsey said, leaning across his body, her face very close to Janie's. "Janie, right?"

Janie smiled a Cheshire Cat smile and just nodded. Janie was no stranger to going up against girlfriends or wives. To her, they were just part of the challenge. "Yes," she said to Kelsey, "I'm an… old friend of Huck's."

"Yes, he's told me." Kelsey leaned even closer to Janie, and the table came to a complete hush. "I'm going to say this only once. If you don't get the message, then that's on you, and whatever shit rains down on you, you brought on yourself, hear me?"

A stunned Janie only nodded. Huck was so shocked he couldn't even jump in, not that Kelsey needed him to.

"Then here it is, Janie. Huck is mine. I don't share what's mine. So…fuck off."

There were snickers around the table, a gasp, probably from Liv, a quiet "You go, girl!" from Alison's direction, and an "Oooh, cat fight!" undoubtedly from Petey.

But Janie smiled, thinking she'd won. Because she knew that Huck absolutely hated when a woman got territorial about him, especially in public. He'd let Janie know that, very sternly, in the past when she'd tried it with him, walking away from her right on the spot.

Except he didn't hate it when Kelsey did it. On the contrary— he absolutely loved it.

He looked up at the smiling Janie with a smile of his own. "You heard my wife. I'm hers. And happy to be so."

All thoughts of questioning a relaxed Jim fled Huck's mind, and he placed a hand on Kelsey's arm, pulling her away from Janie. He then stood up, keeping a hand on Kelsey and urging her to rise as well, which she did.

"Now, if you'll all excuse us, I'm going to take my wife to bed and prove to her just how happy I am to be a married man."

He threw down some money on the table, yanked Kelsey behind him, and walked out the door amidst shouts of goodbye and other, more graphic suggestions from Petey Ryan.

They got in the truck, and he turned to Kelsey.

"I'm so sorry, Huck, I just—"

He put up a hand to stop her. "That was the sexiest thing I ever saw, and I needed to get out of there and bury myself in you pronto."

That shut her up, and she sat back in her seat. This time it was she who was wearing the Cheshire Cat grin.

"I know it's got a biffy and everything, but how would you feel about cutting an hour off the time when I can get my hands on you and going to Sawyer's Ice Cube?"

Her smile got even wider, she nodded, and Huck put the truck in drive, peeling out of the Seafarer parking lot and heading north.

Twenty-Three

KELSEY LOOKED AROUND THE GLOWING ROOM COMING to life as Huck lit candles and turned on a couple of battery-operated lanterns. He asked if she wanted a fire, but the room was warm enough and would certainly soon get much, much hotter, so she declined.

They'd driven north of Copper Harbor, turned onto a dirt road, then left Huck's truck at a large pole barn, taking an ATV from the barn the rest of the way. Although riding through the forest in the pitch dark, only illuminated by the headlight of the ATV, wasn't fun, it was obvious that Huck knew his way well, so Kelsey relaxed, hung on to Huck's waist, enjoying the ride.

And now she was appreciating what Huck had called Sawyer's Ice Cube. At least what she could see of it. No power and very little moonlight on the cloudy night made checking out the place beyond the candles nearly impossible. From what she could tell, though, the views would be amazing, since three of the walls and the roof were made of glass.

Which was very cool. As the candlelight bounced off all the glass surfaces, it created a mild house of mirrors effect.

"Need to use the…biffy?" Huck asked her when he'd finished lighting candles throughout the room. "I'll walk you there. Stand outside the whole time. You can bring one of the lanterns with you inside." He had a smile on his face, which she returned.

"I'm good," she said, grateful she'd taken care of business

back at the Seafarer before he'd hustled her out. He'd suggested a few days ago that they keep a change of clothes in a bag in his truck, and he'd brought both of those duffels plus the bottle of champagne from Jim in with them, strapped to a carrying basket on the ATV.

"Me too," he said, moving to get the bottle out of his bag, then bringing it over to her where she stood at the front of the cottage (was there a front when it was a cube?), staring out to the darkness. She could see her reflection and that of Huck as he moved behind her skillfully unwrapping and uncorking the bottle of champagne.

"Here," he said, handing her the bottle. "Let me go find some glasses or something. I'm sure he's got coffee mugs at the very least."

She grabbed his sweatshirt at the sleeve, pulling him back to her. "If I can use the biffy, I think I can drink from the bottle." Proving her point, she took a deep swallow from the heavy bottle, letting the sweet nectar wash down her throat. "Holy wah, that's good stuff," she said, handing the bottle back to him.

"'Holy wah.' Using the biffy. Swigging straight from the bottle. Why, you're just becoming a bona fide Yooper girl, aren't you."

"If those Yooper girls are Liv, Lizzie, and Alison, then absolutely. If it's Janie Kuurtu, then no thanks."

He took a drink and looked away from her. "Yeah, about that. I'm sorry that she keeps showing up. I would have thought she would have gotten the hint that night at the Cat's Meow. I really—"

He stopped when she held up a hand. "I want to talk about that too. I mean, not necessarily Janie, but how I acted."

"How you acted was hot. Very."

She shook her head. "It was so…out of character for me."

"Still hot."

She ignored that (well, she'd think about it later, not totally ignore it), and continued, "And you've said you don't like jealous or territorial women, so it probably didn't—"

This time it was Huck who held up the hand. "I said I didn't like it in the past. Didn't seem to mind much when you did it."

"But it goes against our, I don't know, message or something. That we got married so quickly, that I bagged the town playboy, because I was so different from the women you're usually with."

"That you are."

She took another drink of the champagne. Not really needing it, as she'd gotten a tiny buzz from the vodka at the Seafarer, but enjoying the fizzy feeling that was slowly going through her, not sure if it was from the continued drinking, or Huck's words. Or from being alone with Huck in the glowing, reflective room, a large platform bed just paces behind them.

"And this just seals it. If any other woman I was with had done something like that, I probably would have been saying goodbye to her."

She raised a brow at that. "In the morning."

He threw his head back and laughed, shadows playing across his face and neck. "Yeah, probably." Then he smiled that grin that reminded Kelsey of the words Deni had said about the Beck brothers' wattage. "Yeah, definitely. In the morning."

"No fool, you."

"Bird in the hand and all that."

She laughed. "So, I guess it worked out okay."

He nodded, took another swig, and stepped closer to her. "But my question is…if you didn't think it was a cool move to make, should I assume that it all came from instinct? That it was what you felt? Really?"

She took a deep breath, her eyes caught by his intense gaze. She reached for the bottle, but he moved it to his side, away from her, with a small shake of his head, like he was withholding the champagne until she answered him. Finally she nodded, and his grin widened. "Now give me back the champagne," she said.

The grin turned positively wicked as he said, "Oh, baby, I am so going to give you the champagne."

He held on to the bottle, but took her hand with his free one and walked her to the bed.

The fizz of the champagne was nothing compared to how bubbly Huck's look made her feel.

HUCK GAVE ABOUT A second's thought to the sheets on the bed and how what he wanted to do to Kelsey would probably mess them up beyond what a mere washing could salvage.

Yeah, it only took a second before he decided he'd buy Sawyer five sets of premium Egyptian cotton sheets to make up for it, because there was no way he wasn't going to lick this very expensive champagne from Kelsey's body.

He walked her the few steps to the bed, then sat down on it, pulling her between his outstretched legs. With the low height of the platform and Kelsey's height, his eyes were right at the zipper of her cargo shorts. Perfect.

As he went for her zipper, she balanced her hands on his shoulders and toed off her boat shoes, kicking them out of the way. The shorts slid easily down her hips and legs, and she kicked those aside too, hands still on his shoulders, though one hand had slid up a little and she started playing with his hair.

Fuck, he loved when she did that.

Her white cotton panties were right in front of him, and he leaned forward, nuzzling into the fabric, smelling her arousal, seeing signs of it as he pulled back. Looking up at her, he said, "Shirt. Gone." His voice was rough with need. She smiled at him and lifted the navy polo over her head, tossing it to a corner of the room, nearly hitting one of the candles.

Which Huck might have let catch the whole damn place on fire, so mesmerized was he by the sight of her standing over him in only bra and panties. White cotton, sure, but damn, she made even those look sexy as hell.

Still… "I know you packed a few lacy underthings, babe. Even some colors. Feel free to pull them out of the suitcase at any time," he said in a teasing voice, which made her laugh. Her head went back, her torso bending a tiny bit at the motion, and Huck hurriedly pulled her panties down, growling at her to take her bra off, which she quickly did and discarded.

"Bend back like that again, babe," he said. "Like you just did when you laughed. But keep your hands on me for balance."

"Balance? You don't think I can keep my balance while I just lean backward a little?"

He smiled up at her, his gaze moving up her toned body. "I'm hoping that what I want to do to you has you nearly falling over."

Her beautiful brown eyes widened, but instead of fear, or even excitement, Huck saw the accepted challenge in her eyes. A challenge he could spend the rest of his life trying to live up to.

He picked the bottle up from where he'd put it beside him on the floor. "You hanging on?" he asked. He felt her hand go around the back of his neck, the other on his shoulder, both holding tight.

"Yes," she said, looking down at him one last time. Then at the bottle. A slow smile came over her, and she leaned back. Not far, but enough to have her hips stick out in front of her a little bit. And enough for the trail of poured champagne to find the target he wanted.

Huck lifted the bottle high, pouring a stream over one of her breasts, causing the nipple to instantly pebble. He couldn't reach with his mouth, but he reached up the hand not holding the champagne and stroked her breast, now wet and sticky, rolling the hardening nipple between his thumb and finger. He did this at the same time he leaned forward, reaching the top of her thigh just as the stream of champagne did, and he lapped up the sweet liquid. His tongue tickled her soft skin where her thigh met her torso, and he felt her shudder, not sure if was from the cold of the champagne he poured on her or his touch.

It didn't matter—he intended to do more of both.

He repeated the stream on her other breast and thigh. Briefly he thought about how expensive the champagne Jim had given them was, and how maybe it shouldn't be wasted in this way. But as he looked up at Kelsey, her head thrown back, her mouth open and breathing heavily, he knew that in no way was this glorious elixir being wasted.

This was what expensive champagne should always be used for.

When both breasts were wet and shining from champagne and Huck's mouth, he then switched the bottle to the middle of her torso, pouring the stream down the center of her body between her breasts. He put the bottle down and grabbed her hips with both hands, as the liquid made its way down her body, some pausing at her belly button, taking a soft turn and reaching her curls at the same time as Huck's mouth.

He wasn't sure which tasted better...the champagne or Kelsey.

No. He knew. Definitely Kelsey.

He devoured her, his tongue tasting and probing, adding champagne to cool her down when he felt her getting close. Or maybe it heated her up, because after the third pour, she grabbed his head with her hands and growled, "Huck. Now."

With that, he turned her, lowering her to the bed, where she stayed for about a half a second before sitting up and grabbing at his shirt, pulling it out of his shorts. The shirt was off, and he rose from the bed long enough to get his shorts and boxers off, pushed to the side along with his shoes. He lowered himself back to the bed, over her, but she shook her head and rolled them both so that she could sit astride him.

Yeah, he was very okay with her taking charge.

For a while.

She looked behind her, grabbed the bottle, then proceeded to do the taste-test routine on him. Sticky and cold. But oh, how her mouth heated it up. Heated him up.

She did his chest, running her hands up and down his arms as she licked, tasted, and nipped at his pecs and nipples, making him almost buck her from atop him, so desperate was he to get inside her.

"Condom. Wallet," he managed to get out. She reached over

him, to the spot on the floor with his shorts, grabbed them, then tossed him the wallet. He pulled out the foil packet, got rid of the wallet, then handed her the condom.

But she didn't open it. She put it to the side of them and took the bottle up again, her aim very pointed, very targeted. She looked to his face, a brow raised.

"Do it," he said in a low, husky voice that he barely recognized.

She put the top of the bottle to the line of hair that ran from his belly to his hard cock, letting the liquid slowly trickle out.

Not a drop fell to the sheets. Her greedy mouth was there to take it all in.

And then she took *him* all in.

Yeah, this was definitely how expensive champagne should be used.

She licked at the underside of his cock, making him even harder. Taking him completely into her mouth, she tickled with her tongue as she sucked him off. His hands went to her head, then down her shoulders, rubbing as she continued on.

"Fuck, that's good," he said when he felt he had enough air to get even those words out. She murmured some kind of answer, but since her mouth was full of his cock, he didn't quite make out what she said.

And he realized he wanted to hear her. Hear her gasps, her moans, every dirty word she might want to utter. He pulled her up his body, capturing her mouth with his. As he kissed her deeply, he savored the taste of champagne from her lips, from deep inside her mouth.

He heard the rustle of the condom wrapper, then felt the latex as she sheathed him. The second it was on, he rolled them over so she was on her back and he was looking down at her as he guided himself to her.

Moans from both of them filled the night as he pushed inside her, so wet, so tight he thought he'd died and gone to champagne heaven.

But it only got better as he moved inside her, picking up

speed, going deeper when she lifted her knees so her calves were against his hips. Her heels dug into his ass, and it was if she was spurring him on. Not that he needed it.

He drove into her, feeling her starting to clench around him, her breath hitching. She was close. He moved his hand down, finger to her clit, which was slick and sticky.

"Huck," she gasped as he circled his thumb around her. She wrapped her arms tight around his shoulders as he picked up the pace.

Her breath hitched once more, and Huck buried himself to the hilt as they both shattered. She bit his shoulder as he ducked his head to her neck, his body convulsing into her.

There were aftershocks and tremors from both of them. Finally, Huck rolled off of her and to her side. He took care of the condom as best he could without leaving the bed. It wasn't like there was a bathroom nearby to clean them both up. Might as well just deal with it all in the morning.

Besides, they'd probably make a few more messes before the night was over.

"Thanks for the champagne, Jim," she whispered as she snuggled close to him, throwing a leg over his thigh and resting her head and a hand on his chest.

"Yes. Thanks, Jim," he whispered back. He'd probably have to get up in a while to blow out the candles, but he was too sated, too wiped out, to move.

And entirely too happy.

Twenty-Four

KELSEY WAS AWOKEN SIMULTANEOUSLY BY HUCK'S kissing of her shoulder and a bright light, which she quickly realized was daylight. Major daylight. Like, three-sixty daylight. She rolled over on her back, and Huck's arm snaked around her naked torso. But Kelsey was more interested (okay, not *more*, but still pretty interested) in finally seeing what had only been hinted at last night by candlelight.

It was amazing. Glass on three sides of the cabin, plus the entire roof. All glass. All spectacular. "Holy wah," she said, using the phrase she'd heard Huck and the other locals she worked with say.

Huck chuckled, his hand running across her stomach and then taking a turn south. "Pretty cool, eh?"

"Very cool." She studied the amazing structure for a few minutes while Huck's hand gently stroked her, working her, getting her ready. It didn't take long. It seemed like she was always ready to take Huck Beck.

He nuzzled at her neck and then threw the champagne-sticky sheet back and worked his way down her body with his mouth while his fingers played a merry tune below. She held on to his shoulders, her arms moving down with his body until his mouth had joined his fingers.

She pushed her head back, pulling the pillow out from under her, wanting to be able to arch her neck with all the delicious shocks that Huck was creating in her.

He licked and sucked, his fingers keeping a tempo inside her as his tongue made magic. Kelsey squirmed underneath him but kept her hands in his wonderful hair, holding him to her. Not that it seemed he wanted to get away.

"Close," she whispered. "So close."

"I'm gettin' that," he said. She could feel his smile against her thigh as he went back to work.

"God, Huck," she said, coming apart. Just as she did, a loud engine roar came from outside, and Huck's head came up as her body started trembling.

"Jesus Christ, what the hell is that?" he said, looking up.

Up? It became obvious to Kelsey that Huck had a better bead on where the sound was coming from as a small plane flew directly over them. A very low-flying plane. As in, they could see the pilot's face. And what was more, the pilot could see them. A very naked them with Huck's head in her crotch.

Huck grabbed the sheet and quickly covered them up, both of them still looking at the plane, which was now past them (a little late with the sheet) and headed toward Lake Superior. It took a turn to the north, but the incline of where Sawyer's cabin sat allowed them to watch it.

Huck grabbed his boxers from the floor, slid them on as he rose from the platform bed, and went to the window wall. Kelsey wrapped the sheet firmly around her and joined him there.

They watched as the plane went about a half-mile up the coast and then made a perfect landing on the water, which was relatively peaceful at this time of early morning.

"A seaplane," she whispered.

"Yeah," Huck said. "Scared the shit out of me."

"Me too," she said, though she had managed to get a mini-orgasm out before the plane had flown overhead.

They watched as the plane rode the water for another couple of hundred yards and then went out of sight around a bend in the cove.

It hit them both at the same moment. They turned to each other, and with "Eureka!" voices said, "A seaplane!"

"Are they common up here?" she asked, moving quickly to her clothes, raring to get going on this new lead.

"They're not uncommon, but no, there aren't a lot of them. So few that it hadn't even occurred to me," he said.

"It wasn't on our radar. Jenkins and Tarrington only talked about boats being under suspicion."

"Yeah, but I should have—"

She put a hand over his mouth, loving the feel of his beard underneath her fingers. So soft for something that looked so rough. But really, the same could be said for Huck himself. "Hey, we're on it now, right? No sense replaying it. No shouldas."

He gave her a nod, and she took her hand away, which he quickly grasped in his own, holding it at their side.

"Let's see if we can't find out from people at the marina more about the plane. We have a good cover for asking—the damn thing nearly scared us to death. We don't want him doing it again…something like that," she said.

He was staring at her, then said, "Shit, I *love* the way your mind works. I'd like to crawl in there and just take my time looking around."

She opened her mouth, stunned at his words, the way he freely threw them out. Her chest got tight, and she quickly tried to hide the swell of emotions he brought out in her by teasingly saying, "You've kind of already done that with my body."

He threw his head back and laughed, and Kelsey admired the strong lines of his jaw, the cords of muscle in his neck and shoulders. And God, that chest. She'd remember that chest forever.

He bent at his knees, put his shoulder gently into her stomach, and lifted, throwing her over his shoulder. He took the four steps back to the bed and laid her down on it, careful to break her fall with a strong hand on her back.

"Yes, I have. Though not nearly long enough. Let's see if we can't find a few nooks and crannies I may have missed. Then we'll go solve this case."

She wasn't sure which thought excited her more—Huck searching every inch of her body or them solving the case.

Probably a tossup.

Twenty-Five

"SO YOU HAVEN'T SEEN ANY SEAPLANES AROUND? Docking here or anywhere else in the area?" Huck asked Frank Belson later that morning. After they'd taken a sauna at Huck's, they'd stopped at the general store in Copper Harbor and bought a few coffees, which they were giving to people they knew at the marina and asking about the seaplane they'd just seen. So far they'd struck out.

Kelsey had been right. People were getting a laugh over why Huck and Kelsey were asking, though Huck only alluded to the compromising position he and Kelsey had been in during the flyover.

"Nope," Frank answered, taking a sip of the coffee Huck had brought him. "There was Bobby Richards a few years back, who would fly up here every now and then. Marquette, I'm pretty sure he was from. Remember him?"

Huck nodded. "I think so. Plane was bright blue with yellow on it or something, right?"

"That's right. You've got a good memory for details, boy."

"Yeah. Can't remember my own phone number, but I remember that."

Frank chuckled. "Oh, you're too young to be getting to that point. Just wait, Huck, just wait."

Huck had a flash of himself as a man Frank Belson's age. Not quite a premonition, maybe more like a wish. In a fraction of a second, he saw himself near the water, surrounded by his brothers, their wives, and children (he saw lots of children—were some his own?). And he saw Kelsey.

Yeah, definitely a wish-list flash. Not a premonition.

"This plane wasn't blue with yellow," Kelsey said, pulling Huck back to the conversation. Although he had enjoyed his flash of an imaginary future.

"No, but maybe Bobby could help you out. He might know more about the seaplanes in the area than anyone at the marina might."

Huck and Kelsey both nodded. "You have a number for him? Richards?" Kelsey asked.

Frank thought, then nodded. "I think I might have it. Let me go check." He moved below deck, and Huck and Kelsey sat at the stern of Frank's boat and looked out at Lake Superior while they drank their coffee.

"Notice anything odd here this morning?" Huck said to her.

She looked around the boat and then the marina. Huck knew the minute she got it.

"The *Mina*'s not at dock."

"Yep."

"But the charter we're doing for Jim isn't due to start for a few hours."

"Yep."

"So…where is it?"

"She. Boats are shes." She'd picked up a lot during their weeks working boats, but not everything.

"So…where is she? And he—Jim?"

"Good question."

"Early morning run of some kind?"

"Or late night one?"

"Shit. We need to start staking out this place at night," she said, confirming what he was already thinking.

"Yep, let me think about the logistics of it. My truck would be seen anywhere close to here."

She pointed beyond the marina to the woods. "Camping out?"

He nodded. "Most likely. Let's do this. Once we get this number from Frank, we drive back to Houghton and get stuff for a few days up here. We tell anyone who asks that we're staying at Sawyer's place. And we will, except for watching this place at night."

She nodded. "That works."

A few minutes later, Frank came back with a phone number that he had for Bobby Richards. "Not sure this is still his number. Or if he even flies anymore. But Bobby had his pulse on pretty much anything going on small-plane-wise, so he might give you some direction."

"Thanks, Frank. I know it's silly to try and chase this guy down. I just want to make sure that, I don't know, he didn't take pictures or anything," Kelsey said.

Frank nodded. "I don't blame ya, sweetie. I'd be a bit put off too, if somebody flew that low over my place."

"He probably didn't even realize he was. Sawyer's place is pretty secluded. But you never know these days. I don't want us on some website somewhere."

Frank shook his head. "Damn, times have changed. And worries have changed too, haven't they?"

Huck thought about his beloved area being a dropping point for drugs to supply meth labs across the U.P. "Yeah, the worries are different, Frank. That's for sure."

After they left Frank, they drove back to Houghton. On the way, Huck called Twain once they got in cell reception range, hoping his brother wouldn't be using a chainsaw or something else loud and not be able to hear his phone.

"Yo," Twain said, and Huck said a silent thanks.

"Hey, need a favor if you can."

"Shoot."

"You still have that drone that you and Matt messed around with?"

"Yeah. It's a piece of shit cheapy compared to the new ones they've got, but it worked for scouting out forest lines and property and that kind of stuff."

"Do you use it on a daily basis? Is it something I could use for a while?"

"Yeah, sure. I only use it when I'm working on a new bid. And even that's mostly in the wintertime. Summertime, I just walk the property line."

"That'd be great, thanks. Is it at T&B offices?"

"Nah, I keep it in my workshop at the Calumet house. You've got keys, right?"

The Calumet house. Not "my" house. Twain had definitely moved in with Liv, even in how he thought about the place he'd made a home for himself and Matt the past seven years. "Yeah, somewhere. Okay if I stop there on our way back up in a couple of hours?"

"Be my guest. I'm at the office now and will be until late. Then going home…to Liv's."

"Got it. Not going back to your Calumet house anytime soon, eh?"

Twain chuckled. "Only to pick up stuff I need and forgot. I imagine it'll be on the market pretty soon."

"That's great, Twain, really."

"Thanks, bro. I think so too. So, how fast did you make the drive back to Houghton last night? I was happy not to see your truck wrapped around Covered Drive on our way home after we left the Seafarer."

Huck laughed. Kelsey, who could hear both sides of the conversation, looked out the side window of the truck, a flush rising up her neck. "We didn't even make it to the highway. We spent the night at the Ice Cube."

"No shit? That's great. Kelsey was okay with the biffy?"

Huck looked over to see Kelsey drop her head in her hands. "It wasn't her most favorite thing, but she's a trouper."

"A Yooper by marriage, if not by blood," Twain said.

"That's my girl," Huck said. Kelsey peeked out from her hands, looking at him. He tried to convey a look that said more than his words had. Or maybe a look that conveyed *exactly* what his words said. That she was his girl.

And he was coming to realize that she might be the *only* girl for him.

He said his goodbyes to Twain, promising him he would talk with him soon.

"A drone? That's genius," Kelsey said.

He shrugged. "Might not amount to anything, but we could probably cover a lot of acreage up there that we wouldn't be able to get to otherwise, acreage that could only be reached by a plane along a shore."

"Maybe that's the answer to surveillance on the marina at night?"

"That's what I was thinking too, but I don't have that figured out yet. We'll have to test it out up at Sawyer's place first. See the range. See how noticeable it would be from the ground. If it even can capture anything at night. Stuff like that."

She nodded, and they drove in silence until Huck thought of something else. "When you talk to Jenkins to tell him about the seaplane angle, maybe he could get us some night cameras that we could put up at the marina. Twain uses those things at his offices at night. Motion detecting. Hunters up here have them out on their trails, too, so we could probably find some if Jenkins doesn't—"

"I'm not going to tell Jenkins about the seaplane angle. Not yet, anyway."

"No? Seems like he might be able to get intel that we're not able to get on registered planes, logged flight plans, that kind of thing."

"First, if planes are flying to Canada to get bags full of Sudafed for meth, they're probably not logging a flight plan."

That was true, but...

"Second, if we tell Jenkins about the seaplane, he's just going to feed that information to his primary agent on this thing. If they were even telling the truth about that in the first place."

Huck was confused. "Wait. You think they were bullshitting about that? That we're the primaries, and we don't know it? That doesn't seem—"

"No. Probably not. It's just with Jenkins, you never know. He's one sadistic fuck, and this is his chance to…"

"His chance to what?" Huck asked.

A shrug from her, and then she turned to look out the window, her face away from Huck. "I don't know. Mess with me, my career. I told you he hates me and has since I beat him in pretty much everything at training."

Huck smiled, thinking of how he could barely keep up with Kelsey on their morning runs. Yeah, an ass like Jenkins wouldn't handle that kind of shit well.

"So how does not telling him help us?"

"Well, it's more that it doesn't hurt us. I'm not sure that he wouldn't throw me—and by extension you—under the bus on this case. In fact, I think he's counting on it."

"Still…"

She turned to look at him. He wanted to pull the truck over, to be able to really study her face when she said whatever she was going to say next. But he didn't. He kept driving, knowing she was likely to say more, keep talking, if he wasn't staring at her.

It had been a short time, but he knew her well.

"I know how much this means to you, Huck. It means just as much to me. I need to prove to my superiors that I'm cut out for undercover work."

"But wouldn't that include keeping your contact well informed?" He couldn't believe he was saying that. Huck was a bit of a rebel, had been known to break a few rules himself. But not something like that. Not something that could so easily blow up in his face, or get him, or his partner, hurt.

"Normally. But because it's Jenkins, not necessarily in this case. I know him, Huck. He'll try to fuck me on this. Use any info we get to help his other agent. No one will ever know our contributions."

"Maybe I could talk to Prescott?"

She shook her head. "Not now. If it comes down to it, and we think we can trust him…"

"I trust Prescott."

"Okay, good. Then when we have something, something really concrete, we take it to both Jenkins and Prescott."

"Cover our asses," he said, getting it. Not particularly liking it, but getting it.

"One thing you'll learn if you go to work for the DEA," Kelsey said, "is that it is a very CYA culture. All of them are. FBI, CIA, DEA, ATF."

That didn't surprise him. Again, he didn't like it, but he got it. He also knew that when doing a joint venture, agencies worked together for the greater good. But there was lots of muscle flexing and power-play bullshit that went along with it.

"Yeah, okay," he said. "We'll play it your way."

She nodded at him, then looked back out the window.

He thought about it all for the rest of the drive to Houghton and as they packed up their clothes, cooler, sleeping bags, and any other camping gear Huck had.

He kept playing her words over in his brain as they stopped at Twain's and put the drone in the back of Huck's truck, then stopped at the Holiday to get batteries and other stuff.

He kept on looking at possible angles Kelsey might be playing as they made their way back to Copper Harbor to be on time for work with Jim and a fishing charter.

And for the first time since the day he'd "married" her, Huck wondered if he could completely trust his new wife.

Twenty-Six

—⚊—

THEY HAD FUN MESSING WITH THE DRONE AT SAWYER'S place, zooming it along the shoreline and over the woods. Both Kelsey and Huck became proficient with it in a short time.

Problem was, it was a pretty low-end model and didn't have night vision, and its mileage radius wasn't enough for them to stay at the Ice Cube and let the drone fly back to the Copper Harbor marina.

So they spent the next week working for Jim for a few charters, sleeping at the Ice Cube for a few hours, and doing night surveillance at the marina. Which meant parking off the road about a half-mile away and walking through the woods to the edge of the marina, where they'd set up in the cover of the trees, staying in sleeping bags, taking shifts watching the marina.

Which never changed from the time workers left, boat lights went out, and everyone left.

No more early morning cruises from Jim—at least no unplanned ones that Kelsey and Huck weren't a part of.

Kelsey was starting to think that Jim had just decided to take the *Mina* out one morning for a ride, nothing more.

She still hadn't called in the seaplane hunch to Jenkins.

And that's all it was, she told herself: just a hunch. Just another possible angle. Perhaps the other agent working this case was already on it. Hell, he could have been the pilot in the plane that flew over Sawyer's place.

Huck had gotten hold of Bobby Richards, who gave him the numbers of two pilots he knew who owned seaplanes in the area. The first was a man who had retired two years ago and sold his plane. The man thought the new owner had taken the plane out of the area, to somewhere in Wisconsin, but he wasn't sure. The second name and number didn't pan out, with the man not answering and no voicemail option.

Kelsey figured she'd soon have to pass those two names on to Jenkins and have the office follow up on them. She could always go through the D.C. office, but she knew she was walking a tightrope with Jenkins anyway. Deliberately going around him would likely push her off the rope altogether.

So, at the end of their scheduled sunset cruise, when Jim asked them if they'd be interested in working an overnight trip to Isle Royale, Kelsey jumped in with an enthusiastic yes before Huck could even think about it.

She was sick of sleeping in the woods, being eaten alive by the ever-present mosquitoes, and coming up with nothing.

At least on this trip, she'd be able to sleep for more than three hours at a time.

"Wait," Huck said. "Which night, exactly? We've got that reception that Liv is throwing so everyone can meet Kelsey. That's Saturday night."

Jim was already nodding. "Right. I remembered, and I plan on attending. Thanks for the invitation." Huck and Kelsey both nodded. "We'll leave Friday early and spend the day at Isle Royale. I think these are hikers or something, or maybe they are just sightseeing. They didn't want any fishing time. We spend the night—they have a room at the lodge, and we'll stay on the boat. We head back Saturday midmorning. That gets you back in time to get down to Houghton, get cleaned up, and make it to your reception. I'll take care of the boat and head down later."

Huck looked at Kelsey. She could see him going over the

timeline in his head. If they had boat problems, or anything else, Liv would be standing at a reception by herself with no guests of honor.

"I'll understand if you don't want to chance it," Jim said. "It's a last-minute thing, but I didn't want to turn them down. It'll be my first Isle Royale charter of the season."

Kelsey deferred to Huck with a small shrug. She could see him weighing it out. A chance to look around Isle Royale, as well as to spend a night on the boat. So far, Jim was still their only real suspect. They both had come to believe that Jim wasn't involved in the muling of Sudafed or anything else, but still, it was the best lead they had.

"Sure, we'll take the charter. Thanks, Jim."

"Thank you. You guys have been great with last-minute scheduling. It's appreciated."

He did appreciate them, Kelsey knew. He always gave any kind of tip that they received for a charter completely to Huck and Kelsey, not taking a cut for himself, which made the argument stronger that *if* Jim was involved in something illegal, it wasn't solely for the money. Could he be being blackmailed into letting someone use his boat?

That night while in the woods, between shifts and bouts of spraying themselves liberally with Off, they discussed that fact, adding it to all the others they routinely talked about.

To Huck's credit, he didn't ask her again if they should call in Jenkins on the seaplane. Of course, Kelsey thought as she swatted another bug off her hand while looking through night binoculars at the deserted marina, he *could* have gone behind her back and taken it straight to Prescott.

It would help him in his cause to get back in with the DEA. Prescott would love for the DEA to come up with the intel and show up the FBI.

And Kelsey knew how badly Huck wanted in. Badly enough to undercut her? And yeah, it wasn't lost on her that she was close to doing the same thing to Jenkins, but that was…different. Definitely different.

A soft buzzing went off, and Huck woke to his alarm. He rubbed his hands over his face, waking himself up and looking to Kelsey. She shook her head—nothing to report.

They quietly squirmed around, with Huck coming out of his sleeping bag and sitting cross-legged on the top of it. Kelsey handed him the night binoculars, then shimmied into her own bag. No words were passed, no sounds made. But just as Kelsey was drifting off, Huck's hand gently stroked her hair, and she pushed her head into his touch, missing it. Needing it.

They'd had sex in the past week since the first night at the Ice Cube, but it had been hurried, frenzied, done only when they had time to spare between working at the marina and returning to stake it out.

Not that it hadn't been fantastic, but Kelsey missed the small touches, the lingering in bed with limbs entwined.

And she was desperate to again spend the night in Huck's arms.

Strong as that feeling—that *yearning*—was, perhaps it was best that they'd had to cool it on the intimacy, if not the actual sex.

Way in the back in her mind, where she squashed down the idea of Huck going to Prescott behind her back, she had pushed down the fact that she was on the clock with Huck. That soon, though she didn't know when, she would be going back to D.C. and Huck would either be staying here or going through DEA training and beginning a new chapter in his life. One that wouldn't leave room for a wife, fictional or otherwise.

The main headquarters of the DEA was in Arlington, Virginia, but they had offices all over the world, and Huck had no idea where he'd be placed if he even got back in and made it through training.

She moved her head so her face was at Huck's palm, and gave

his hand a soft kiss. Then she snuggled into the sleeping bag and tried to turn her damn brain off.

Twenty-Seven

⸻

HUCK HADN'T SPENT THE NIGHT ON ISLE ROYALE IN A
few summers. Once they had their charter couple settled at the
Rock Harbor Lodge, Jim, Kelsey, and Huck had dinner on the
boat, enjoying the chance to split a bottle of wine and a few after-
dinner drinks. They were off the clock with no chance that Jim
would have to captain, so they enjoyed the evening. Jim went
below to one of the cabins around nine. There were two other
cabins below, but Huck asked Kelsey if she wanted to take their
sleeping bags and stay in one of the many wooden shelters on
the island. He thought she'd opt for the boat, seeing as it would
be more comfortable than being outdoors, but was pleasantly
surprised when she said she'd like to spend the night off the boat.

And even more pleasantly surprised when she whispered,
"That way we won't wake up Jim if we're…noisy."

He smiled at her and said, "No, but you might attract some
wolves the way you howl."

She laughed and started gathering up some stuff for them to
take. "Me? Your moans could be confused for a moose call, for
sure."

He wrapped an arm around her, pulling her close and sliding
his hand down to her ass, which he gave a long squeeze. "Are you
complaining?"

Her breath caught, and Huck wondered if maybe they
should skip the campout and get right down to business here in

their cabin. Just as he was about to back her up to the bunk, she whispered, "No complaints. None." She took a step away from him, even though he kept his hand on her ass. "Now take me to this place where we can make animal noises all night long."

"I can do that," he said, finally letting her go, but knowing it wouldn't be long before she'd be back where she belonged—in his arms.

He grabbed another bottle of wine, marking it down on a note for Jim and letting their captain know they were going to camp out and would be back early in the morning. He threw some other essentials in his backpack and took one sleeping bag under his arm. Kelsey took the other, and he led her, flashlight in hand, to a shelter that he remembered on a part of the island away from the marina. With the Keweenaw Peninsula being so far west, and yet still on Eastern time, there was still daylight this late in the evening.

He explained that the shelter campsites were on a first come, first served basis. Since Jim had already paid their daily park fee usage, they were free to stay at whatever campsite they found. He had one in mind, and it was only about a half-mile hike from the Rock Harbor marina. There were no campfires allowed on the island, but the rustic campsite had running water, a lean-to for shelter from the wind, and outside johns, which they were both getting used to, having spent the week at Sawyer's place.

"I NEVER THOUGHT THE smell of Off would be such a turn-on," Kelsey said later—much later—when they had made several animal calls into the wild. Huck wasn't even sure what animal he'd sounded like when he was buried deep inside Kelsey and she had clenched around him.

But damn, it felt good, and he'd let out a howl to that effect.

Now, lying on the hard wood floor of the shelter, their sleeping bags zipped together to create one large cocoon, Huck held Kelsey in his arms and thought about how much he'd missed doing that since that first night at the Ice Cube.

And how much he never wanted to let her go.

She rolled on top of him, putting her hands high on his chest, resting her chin on the back of them. "Penny for your thoughts," she said.

He knew she meant about the case. It wasn't all they talked about, of course, but he knew it was always on her mind, as it usually was for him.

But it wasn't now. No, now his thoughts went to his feelings for Kelsey. In the midst of all the lies they'd been telling—hell, *living*—he knew one truth. Absolutely and positively.

"I love you," he said. It was a thought heftier than a penny, for sure, and he was shocked he had let it slip out.

Except Huck didn't let shit just slip out, and he wouldn't cop out on that now.

He'd meant it, and he wanted her to know. He didn't know how long they had together, but he wanted her to know, even if she got called back in tomorrow.

He wanted her to hear something he'd never said to another woman.

And not because he wanted to hear it back. He'd heard it before. He didn't need to just hear the words; he needed them to *mean* something. From Kelsey's startled face, he knew he'd surprised her. From the way she dipped her head, he knew she wasn't going to respond in kind.

But when she lifted her head up to look at him, unshed tears pooling in her eyes, whispering only his name, he knew that even if she didn't say the words, even if his had spooked her, she felt the same way he did. He moved his hand up her naked back to the top of her head, and gently tucked it down to his chest, giving her an out, not making her embarrassed that she couldn't say the words back.

He'd almost drifted asleep, happy and content, when she said softly into his chest, "I could get called back to D.C. any day."

"Yep," he said. His voice was husky, but he wasn't sure if it was from the near sleep or the deep emotions that were roiling inside of him.

"And you don't have any idea what's going to happen next for you," she said, head still buried in his chest. He could feel the words she spoke as well as hear them.

"Nope," he said.

"And...I love it here, I really do. I'm surprised how much. But I love what I do, too. Really love it. I could never—"

"Shhh," he said, rubbing her shoulders, feeling them tense up as she talked. "I know, baby, it's not meant to be. But we'll just enjoy our time left together."

Silence from her, then a tiny nod into his chest, and he tightened his arms around her.

"Sleep, Kels," he said. Another nod from her. They lay in silence for a while, with Huck not knowing who finally fell asleep first.

Twenty-Eight

—ɯ—

KELS. HE'D CALLED HER KELS. A NICKNAME SHE'D LOVED
as a kid, had shed when she joined the FBI, and had absolutely
abhorred for the past two years.

And Huck had called her that after he'd told her he loved her.

If nothing else, she could take away from this assignment the
fact that he'd given her a beloved nickname back.

But he'd given her much more than that, and she knew it.

She just couldn't handle it.

Kelsey Cameron, tops in her FBI training class, valedictorian
of her high school, honors at Harvard.

And she runs when a man tells her he loves her.

Literally runs.

She woke before Huck in their little shelter and decided to
take a quick run before they'd head back to the boat and start to
prepare for the trip back to Copper Harbor.

She could have woken up Huck to join her. He'd been with
her on all her other runs after that first one in Houghton.

But she hadn't. She'd needed to be alone for this run and
think about what Huck had said to her.

He got around, that was undisputed. What had Tarrington
called him? Oh, yeah, the town player. Janie Kuurtu and others
Kelsey had met could attest to that.

And yet Kelsey would have bet her badge and Glock that
Huck didn't tell those women that he loved them.

He didn't need to, not just to get someone into bed. Hadn't needed to with Kelsey either. But it wasn't a get-her-into-bed move. The words would mean too much to Huck to just throw them out willy-nilly.

He was…interesting. By no means a Dudley Do-Right, and yet she knew he had a strong moral code, just one of his own making. Huck Beck would never tell a woman he loved her if he didn't mean it.

The question was, could she say it back?

She loved him, of that she had no doubt. Had been falling in love with him from that first day when he'd prowled her apartment, getting to know his new wife in his own way.

No, it was probably before that. Four years ago.

She wasn't a believer in love at first sight. Or, at least, she *hadn't* been. But he'd definitely had her interested four years ago. Enough that she thought about him every now and then. Even pulled the sketch of him out of her jewelry box every once in a while.

And he remembered her too from all those years ago. That. That might have been the clincher, the final thing that threw her into the abyss of loving Huck Beck—knowing he'd thought of her too.

And it was an abyss, loving Huck. There was no future for them.

She was going back to D.C. soon. And if she could make some headway in this case, even solve it for Jenkins, there was no way they wouldn't give her more undercover work. Even Jenkins would have to concede she'd done a good job.

And Huck? Well, Huck would either be spending his life here, as he was doing now, or he'd be starting his career with the DEA, doing his own undercover work.

She reached a high point on the island and stopped running, hands on hips, bent at the waist, trying to catch her breath.

She never got this winded on a run, but this morning she was really pushing herself.

Pushing herself or punishing herself? Punishing herself for being too chicken to have answered Huck last night with the words he wanted to hear.

Words she wanted to say.

Standing straight, she surveyed the landscape in front of her. The island was beautiful, and she wished she could have spent more time on it. But who knew. If the case went on, perhaps they'd get more overnight charters, she and Huck could spend another night in a onesie sleeping bag, and she'd finally be able to voice the feelings she so deeply felt.

With that thought dangling, she looked down to the shoreline, which was around a large bend from Rock Harbor, out of sight from the marina and the populated areas.

And saw the same damn seaplane that had flown over the Ice Cube.

She pulled her phone off the Velcro thingy on her shoulder where she automatically kept it while running, whether listening to music or not. Taking photo after photo, she captured the plane's N-number and other identifying marks.

Crouching now so the pilot wouldn't see her if he happened to look to the high areas of the island, Kelsey waited, hoping whatever might happen (*if* anything happened) would happen quickly so that she could get back to Huck in time to leave for work.

Not that she wouldn't miss reporting to the *Mina* to see what the hell this plane was up to.

Much like it had the morning at Sawyer's place, the seaplane was slowly moving along the shoreline of a very remote area, with no other vessels, or people, in the vicinity.

And just like that, like she'd conjured it up with her thoughts, a boat rounded the bend in the cove where the plane sat, and Kelsey started snapping more photos.

She was far enough away that she wouldn't be able to get good photos of the people inside the plane or boat, but she'd be able to get generalities—gender, height, coloring, stuff like that.

She watched as the boat drew near to the plane, and the pilot stepped out of the door and onto the float. The boat wasn't as large as the *Mina*, but large enough to weather Lake Superior and make it to the island. But were they coming from the U.S. or Canada?

After a bit of maneuvering, the boat came side by side with the plane, and someone threw a rope over the side of the boat, which the pilot caught and tied to the plane.

Then, holy shit, six—no, seven—garbage bags were taken from the boat by the only person Kelsey could see on the boat, a blond man, and handed down to the pilot of the plane, who promptly placed each bag inside the plane.

Kelsey caught it all on her phone. Video of the whole thing, zooming in on the faces of each man, though they were still too far away for a solid identification.

But this would be enough. She had the N-number of the plane and the registration number of the boat, both of which she typed into the Notes app on her phone just in case the pics alone didn't do it.

There were some words spoken that she couldn't hear, but she could tell were happening by gestures the men made. Then they both headed back inside their vessels. The boat headed one way (toward Canada), and the plane took off, heading toward the U.S. through the air.

Kelsey got some more pics as they both headed in opposite directions, careful to put in Notes the time, date, and anything else she could think of that might be pertinent later on.

Then she turned and started running back to the shelter, which was empty by the time she got there, a note from Huck on the ground with a rock on top of it saying he'd meet her at the boat. He'd taken her things with him, so Kelsey picked up the note, putting it in the waistband of her running leggings, and continued with her run, exploding with excitement to tell Huck about her discovery.

But when she got to the dock, Jim was already up, and he

and Huck were working side by side, prepping the boat for their return journey.

"Good run?" Huck asked her as she came aboard.

"*Very* good run," she said, hoping her voice would clue him in. He did look at her for a moment, studying her, and took a step away from what he was doing on the other side of the deck from her.

"Well, there they are," Jim said from above her, and Kelsey turned to see the couple who had chartered the *Mina* approaching down the dock.

Well, it would just have to wait until they were back in Copper Harbor, driving back to Houghton for their reception. She'd have the whole hour drive to tell him about seeing the exchange this morning.

Except, after thinking for the entire boat ride back to Copper Harbor, she didn't tell him on the drive home.

Or while they were getting cleaned up and dressed for the party.

Or even while driving to the restaurant where Liv had booked a private room for the small reception.

Kelsey didn't say a word about what she'd seen that morning.

Twenty-Nine

"AT FIRST, I DIDN'T SEE IT," SAWYER SAID WHILE ALL three Beck brothers stood at the bar during Kelsey and Huck's reception. "But seeing you two together tonight makes me think I was wrong."

"You were wrong," Huck said.

Sawyer tipped his bottle of beer toward his little brother, and Huck nodded, accepting the apology, such as it was.

The reception went well, and was now winding down, a few couples still on the dance floor. Kelsey sat chatting at a table with Liv and Deni. She wore the red dress he'd had her pack from her closet.

And he was oh so glad he had.

She'd been great meeting all the people who had come that she hadn't met before. Which really weren't that many, between Liv (thankfully) keeping it very small and Kelsey having spent three weeks in the Copper Country working and living amongst Huck's friends and family. But she'd been a trouper, taking in all the congratulations headed their way, talking with everyone just like a bride would do at a real wedding reception, and setting his heart on fire by doing it all in that red dress and spiky sandals.

Jim came and even danced with Kelsey once before heading back to the Harbor. Good food, lots of booze, and even a small wedding cake. They got a huge round of applause when they were introduced as husband and wife by Sawyer.

And another huge round of applause came later in the evening as Twain announced his and Liv's engagement and the impending arrival of the newest baby Beck.

Now Huck was wondering how long the guests of honor had to stay before he could take Kelsey home and have their "wedding night."

But before they dove under the sheets, Huck was going to sit Kelsey down and ask her what was bothering her. She'd been off all day, starting with leaving him alone at the campsite this morning, all the way through walking in the door of the reception. Once there, she seemed to drop whatever had been on her mind in order to play the loving wife. The way she'd looked at him the few times they'd danced had him convinced that she wasn't playing the "loving" part.

"Yeah, you did good, Huck," Twain said, as they all looked at the table where the women sat. The women must have been talking about the brothers, because they were all looking at each other and then burst into laughter.

"Think we're being talked about," Sawyer said.

"Yep," Huck said as he shook his head and rolled his eyes at all the women, which only brought about another round of laughter.

"Thanks. I know I did good," he belatedly answered Twain, though it was a statement that needed no answer.

"She seems really good for you," Twain added, and Huck only nodded.

"I love her," he said. It was newsworthy coming from him, since he'd only said the words to her last night, but his brothers nodded like they didn't need to be told that bit of obvious information.

He turned from looking at the party toward his two brothers, the two most important people throughout his life. Followed closely by Liv and Matt. He thought about the lie he was telling them, the many lies he'd told lately. He couldn't—wouldn't—come clean about Kelsey and his marriage, but there was something else—another lie—that he needed to make right. He owed it to them.

"Listen," he said, stepping closer to them, his back turning to the rest of the room. Sawyer instinctively moved a step away from the bar and created a circle of just the three of them. Tight, solid, not letting anyone else in. "There's something I need to tell you both. Something that's been eating me up for a while now."

Sawyer put his hand reassuringly on Huck's shoulder, and Twain straightened away from the bar which he'd been leaning against. "What's up?" he said softly to Huck.

"It's just that, I mean, I love you guys, and I'm sorry I didn't say anything sooner." He saw Sawyer and Twain exchange puzzled looks and cleared his throat to go on. "I have to let you know that—"

"Babe, I think it's okay if we take off now," Kelsey said, running her hand up Huck's back, under his suit coat and under his shirt. She squeezed into the circle between Sawyer and him.

"Umm, yeah?" he said, looking at Kelsey, who was giving him a pointed stare. Huck knew it meant something, he just wasn't sure what.

"Yes. Liv said we didn't have to be the last ones to leave. If this was our actual wedding reception, we probably would have left a while ago."

"Okay. I was just—"

"You'll excuse us if I drag my husband home, won't you, guys?" she said to Sawyer and Twain. "These shoes are killing me. So not my style."

"But they look great," Liv said, entering the circle at Twain's side.

"Sure do," Deni added, as she joined the little group. Sawyer slipped an arm around her waist.

"Maybe you two ladies could walk Kelsey to the car? We just want to wrap up with Huck," Sawyer said to Deni and Liv.

Huck felt a pinch at his back, a sign (warning?) from Kelsey. He waved a hand of dismissal in the general vicinity of his brothers. "You know what? Don't worry about it. Not a big deal. It can keep."

"You sure?" Twain said, concern in his eyes.

"Absolutely. I'm going to take my wife home and happily take those killer sandals from her aching feet." Kelsey playfully swatted him, and he slipped an arm around her and kissed her forehead, which was even with his, given the height of her sandals.

They said their goodbyes to his brothers, Deni and Liv, and any others still at the party. They thanked Liv profusely for hosting the evening for them and then took off.

Another ride in silence, with Kelsey saying nothing.

When they got home, he asked if she wanted a drink, but she just shook her head and went upstairs. He had one beer, then followed.

When he got upstairs, she was sitting up in bed, the lamp on her bedside table still on. She looked adorable in her Harvard tee, face freshly scrubbed free of the makeup she wore to the party.

And angry as hell.

"Just what exactly were you about to say to your brothers?" she asked. Before Huck could say a word, she added, "And it better not be what I think it was."

Thirty

"WERE YOU THINKING I WAS JUST ABOUT TO TELL MY brothers that I am only their half-brother?"

Umm, no. That wasn't what she'd been thinking.

"What?" she said, feeling like shit. She'd mistakenly thought he was about to tell his brothers the truth about his and Kelsey's relationship. She'd been shocked as she'd neared him and heard what he was saying, and had jumped to the easiest conclusion, even though she hadn't really believed it of him.

"I'm only their half-brother. John Beck is not my father. Now, if you don't mind, I'd like to get out of these clothes. They aren't spiky, high-heeled sandals, but my shoes are killing me, too."

She waved for him to go ahead, stunned. Waiting for him to change and then use the bathroom was excruciating with Kelsey wondering what she should lead with—an apology or soothing him over the pain that his declaration obviously gave him.

"You don't need to apologize," he said when he came out of the bathroom wearing only the cut-off sweats he slept in. Or at least the shorts he started the night sleeping in. He seldom ended up with them on. Same with her Harvard tee and men's boxers, though she still had those on.

"I am sorry, though," she said.

"I know," he said, climbing into his side of the large bed. He stopped, staying on his side, not moving to the middle like he usually did. "If I had walked up when you did and heard the lead-in I was giving them, I'd think the same thing."

"I should have known you'd never blow our cover. I *did* know it. I just was caught off guard."

He turned on his side, facing her but still so far away. It reminded Kelsey of their first night together in this bed, when they'd ever-so-slowly slid their hands toward each other, meeting in the middle.

"Tell me," she said softly, sliding her hand toward him, hoping he'd now meet her halfway.

He did, his hand taking hers, entwining their fingers. "I found out four years ago."

"Four years ago?" she asked, the timing of that tickling something in her mind.

"Yep. And yes, it was the reason I quit the DEA training."

She knew something big had to have happened for Huck to leave. She just couldn't imagine that he'd washed out. Not after getting to know him and seeing how good he would be at this.

He took a deep breath, then let it out. Kelsey waited, just holding his hand and meeting his eyes with her own.

"One of the weekends we had off, I took a train up to Boston to see my dad. I hadn't seen him in a long time. Years. We didn't have the best of relationships with him—my brothers and I."

"Because he left you, left his family."

"Yeah. And I was so young at the time that in my head I thought it was something I'd done."

"Sure, you were a kid. But you must have seen that you hadn't done anything wrong when you were older. When you understood about divorce."

He laughed, but the sound was pained, not jovial. "That's just it. I did understand by then. And I guess I wanted to show him that I finally got it. I was almost due to graduate from the training, become a DEA agent...really had my shit together."

"Right, that's good," she said, sensing that the story wasn't going to turn out well.

"Yeah, sort of. But part of it was a 'fuck you' to him, too. Letting him know I hadn't needed him. That I was doing just fine. Twain was divorced, Sawyer was basically a hermit, but I was fulfilling my dream." She rubbed her thumb along the top of his hand, loving the feel of his rough skin.

"And he let me have it. He was drunk—turns out he's a drinker, but I hadn't known that when I was a kid. Sawyer, my mom, Twain, none of them ever mentioned that fact."

"What do you mean let you have it? Did he...did he hit you?" The thought made her blood run cold, especially because she knew Huck wouldn't have retaliated, wouldn't have defended himself against his older, drunken father.

He shook his head against the white pillow. He'd shaved his beard for the party tonight and trimmed the goatee close, so it was almost nonexistent. She loved him with whatever facial hair he chose to wear, but this clean, neatly trimmed look made him devastatingly handsome.

"No, he didn't hit me. I don't think he had the coordination to pull it off, drunk as he was. Besides, John Beck's weapon of choice was always words, not fists."

"What did he say?" she asked, and then held her breath.

"Not much, really. Just four words: 'You're not my child' was pretty much it. He went on, of course, but those were the killers."

"Almost seems like you should be glad that asshole isn't your father."

"Yeah, except then it played on my old self-doubt. It called up all those emotions from being a seven-year-old kid and thinking his dad leaving was his fault."

"How?"

"Because it *was* my fault. Me being conceived. My being born was what did them in."

"But you were seven when he left. That doesn't make sense."

He shrugged a shoulder. "He said he knew it the moment I

was born. Knew I was the result of my mom sleeping with some guy John worked with. That he pretended not to know, was convinced that the affair was over. And maybe it was, but he let it fester, let it burn a hole in him. They fought for the next seven years, and he drank. Then he finally couldn't take it any longer and left. Left us all. Even his…real sons."

"But that still isn't *your* fault," she said.

"I know. Or at least I know that now. But it really fucked with my head at the time. He said the guy who was my real father had killed himself a few years after John had left. That he'd never come to terms with the end of his and my mother's affair. Apparently they really had ended it when I was born, and the guy thought he stood a chance once John left our family. But my mother wasn't interested. John laughed about that. Laughed about my real father killing himself."

"Jesus, what a dick."

The laugh was real from Huck this time, but small. "That he was. Is, I'm assuming. There was this tiny part of me that was so gleeful he wasn't my biological father, and that there might be a man out there somewhere that I could find and perhaps have a relationship with. And then John tells me the guy is dead. And laughs about it."

"God."

"Yeah. Anyway, on the train back from D.C., I let his words, his disdain for me, really mess with me. I went on a bender that night. Missed training the next day. Prescott pulled me out of a hangover the second day, was willing to let me back in, but by then my mind was so fucked with that I walked away."

"Huck," she whispered, stroking his hand.

"I regretted it almost immediately, but my pride wouldn't allow me to go begging to Prescott. Not that he would have taken me back anyway. I spent the next six months at the bottom of the bottle."

"What happened to change that?"

"Matt called and asked if I could come to his birthday party. I did, but I was a mess. Sawyer and Twain called me out on it. I told them to go fuck themselves, but after another week of wallowing, I realized they were right. Cleaned up my act after that. The rest, you pretty much know. It's exactly what I'm still doing today."

"You know, Prescott probably would have taken you back after you left. If he remembered you so much that he's giving you this chance now, then you must have really impressed him."

"Maybe. Probably. But I wasn't seeing that clearly at that point."

"No, probably not. I'm sorry that all happened to you," she said.

"Thanks. I'm starting to think it all happened for a reason, though I'm not a big believer in that kind of destiny shit."

"So what was the reason it happened, do you think?"

Another long breath, which he exhaled before continuing. "I don't know if I was ready then. Just out of college, totally gung-ho. I lacked maturity, life experience. I think I would have ended up like Jenkins, a smug, power-hungry asshole."

She snorted, and he smiled. "Plus," he continued, "I wouldn't have met you again now. And if I had somehow found you back then, after that day in Quantico, I probably wouldn't have been ready for you, either."

Now she was the one to take the long, shaking breath, slowly letting it out. "Huck," she whispered.

He was shaking his head. "Don't worry, Kels. I know I freaked you out last night. I'm not looking for anything more than the days we have left together. But I wanted you to know how I felt. How I feel."

"I…I don't know—"

"So anyway," he said, bulldozing over her stammering, "that's what happened four years ago. I've been wanting to say something to Sawyer and Twain for a while now, figuring they have a right to know. But we haven't all been together much over the past couple of years. And I was feeling particularly close to them tonight. And since I can't tell them the truth about what's going on, I just thought…"

"I'm so sorry I interrupted you," she said.

"That's okay. It probably wasn't the time or place to do it. I'll tell them soon." He looked deeper into her eyes and added, "Probably when I tell them that you left me."

"Do you think you'll tell them the truth about us, after I… leave, even if you aren't asked back by Prescott?"

"I'm not sure. I think it might just be easier to tell them we split up. That we married too soon."

"If you do, pin it on me. Say I was, I don't know, cheating on you, or missed home too much, or that I was the one who talked you into getting married so soon and then freaked out about it, or something."

He smiled at her. "Thanks, but they would more easily believe I fucked us up somehow."

"That's not fair," she said quietly.

"No, but it would be easier for me in the long run. They were so proud when I got the call that I was in DEA training four years ago. And so disappointed when I came home, having quit. I'll never forget the look in Sawyer's eyes when I told them I'd quit. Disappointment, major disappointment, but also pity."

"But you didn't tell them why you'd quit, what had happened with your father."

"No. I wasn't ready to then. I wished I had, so many times. But that look in Sawyer's eye stayed with me. And I just can't see that look again over something like Prescott not taking me back. I'd rather see that look over fucking up my fictional marriage. At least I'd know the truth."

She didn't say anything more to that. There wasn't anything she could add, anything that could make the situation better. The fact was she would leave, and Huck would have to deal with the fallout. In whatever way he felt he should do it.

He'd been so honest with her about his past, telling her something he'd never even told his brothers. She wasn't able to say the words "I love you" to him, but she could try to show it by telling him something about her no one else knew. Or at least no one who mattered to her.

"I slept with Jenkins," she said quickly, getting it out before she thought too much about it.

"What? When? What the fuck, Kelsey," he said, moving the distance between them on the bed, unclasping his hand from hers and putting it on her upper arm.

"Two years ago," she said, and his hand relaxed. "Two years ago," she repeated. "And only once. One stupid, drunken night."

"You don't have to tell me this. It's none of my business," he said, and she fell a little more in love with Huck Beck.

"I know. I just want you to have the backstory of why I haven't...why I've been...reluctant to share everything with Jenkins."

He slid his hand down her arm to her hip where he held her, moved closer, and then nodded for her to tell her story.

It certainly seemed to be the night for True Confessions.

"We were in training together, you knew that. And we were both stationed in the D.C. office, which was the best assignment you could get, the one I wanted most." She looked away up at the ceiling, not wanting to look into Huck's cool blue gaze as she told this story. "He was an ass in training, always trying to best me. And I admit, I loved the competition, because it pushed me, but mainly because I always won.

"Back then the newer, younger agents went out a lot after work. No one was married, no kids yet, just mid- to late twenty-somethings who had high-stress jobs and wanted to blow off steam."

"That makes sense," Huck said, and she glanced his way to see understanding on his face, then looked back to the ceiling.

"Jenkins was always saying stupid stuff, inappropriate for

sure, but I always blew him off. I was the only female agent in the office under forty, and I didn't want anyone to think I couldn't handle him. I *could* handle him."

"Kels, did he...hurt you?" Huck said, and she could feel his body tense, his hand on her hip flexing.

"No. Nothing like that. We got really drunk one night, and I went home with him. I blame the alcohol, a dry spell, and Jenkins' trash talk finally getting to me. I regretted it almost immediately. I mean, like while we were still in bed."

"Everybody's had one of those nights, a night they regret. You shouldn't feel too bad about it."

She shook her head. "I don't. I didn't. I didn't lie when I told you I'd never had a one-night stand with someone I didn't know. But I had a one-night stand with Jenkins."

"And he was an ass about it afterward," he guessed. No, he knew. Huck Beck was a good detective, and he knew Kelsey well.

"As assy as they come," she said, nodding. "I didn't say anything to anybody. Yeah, I could have filed a complaint, but I was still trying to fit in in a boys' club. I didn't want to be known as the person who couldn't 'take a joke,' as they would surely see Jenkins' bothering me. Plus, I desperately wanted to keep my coworkers from finding out that I'd slept with Jenkins. I was so ashamed, and of course they did."

"From Jenkins himself, no doubt."

She nodded. "Yeah. Still, I pretty much ignored him, his advances, his insistence that it had been just the beginning of something more. He was delusional and then pissed, with his jokes becoming more like taunts."

"That fucker," Huck said, and she smiled at him.

She kept her eyes on him as she continued, the worst behind her. "I handled it. Was handling it. Finally, a couple of my colleagues reported Jenkins to our superior. They thought Jenkins was bordering on dangerous."

"Good for them," Huck said.

"Maybe. Maybe not. I was called in and asked a bunch of questions about it all. I confirmed that Jenkins and I slept together once and all the other stuff that happened after. Honestly, I don't think they cared about it. They were only concerned with a possible lawsuit. So they transferred Jenkins to the Chicago office."

"That's good. I mean, they should have fired his ass, but at least he was out of your hair."

"Yeah, that's what I thought. And he was. But I found out a few months later that he'd actually gotten a promotion when he was transferred, and I became a leper in the D.C. office, passed over for lots of undercover opportunities."

"Christ, that's bullshit," Huck said.

"No, that's office politics."

"Fuck," he added.

"Yep," she said, stealing his standard answer. "It would have been better for my career if it had never been reported, and I knew that, which is why I was pissed at my coworkers who reported Jenkins. Who were, in turn, pissed at me for not being grateful to my knights in shining armor."

"Shit."

"Yeah, let's just say it's been a long two years. That's why I was so happy to finally get this case and the opportunity to do undercover work. And it's also why I flipped when I realized Jenkins was my direct supervisor on this case."

"And he certainly enjoyed that. It was obvious to see that day in the office."

The day they "got married," but she didn't say that out loud.

"So," she said after a minute passed with neither of them saying anything. "There's my deep, dark secret. It can't beat finding out about your father, and suicide, but it still…"

"Shh," he said, pulling her close to his warm body, her body sliding against the soft cotton sheets. "It's over. My shit. Your shit. We both survived and came out the other side. The best thing we can do now is…win."

"Yeah, how we do that?"

He grinned, and his hand slid from her hip around to her front, slipping into the fly of her boxers. "I'll tell you in the morning. Right now we're going to have a wedding night like no other."

She wrapped her arms around him and hung on, hoping his words would be true.

They were.

Thirty-One

HUCK SAT AT HIS KITCHEN TABLE THE NEXT MORNING drinking a cup of coffee. For once, he'd awoken before Kelsey. But it wasn't because she was extra tired (they had worn each other out the night before), or he was extra alert. No, it was because he needed to talk to her, and he wasn't sure how to start.

She'd handled his confession about his father and why he'd left the DEA four years ago, but that hadn't directly involved her.

What he had to tell her this morning most certainly did, and he wasn't sure how she'd take it.

She entered the kitchen while he was on his second cup. "Morning," she said, and waited in the doorway until he looked up at her. She had put on her Harvard tee and her boxers after sleeping pressed up against him in the nude.

"Morning," he said, trying to smile at her. He wanted to smile at her, but his stomach was in knots from knowing she may never look so tousled and...well used in his house again after he told her what he had to say.

She held up a finger in a "just a minute" way and took a step back out of the doorway, out of his line of sight. But he could still hear her, and it sounded like...was she undressing?

Aw, shit. She wanted to go again just when he needed to be honest with her. Could he be with her again knowing what he knew? It hadn't slowed him down last night, so maybe.

But she wasn't naked when she walked back into the kitchen.

It was even better. She was wearing the red bra and panty set that she'd reluctantly packed in her apartment and had yet to wear once in Michigan.

He stuck an arm out, but she ignored it and instead went to the counter, where she kept her back to him and fiddled with something that didn't need fiddling with.

He laughed when he finally got it, and she looked over her shoulder at him, smiled, and then faced the counter again.

It was exactly the way he'd asked her to pose for the photos they were taking back in her apartment. In her bra and panties, at the counter, pretending she didn't know Huck was taking a pic.

He thought it would be sexy as hell and that it would prove their intimacy more than even the bed shots did. Plus, he desperately wanted to see her just like she now stood.

She was magnificent. He knew every inch of her body, but to see her standing like that, her long legs strong and firm, her incredible ass barely covered by the red, lacy, high-cut panties. The strips of red bra straps highlighting her creamy shoulders. Yeah, magnificent.

He didn't even bother reaching for his phone. He didn't need a picture. He'd remember it forever.

After he voiced a husky "Thank you," she smiled and collected her pajamas, slipping them on over the red undergarments. She went to the coffee maker and poured herself a cup, looking to Huck to see if he wanted more. He shook his head, and she came to the table and sat down across from him.

"Last night was amazing," she said, and he nodded. "And we're good, right? With everything?"

Not everything, no. But he nodded once as he said, "With what we said last night? Yeah, I'm good if you are."

"I am," she said, and they both looked at each other as they took a drink from their cups and then put them on the table. "Good," she said, "because there's something else I want to say."

Oh, God, he couldn't stand it. He couldn't let himself be sidetracked again. It was killing him. "Actually, can it wait? There's something I need to tell you."

"I think I better go first," she said.

"But I really think…" They stared at each other, and Huck knew he couldn't let her beat him to the punch, or there was a good chance he would sit on what he needed to say for another day.

"I saw the seaplane yesterday," he quickly said at the same time she blurted, "I saw the exchange of drugs yesterday."

They both were silent and stared at each other.

HUCK HAD GONE FOR his own run while Kelsey was on hers. He had packed their stuff, left her the note, and gone to the boat first. Then he took the low trails, thinking he might find her and join her. Taking the lower, straighter route explained why he had gotten to the bend around the same time she did. He would have been below her, and maybe a few hundred yards back, on a different trail while she was crouched down snapping photos and taking video.

She ran upstairs and grabbed her phone so they could compare what they'd each gotten. She came back to the kitchen, and they exchanged phones, his already called up to the pics he'd taken.

"Unbelievable," she said as she scrolled through his photos and played the video he'd taken, while he did the same with her phone.

"Why didn't you tell me this yesterday?" she asked. No accusation in her voice, because how could she accuse him of anything when she'd done the same thing?

"I wanted to. But we weren't alone until we got in my truck, and by then I'd realized that you were acting weird. I assumed it was because of me telling you…of me saying what I did the night before, so I decided to wait until after the party. And then… Well, then we talked about other things."

"Right," she said, nodding, replaying the day in her head. He hadn't known she'd seen the plane and boat too, so it was a logical assumption when he read her mood to chalk it up to her being spooked by him telling her he loved her.

And that part was true, which was why she'd gone running in the first place.

"Why didn't you tell me? I'm guessing that's why you were acting so weird, and not because of what I said. So why didn't you say anything?" he asked.

"I was trying to figure out the endgame first. I wanted to be able to tell you when I had a clear plan in mind."

"Because you didn't want my input? Or because you didn't trust me?"

"Neither," she quickly said, reaching across the table and grabbing his hand. "Because I didn't want you to get caught in any crossfire that might come from Jenkins and me. I'm just not sure how to play this with him yet."

"It's easy now. You call him while we're both on speaker, so he knows I know you gave him the information to break the case. There's no way he can cut you out or throw you under the bus."

She chuckled a little. "You don't know Jenkins like I do. He wouldn't have put me in place without some kind of plan to screw me over."

"He screwed you over by not giving you any good information. Nothing to go on. Telling you to stay in the background. Not even telling you who else was working the case. And possibly sending us on a wild goose chase. That's where he thought it would end, with us providing no real information, which he'd be sure to pass on to Tarrington and your boss in the D.C. office."

"Maybe," she said, hoping what Huck said was true. She felt helpless, the thought of Jenkins having any effect on her career again sickening to her.

And then another play came to mind. One that wouldn't help her, but she figured she might be beyond helping on this case. At least she could help Huck.

"We'll call Prescott instead," she said.

Huck gave his head a small shake. "We were told to report

directly to Jenkins. It's the FBI's case."

"Yes, but that wouldn't stop Prescott from stepping in if he had pertinent information that had a shelf life on it."

"We don't know our intel has a shelf life. We don't even know where the boat and plane are right now."

"Yes, but Jenkins doesn't need to know that. Nor will he find that out."

He shook his head again. "I don't know, Kels. I mean, it would be great for me. I'm sure Prescott would love to burn the FBI."

"Of course he would. They all live for that kind of shit," she said.

"But you'd get it from Jenkins, and you know he wouldn't be quiet about it. You'd be burned for sure."

"I can handle it."

"No. No way do we take that chance. This is your career at stake. I know you want to fuck over Jenkins, and I don't blame you, but you can't put your career in jeopardy."

She squeezed his hand. "But it will make *your* career. Mine will survive. It survived before."

"Or it will be strike two for you. And you might not get a third pitch. What if you bypassed Jenkins and called Tarrington directly?"

She shook her head. "Won't work. He'll be pissed I went over Jenkins' head, and let Jenkins know about it. He's Tarrington's boy."

She was growing more and more convinced this was the route to go. She was leaving Huck. Returning to the job she loved. She could at least give him the best possible shot at living out his own dream.

"No," he said again. "Absolutely not."

She let out a loud sigh. "Okay. Fine. Give me my phone. I'll call Jenkins."

Satisfied, he slid his phone back to her. She moved his phone to the side but not across the table to him. She picked up her phone, dialed, put it on speaker, and then put it back down on the table.

"Prescott here," the voice on the phone said, and Kelsey slid her phone back toward her, out of Huck's reach.

"Sir, this is Kelsey Cameron calling."

"Is Beck all right? Is he hurt?"

"No, sir, Huck is right here with me. We have some information to give you, sir."

"Give *me*? Have you given this information to Agent Jenkins?"

"No, sir, we haven't. Huck found this information himself. I thought it only fair that he call it into his superior. As of now, Jenkins is not involved."

A long pause on the phone as Prescott weighed the pros and cons of cutting Jenkins—and the FBI—out of their joint operation. Kelsey didn't look up at Huck, but she could feel his glare burning into her.

"Beck, are you there?" Prescott finally asked.

"Yes, sir. I'm here," Huck answered. Kelsey risked a look at him, hoping his eyes had dropped to the phone. Nope, still on her, and still steely. His eyes definitely more gray than blue right now.

"And you found some information that would help?"

"Yes, sir. But so did Agent—"

"I'll text you the photos and video from Huck's phone right now," Kelsey said, grabbing Huck's phone and beginning to do just that, finding Prescott's name in his contacts.

"Video? You have video?"

Huck proceeded to tell Prescott what he'd seen yesterday morning while Kelsey sent the pics and video to Prescott.

"I just received them. They— Holy shit. This is good. Very good, Beck."

"It was a team effort," Huck said, glaring at Kelsey again. It didn't matter. Kelsey was getting a warm glow all around her just hearing Prescott's words of praise for Huck. Words she never would have gotten from Jenkins if they'd called him instead.

They sat through another few minutes of silence while Prescott presumably looked through the video and photos. Huck had gotten pretty much everything Kelsey had. She'd keep her information on her phone in case they needed it for backup for getting a search warrant or something. But if they didn't, she'd never let anyone know she had the same information. Not showing anyone that she also had the photos was a way of protecting herself from Jenkins' possible backlash.

"Okay. We're going to move on this. Are you expected in Copper Harbor today?"

"No," Huck said. "We don't have another scheduled charter to work until Wednesday. Usually if that's the case, we still go up there to see if any other boat needs help."

"Don't do that tomorrow," Prescott said. "Stay in Houghton. We might be able to wrap this up in the next day or two, and I don't want you anywhere near there if arrests are made."

"We'd want to be in on any arrests," Kelsey said.

"We don't want to blow your cover, Agent Cameron. Just in case we need some follow-up work done. And we especially don't want to put Beck in danger by word getting out that he was instrumental in the arrests of possible locals."

"Right," she said. It made sense. As much as she'd like to be a part of the takedown, she knew Prescott was right. Seldom did the undercover agent get to be in on the arrests. It was just too dangerous to any ongoing investigation and to the agent.

"So sit tight today. If you don't hear from me before then, don't go to Copper Harbor tomorrow either. Got it?"

"Got it," they both said.

"Good. And good work, Beck," he said.

"Thank you, sir."

"You too, Agent Cameron. I won't forget who made this phone call, even though I will say it was Beck."

"Thank you, sir," Kelsey said, grateful that Prescott would cover for her. Though that might not be enough.

Kelsey hung up, and she sat in her chair, being very still, waiting for Huck to let her have it.

When he said nothing, she looked up at him, bracing for the steely stare. But his face was soft, his eyes blue and warm.

"I love you," he said.

She didn't hesitate, didn't even think about it. "I love you too."

He smiled, got up from his chair, touched her head as he walked past her, and left the room.

Thirty-Two

—☙—

AT NINE THAT NIGHT, PRESCOTT CALLED HUCK'S PHONE, telling him to put it on speaker so he could speak to the both of them.

"Good work both of you," he said. "Our team found the plane via satellite along the shoreline by Marquette. We found the boat near Grand Portage, Minnesota, about to make another delivery. When we got a team there, the plane still had the bags of Sudafed on board. Both parties have been taken into custody, and the plane and boat have both been seized by the DEA."

Huck shared a look with Kelsey, once again across from him at the kitchen table, their Commodore pizza box shoved to the side. Huck then looked at the clock on his microwave. "That was an eventful twelve hours," he said, and Kelsey smiled.

"Yes, it was. But a fruitful twelve hours. The boat captain is lawyering up, but the pilot seems willing to give up his supplier and the names of those who he delivered the junk to in hopes of lesser charges. Hopefully we'll be able to follow the trail now and get these meth labs taken care of."

"That's great," Kelsey said. Huck studied her. There was no emotion in her voice. Concern about the aftermath of what she'd done, the sacrifice she'd made for him and the revenge she got on Jenkins, had set in a few hours earlier. But she hadn't said anything about regretting it, and had even suggested he run to the Commodore to get her new favorite pizza, which he had.

"Your hunch was right, Beck—neither were locals. At least not from the Copper Country. One was originally from Marquette, but hadn't lived there in years. The other from Minnesota. We're digging deeper on how the original contact was made, but it doesn't look like there's any local connection."

Huck sighed, a big sense of relief coming over him. It wasn't so much a hunch as a desperate desire that this mess not be caused by the people he knew so well. Kelsey looked over at him and gave a nod and small smile, happy as well that he wouldn't be disappointed in one of his own.

"Again, really good work," Prescott said. "Beck, you've given me something to think about. I'll be in touch. Cameron, I'm sorry to say my next call will be to Tarrington, to inform him of all that went down today. I'll try to downplay your role in the DEA taking the ball and running with it."

"That would be appreciated, sir, but I understood what I was doing," Kelsey said.

"I get that. Even more reason to protect you if I can," he said. "If you're ever interested in playing for the other team, Cameron, give me a call."

A small, sad smile played across her face, and Huck reached out to squeeze her hand. She squeezed back and then slid her hand away. "Thank you, sir," she said, and Prescott signed off.

Huck rose from the table, went behind Kelsey's chair, and rubbed her shoulders. "Why don't we go to bed," he said. "Make it an early night. We've had a long day of doing nothing but worrying."

"Not yet," she said, and Huck didn't push. Instead, he put the leftover pizza in the fridge, made Kelsey another vodka tonic, and grabbed another beer for himself, which he took swigs from as he cleaned up the kitchen.

Kelsey sat at the table, taking an occasional sip from her drink but mostly just staring at her phone. When it did ring a half-hour later, she jumped and then reached for it. Huck made his way back over to the table.

As an afterthought, Huck grabbed his phone and set it to record their conversation. He was learning fast about the Cover Your Ass culture of federal agencies.

"Kelsey," Jenkins said when she answered the phone.

"Yes. You have me and Beck on speakerphone."

"Take me off speakerphone, Kelsey," he said, his voice low and menacing.

"I prefer to stay on," Huck said. "It was my information and call to Agent Prescott that got the ball rolling this morning."

"Oh, was it?" Jenkins said.

"Yes," Huck said, his tone confident, unbending.

"Okay, then. Here's the deal. Agent Cameron, you're booked on the morning flight out of Marquette. A nine-ten departure. Connection in Detroit, arriving at Dulles at six twenty-nine p.m. Is that understood?"

"Understood," she said, not meeting Huck's eyes, looking down at her phone.

"You can board as an agent, with your badge and gun. Beck won't be traveling with you, so there won't be any questions about why he'd be with an FBI agent."

"Good," she said, and he realized that she was once again protecting him.

"Don't know what's going to happen with you, Beck," Jenkins said. "That's up to Prescott."

"Right. Understood," Huck said.

"But I will be recommending to him that you not be asked back to the DEA Academy. You went rogue on this, and there is no place for rogue agents in either the DEA or FBI."

Across from him, Kelsey's shoulders sank, and Huck touched her hand so she would look at him. When she did, he shrugged and mouthed, "Don't worry about it." She nodded back to him.

"And the primary agent on the case? Were they able to find anything?" Kelsey asked.

A long beat of silence before Jenkins said, "No. He was focusing on the L'anse/Baraga area the past week. Tomorrow he's

joining the DEA on the questioning of the suspect in Minnesota."
A smile flashed over both their faces that they had bested the
primary investigator. "I'm assuming you can find your own way
to the Marquette airport in the morning?" Jenkins asked.

"I'll drive her there," Huck said.

"Fine. I'll be making a report to Grimes in the morning."

At Huck's questioning look, Kelsey mouthed, "My boss." He
nodded.

"I understand," Kelsey said.

"Sure you don't want to take me off speakerphone?" Jenkins
asked.

Kelsey made to grab her phone, but Huck quickly said,
"We're sure."

They heard a long sigh on the other end, then Jenkins said,
"I know you fucked me over on this, Kels. Prescott seems to be
covering for his boy and for you. But I know the truth."

"I'm not sure what you're talking about," Kelsey said in an
even tone, and Huck's admiration of her went up even higher,
though he wouldn't have thought that possible.

"Yeah, I know you think you fucked me good. But we both
know who fucked who the hardest. And we both also know we
have long memories. Don't be looking for any help from the
Midwest Bureau on any of your cases."

"Duly noted," she said, warning in her eyes for Huck not to
say anything. This was her battle, and as much as Huck would like
to reach through the phone and strangle Jenkins, he'd let Kelsey
handle it. She was more than up to the task.

She was his hero.

"Oh, and Jenkins?" she said.

"What?"

"Go fuck yourself."

Huck's smile was wide, and hers quickly joined his as she
ended the call.

"Now it's time for bed," she said, rising from the table.

He was right behind her.

He made love to her slowly and tenderly, and Kelsey's emotions were such that she almost would have preferred a fast and furious coupling. They'd had plenty of those the past few weeks, and they'd been deeply satisfying.

But they had not been nearly as good as having Huck hold her face in his hands while he moved inside her. Or him calling her Kels as he looked deeply into her eyes, wiping out the memory of Jenkins using that name earlier.

He didn't tell her he loved her again. That would have been too much for her, knowing she had to leave in the morning. Leave *him* in the morning. He seemed to sense that, and that only made her love him more, though she didn't say the words again either.

Later, when she wasn't sure if she was more physically or emotionally drained, as she lay in his arms, he said to her, "You know, the FBI motto is Fidelity, Bravery, and Integrity."

"I'm aware," she said.

"I think what you did today, shit, during this whole investigation, embodies all three."

She lifted up her head from his chest. "Are you kidding me? I was hardly loyal to my agency. Bravery is debatable, and I feel slimy about the whole thing. Not really full of integrity."

He pushed her head back to his chest, and she heard his words rumble through him as he spoke. "You were loyal to me—somebody you got saddled with. Not a full agent, not quite a confidential informant. Someone whom you protected, even at peril to your own career—that's the bravery part.

"And putting yourself on the line for what you believed was the right thing to do shows incredible integrity."

"Before you build a shrine to me, let's not forget that one of my motivating factors, maybe *the* motivating factor, was petty revenge on a guy I made the mistake of sleeping with two years ago."

"Mere details," he said, and they both laughed. His whiskers scratched her forehead, and she nuzzled in deeper, loving the feel of it. The feel of him.

Her last thought before drifting off was to savor that moment, because she knew she would never have it again.

HUCK WOKE UP TO KELSEY gently nudging him. He turned toward her side but realized she wasn't in bed and had been nudging him from the other side. Where she stood, fully dressed.

"We need to leave in about twenty minutes for Marquette," she said, and he nodded.

He wanted to pull her back into bed, have a proper farewell, but as soon as he'd indicated he understood her, she turned and walked out of the room. She was pulling a suitcase behind her.

She'd packed already? And showered and dressed? Holy wah, he must have been dead asleep not to hear her.

Which didn't surprise him. He was exhausted. The thought that after he got home from Marquette he'd have nothing to do until Wednesday and could sleep for two days did nothing to help the mood he was in.

"Leave your bags at the top of the stairs," he called after her. "I'll carry them down."

"Thank you," she said from the hallway. Then he heard her descend the stairs, and he reluctantly hauled his ass out of bed.

She was waiting for him at the door when he got downstairs with her bags. Holding two travel mugs with what he assumed, and prayed, was hot, strong coffee.

She put the cups down on the hallway table and opened her gun case, which she'd obviously brought down from the attic. She placed the gun at the small of her back, in front of her blouse, but covered by the suit jacket she wore. After putting the case in the front zip of her carry-on, she took the badge and slipped it into her back pocket.

Huck was pretty sure it was the same suit she'd been wearing the day he met her in D.C. at the FBI office. Although he'd seen her closet. She had a bunch of those severely cut, dark suits.

She looked to him and nodded her readiness to go, then picked up her messenger bag, slung it over her shoulder, took the coffees, and led the way out of Huck's house.

Totally Agent Cameron.

Kelsey Beck had disappeared.

They rode in silence the two hours to Marquette. The only diversion was him taking a loop around Chassell so she could get a better look at her mother's hometown. The signs for the Strawberry Festival were strung everywhere, announcing the schedule of events, which would begin in four days.

He remembered driving into town in the dead of night with Kelsey by his side and mentioning that he'd take her to the Strawberry Festival if she were still there.

They'd almost made it.

She said she preferred to say their goodbyes in the truck and for Huck not to escort her into the airport. He thought that was a good idea, so they could have more privacy. But after he put her luggage onto the curb and climbed back into the truck, he found he didn't have much left to say.

"Obviously it is preferred that you don't mention my being an agent, or the investigation in any way," she said. "We understand if you need to tell your family about my involvement, but please make sure that they keep it confidential."

He nodded, still not sure what he'd say to his brothers. Possibly because he barely believed himself that he and Kelsey were over?

"Good luck to you, Huck," she said, sounding a little less formal. But then she ruined even that much by sticking her hand out to shake.

"Christ," he said under his breath, but shook her hand. She quickly pulled hers away from him and exited the truck before he could even open his door. He knew she was protecting herself, pushing her emotions to the back, letting her professionalism get her on the plane. He should thank her for that.

But to be denied holding her one last time? To not get a goodbye kiss?

He scrambled to get out of the truck, but when he came

around the front, she was already wheeling her luggage into the small airport and holding a hand up behind her.

He stopped as she wanted, once again deferring to the agent in charge.

And mentally kicking himself the whole drive back to Houghton that he'd done so.

Thirty-Three

—∽—

"YEAH, WE KNEW THAT. SO WHAT?" SAWYER SAID TO Huck two months later.

They were in what would be the nursery at Twain and Liv's house, painting the walls a soft, gender-neutral yellow. Liv and Deni were out shopping for furniture for the nursery, and Matt was at a friend's house. Ever since she'd passed into her second trimester, Liv had gone into nesting mode and had been bugging Twain to get going on the nursery. Twain had enlisted Huck and Sawyer on a rainy September Sunday to help him out.

Liv had made her famous lasagna for later, and they were all staying for dinner. Huck took advantage of having just his brothers in the house to finally tell them about John Beck not being his real father.

Which apparently they already knew?

"What do you mean, you knew?" Huck said, holding the paintbrush he'd been using over the can.

Twain shrugged, setting his roller down into the pan of paint. "We knew. We've known since you were a kid. It didn't matter to us."

Jesus Christ, he couldn't believe what he was hearing. "And you never thought to tell me?"

Sawyer put his brush down as well and stretched, twisting at the waist. "We weren't going to tell you as a kid. That would mess you up. Then, later, it didn't seem relevant. None of us had a relationship with Dad, anyway."

"Umm, it messed me up as an adult. Finding out from a drunken, and joyful to spill the news, John Beck."

"That prick," Sawyer said under his breath.

"When did you find out?" Twain asked.

Huck took a deep breath, trying to digest the news that his brothers had known about his parentage all this time. "Four years ago."

Twain and Sawyer looked at each other. "Four years ago. That have anything to do with you quitting DEA training and spending the next few months at the bottom of a bottle?"

"Yeah, a little bit," Huck admitted.

Sawyer walked toward Huck, laying a hand on his shoulder like he used to do when Huck was a kid and Sawyer would have to discipline him. "Wish you had told us then. Maybe we could have helped you through it."

Just like that, any animosity he might have felt for his brothers not telling him the truth earlier dissipated, and Huck felt nothing but love. "I wish I had, too," he admitted.

"And we should have told you sooner, when you were an adult. You didn't need to hear that news from Dad. I can only imagine how hatefully he spun it," Twain said.

"Yeah, he kind of did."

"That prick," Sawyer said again. "That's on me. I should have told you, but I had, you know, pretty much checked out by then. It never occurred to me that you'd get in touch with Dad. It should have. You should have heard it from us, not from that bastard."

Huck remembered ten years ago when Molly had died and Sawyer had retreated into his shell. A shell he was now fully out of, thanks in most part to Deni.

"And honestly," Sawyer added, "it never mattered to us, Huck. Never. Full, half, that's all bullshit." He moved his hand from Huck's shoulder to the back of Huck's neck, pulling him close. "You're our brother, man. You're a Beck. You're...ours."

At the slightest pull from Sawyer, Huck went into his brother's arms, letting his big bro hug the shit of him. Loving it, actually.

Twain came next, giving him a bear hug and a squeeze that made Huck feel like a maple tree that Twain was wrestling to the ground. A match Twain would surely win.

"We cool?" Twain said when he pulled back.

"Yeah," Huck said, being completely honest.

"*You* cool?" Sawyer asked, studying Huck.

"Yeah," he said again.

"Good," Sawyer said, and then swatted Huck on the back of the head, another move from their childhood. "Then tell us why the hell you've been sitting around here for the last two months while your wife has been in D.C."

When Prescott hadn't called him back, he'd decided not to divulge the facts that the marriage had been a sham and he'd done it with the hope of getting back into the DEA Academy. When that didn't look like it was going to happen, he was glad he hadn't mentioned it at all. He'd told them at first that Kelsey had gone back to D.C. to tie up some loose ends at her former job and with her apartment. They'd bought that. A couple weeks after that, he told them that she decided she needed "space" and that she would be staying in D.C. for a while. They hadn't mentioned it since then, for which he was grateful.

"I needed to fulfill our commitment to Jim," he said. Which had been true. Huck had felt like shit giving Jim no notice of Kelsey leaving. He had hustled his ass to try to make up for her absence. Jim had seemed to appreciate Huck's efforts. Huck even learned that Jim often went on early morning rides when he didn't have a charter booked to look at lakefront lots and homes because he was interested in buying, which solved the mystery of where he'd been the morning Kelsey and Huck had noticed the *Mina* missing. Huck hadn't heard from Prescott, so he needed the work with Jim.

When Huck had gotten back from dropping Kelsey off in

Marquette, he found she'd put her share of the tip money they'd earned in an envelope for Huck and left it on the kitchen table. He'd understood, but it had still pissed him off.

"Fine. But charter season is over. What's keeping your ass here now?"

Huck shrugged. "I'm not sure she wants to see me."

Twain laughed. "Since when has that ever stopped one of us?"

"Yeah, but this is different. She's different."

He looked at his brothers, hoping they'd let it drop. But instead, they looked at each other, a private joke passing between them.

"Build her something," they said at the same time, and then both burst into laughter.

"What the hell?" Huck said, shocked to see his usually stern brothers yukking it up. They had changed a lot since falling in love. For the better.

Twain pointed to Sawyer. "When I was trying to win Liv back, Sawyer told me he'd built something for Deni when he'd messed up, and it had worked." He walked over to the corner of the nursery and took a drop cloth off a beautiful cradle made from a wood burl. "So I made this for Liv, and damned if it didn't get my foot back in the door."

Huck admired the craftsmanship of the bassinet. "Beautiful," he said to Twain, who took the compliment with a smile and a nod. "What did you build Deni?" Huck asked Sawyer.

"Picture frames," he said. Twain's smile was catching, and Sawyer grinned from ear to ear.

"Picture frames?" Huck said, looking back at the spectacular piece that Twain had created. "Kind of lame, isn't it?"

Sawyer shrugged. "They had their own special meaning. And it worked."

Apparently so, if his smiling, happy brothers were any proof.

"Umm, there's nothing that I can build Kelsey. Nothing that I could think would mean anything to her." A jewelry box, maybe? To replace the one that held his sketch? But no, if she'd hauled it from D.C. to Houghton, she was attached to that one.

"Think of something. It'll come to you."

He wasn't headed in the right direction. He was supposed to be preparing his brothers for the fact that Kelsey wouldn't be coming home, that she and Huck had split for good. And now he was contemplating what he could build her to win her back.

Before he could get them back on track and start prepping them for the news of his impending "divorce," Liv and Deni came home and oohed and ahhed over the color of the nursery.

"Cocktail hour shortly," Liv announced. "I'm throwing the lasagna in the oven now." The baby was now showing, and Huck watched Twain watch his soon-to-be-again wife with a sappy look on his face.

Huck's heart lurched as he watched both couples walk out of the nursery and down the hall.

He wanted that. All of that. He wanted it to be with Kelsey.

And this time, he wanted it to be real.

Thirty-Four

—◊—

"WHAT ARE YOU DOING HERE?" KELSEY SAID TO HUCK as she waited for him to go through the metal detectors in the reception area at her office.

It was mid-September, and she hadn't heard from him since the day she'd left the Copper Country. When she'd gotten the call from reception that she had a visitor and then learned it was Huck, she was shocked.

"Are you here because you're in the DEA Academy?" she asked hopefully.

He shook his head as he was patted down by security. "No. I haven't heard from Prescott."

"Still? I would have thought…" Huck shrugged, and Kelsey felt like crap for bringing it up. She'd called Prescott after she'd gotten back to once again make Huck's case on why he would be a good candidate for the DEA. Prescott had thanked her for the call, but hadn't given anything away about Huck's future.

And then Kelsey had tried to forget. Forget the way Huck held her as she slept. The way he looked at her with pride and admiration when they talked about the case they'd worked on. Forget his loving family, whom she'd quickly come to love, too.

She hadn't forgotten, of course. The memories were still fresh and raw, as was her pain. So she'd spent the last two and a half months burying herself in her work even more than usual. Coming home so exhausted that she wasn't even able to think about Huck as she lay in bed at night. But that hadn't worked either.

Her superior, Agent Grimes, had read her the riot act for her part in the DEA breaking the case and making the arrests. Or rather, for her supposed part in it. Nobody could prove that Huck wasn't the one who had supplied the information to Prescott except for herself, Huck, and Prescott. And none of them were talking.

In the end, Grimes had cut her some slack, even mentioning that he regretted how he'd handled "the situation" two years ago between her and Jenkins. She hadn't been faced with any disciplinary action; nothing was put in her file. But she hadn't been offered any more undercover assignments.

Basically, she was right back where she'd been three and a half months ago.

Except for the unbearable heartbreak of missing Huck.

"Yeah," he said as he made it through the security gauntlet and she signed him into the building, giving him a visitor's badge. "Doesn't look like your sacrifice is going to have been worth it," he said softly, for her ears only.

"It was worth it," she said. Once he had his badge, she led him to the elevators and up to her office. She ignored the stares from her coworkers as she escorted Huck to her office, where she closed the door behind them.

"Is something wrong with your family? Your mother?"

He shook his head. "No. She's fine. Everybody's fine. I'll probably stop by and see my mom tomorrow. She and Gary just got back from their cruise a week ago."

"So you're here to see her?" she said, finally getting it. He came to visit his mother a few times a year. Was he thinking she'd be his girl in the D.C. port? Because, lovely as it would be to spend a few days in bed with Huck a couple of times a year, she just wasn't built for that kind of casual relationship.

"No," he said. "That's not why I came. But I will try to get out to Alexandria while I'm here."

She stared at him as she started to move to her desk. Stopping herself, she instead turned and sat at the visitor's chair next to the one where he sat. She wasn't sure why Huck was there—in D.C. or her office—but she didn't want a big desk between them while he told her.

"I'm here to see you, Kelsey. Only to see you."

"Oh," she said. She could feel her eyes growing wide and a flush creep up her neck. His eyes were so intense, the blue seeping into her soul. He'd shaved close, like the night of their reception. He was wearing the chambray shirt and sport coat that he'd worn the day they'd met, right here in this building in one of the lower-floor conference rooms.

God, he was beautiful.

"I never told my brothers the truth about us. I just let them believe we were splitting up."

"Oh," she said again.

"Yeah. Well, recently they told me that if I wanted to get you back, I should build you something."

"Build me something?" He chuckled and proceeded to tell her about both Twain and Sawyer building something for Liv and Deni when they'd hit a rough patch.

Why was he telling her this? "That's really sweet. But I don't see how—"

"First, I had to decide if I was willing to put myself out there, take the chance."

"What chance?" she asked, but she knew. Or at least she hoped she knew.

"The chance that you might want something more, something real…with me."

She stared at him. All the good reasons why she'd been so cold to him that last morning, all the reasons why she knew she and Huck couldn't work, were sent scurrying from her brain.

Which scared the crap out of her. She was an analyst, for God's sake. A good one. You didn't just throw out good data based on hunches. Or worse, feelings.

"I do want something real with you," she said, surprising herself. "But I don't—"

"Good. Great," he interrupted her. "So then I started wondering what I could build you. You know, I have to keep up a Beck brother tradition."

She looked at him more closely, seeing if there was room in his jacket for, like, a birdhouse or something. That was the only thing that she had any experience with building, having made one in woodshop in seventh grade.

"And then I thought, no. I don't have to build her anything."

She didn't need a birdhouse, that was for sure, but she found herself irrationally peeved that he hadn't made her one.

"*We* need to build something. Together."

Oh. Yeah, that might be better than a birdhouse.

"We need to build our careers, whatever mine turns out to be, and wherever yours takes you."

"There are lots of boats in the area," she said, and he laughed.

"Exactly. We'll figure that out together." He smiled at her, and for the first time in months, she thought things might be okay. "We'll also build our relationship. Together."

She nodded but didn't say a word. She didn't want to make any jokes about their relationship. It was too precious to her.

"We'll build our home. Together."

"My apartment's big enough for two," she said, and again he flashed that devastating smile.

"And there's my place in Houghton for vacations," he said.

"I really did love it up there."

"Good, 'cause I'm a Yooper through and through. I could never give it up entirely."

"I wouldn't want you to. I love your family, too."

He nodded. "They're crazy about you."

"Probably not right now," she said.

He waved that away. "They assume I messed up, thus the building something to get back in your good graces. You show up with me again, they're going to be ecstatic."

She smiled at that thought. Liv was probably showing now, and maybe she and Twain were already married. Before she could ask, Huck moved to the edge of his seat, twisting so he was completely facing her. He took her hands in his and looked at her for a long time before he spoke.

"But most importantly, Kelsey Cameron, I want to build a life with you. Together."

She felt her cheeks getting wet with tears. Damn, she'd never cried at the office. But today she didn't care about that. Not when Huck added, "Do you want that too?"

She said the words to him that she'd said over three months ago, if only fictionally.

"I do."

Epilogue

—ᴍ—

"MY GOD, IT'S GORGEOUS," KELSEY SAID TO DENI, admiring her newly acquired engagement ring. "I'm so happy for you both," she said, giving Deni another hug.

They'd all hugged when she and Huck had arrived at Liv and Twain's house for Christmas dinner. She and Huck had just flown in that morning, nearly not making it at all because of the poor weather.

They'd spent Thanksgiving at her parents', with all of her family finally meeting Huck. But they probably should change that up next year and go to Houghton for Thanksgiving, and to Westchester for Christmas to possibly have better weather.

Or maybe next year they'd just stay in D.C. and have a quiet Christmas, just the two of them.

Next year, the year after. It felt like heaven to Kelsey to be able to plan on a lifetime with Huck. The life they were building. Together.

"And ours wasn't even the biggest news of the night. When we got to Petey and Alison's party, ready to drop the bomb that Sawyer had just popped the question, we were totally upstaged by our hosts having a surprise wedding," Deni said.

"Petey Ryan got married?" Huck said. "Wow, that's kind of shocking."

"No less shocking than when you came back to town last May with a bride," Twain teased Huck.

They had told his family about their ruse. It had been easier for them to take when they also shared the news that Huck was now in the DEA Academy. That, and the fact that they were giving their relationship a try. For real.

They'd told them all that in October when they'd flown to the Copper Country for Twain and Liv's wedding. It had been small, just family and close friends, and the reception had been at her family's restaurant in Calumet. Huck had driven north after they'd left the party, and they'd spent the night in Sawyer's Ice Cube, though it was a much different stay in October than it had been in June. Kelsey had to admit the fireplace had been delightful and the sauna more welcoming in the cold fall. The trips to the biffy were a different kind of hell, though.

And the fall colors of the trees along Covered Drive took Kelsey's breath away.

"Liv and I are sick we missed Petey's party—his wedding," Twain said. "He called when he'd gotten our regrets that we couldn't make it and tried to talk us into it. But we had a Koskela family gathering that night that we couldn't miss. Liv's parents were leaving the next day for Florida for the winter."

"It was really lovely," Deni said, and then turned to Liv. "Not as lovely as yours, of course."

Liv laughed. "Of course not." Liv patted the spot on the couch beside her, and Kelsey went over to join her, Deni moving to sit on Liv's other side. "She's kicking," she said, and took Kelsey's hand to place it on her huge baby bump. She was due in two weeks, and they were hoping for an early delivery and perhaps a New Year's baby.

The baby kicked, Liv laughed, and Kelsey gasped at the beauty of Liv and Twain's love creating such a tiny miracle.

Thoughts of where she and Huck might be spending the holidays next year were expanded to include the possibility of them spending it preparing for their own tiny miracle.

HUCK WATCHED KELSEY laugh with Liv, her hand on Liv's

baby. A lump caught in his throat as he imagined Kelsey and Liv trading places, with Kelsey as big as a house with his child.

They'd talked about it and had decided to table the discussion for a year, but the look in Kelsey's eyes now as she placed a second hand on Liv's baby had Huck thinking that their timetable might just move up a bit.

Which he was more than okay with, even though he wasn't positive where he'd be in a year. But they were determined to build that life. Together. So they'd figure out a way to make it all work.

Two days after Huck had gone to Kelsey's office, he drove out to Arlington to pay Prescott a visit. He told Prescott that he couldn't wait around anymore, but he felt he deserved to be given the chance to rejoin the DEA Academy. Turned out Prescott was waiting to see if Huck would fight for his second chance. He said he had waited for Huck to come back and fight for his spot four years ago and was disappointed that he hadn't.

Huck knew he was a different man four years ago. After finding out about his father, he questioned everything, including himself and his abilities. Thanks to working with Kelsey, he now knew he was good enough to make it in the DEA, and wanted to prove it to Prescott, Kelsey, and his brothers. But most importantly, he was going to prove it to himself.

Prescott had also mentioned that he'd like for Huck to stay at the Arlington DEA office with him for the first few years after training, and Huck had quickly agreed and said that he'd jump at the chance to work closely with Prescott.

Now Huck was in the middle of his eighteen-week Basic Agent Trainee class at the DEA Academy. They had a two-week break for the holidays. This time around, he was about the same age as the other BATs, but still had less experience than the majority of them, who mostly came from law enforcement or military backgrounds.

Huck realized now that Prescott had indeed seen something in him back then to have placed him into training right out of college.

This time, he wasn't going to let the man down.

"How about a toast to the newly engaged couple," Twain said, coming out of the kitchen with several champagne flutes on a tray. He set the tray down on the coffee table and handed out the flutes. "A sip won't hurt," he said to Liv, but also had a flute with water in it, which he set on the table in front of her.

As they held their champagne, Huck's eyes went to Kelsey's, and he realized she was also remembering the night at the Ice Cube and Jim Peterson's gifted champagne. And everything he did to her with it. A cute flush crept up her neck, and she quickly looked away from Huck.

"To Sawyer and Deni," Twain announced, holding up his glass.

"To Sawyer and Deni," they all chimed in.

"No more Bad Luck Beck brothers," Sawyer said, looking to his two brothers.

Huck nodded, returning the sentiment. "No. No more. Here's to the Crazy In Love Beck Brothers," Huck toasted, and they all joined in. Twain had even let Matt have a champagne flute.

"Cheers!" was shouted, glasses clinked, and Huck looked around at everyone he loved most. He was moved to his core at all of them being in the same room.

"One last toast," Huck said, standing up, looking at Kelsey for confirmation that she was ready for him to tell their secret. A nod and a smile from her had Huck raising his glass. "Not so much a toast, as more of an introduction."

Everyone looked puzzled, exchanging glances with each other and then looking at Kelsey, who sat smiling, looking at Huck.

Like she would for the rest of their lives.

"I did this once before. In this very room, as I recall. But this time is different. This time is for real. Forever."

Gasps from Liv and Deni. The women always were sharper at picking up on that kind of stuff.

"May I introduce you to my wife, Kelsey Beck."

252 ❧ MARA JACOBS

They had gone to City Hall three weeks ago. The same City Hall that they'd told his family they'd married at in the first place. He had asked Kelsey's father for his permission when they'd gone to Westchester for Thanksgiving.

They did take pictures, and Kelsey wore her red dress. It was off her three minutes after they returned to her apartment.

He tipped his glass to clink with his wife, who had left the couch and was now standing by his side. She smiled at him as he wrapped an arm around her waist. "Hear, hear," she said, raising her glass, taking a drink, and then lifting her mouth to his to kiss. Which he did. Gladly.

She tasted like champagne. And the future.

~*~

Acknowledgments

A huge thank you to Lisa Braedon, who shared with me the story of how she met her husband, Evan, and gave me permission to use it. Although it was for a class, not FBI training, Lisa and Evan had to partake in the exercise Kelsey and Huck did in the prologue of Worth The Lies. They had to stare at each other's faces for a period of time without saying a word. And, just like Kelsey and Huck, they fell madly in love.

Beta readers Holli Bertram, Liz Kelly and Patti Kearly were invaluable in their feedback. The editing at Word Wolfe and Editing 720 was, as always, top notch. And a big thank you to my last-look editor, Margo Burrage.

The Worth Series continues with

WORTH THE FLIGHT
THE WORTH SERIES BOOK 7

Try Mara's New Adult Romance Series

IN TOO DEEP
FRESHMAN ROOMMATES TRILOGY, BOOK 1

IN TOO FAST
FRESHMAN ROOMMATES TRILOGY, BOOK 2

IN TOO HARD
FRESHMAN ROOMMATES TRILOGY, BOOK 3

Mara Jacobs is the *New York Times* and *USA Today*
bestselling author of The Worth Series

After graduating from Michigan State University with a degree in
advertising, Mara spent several years working at daily newspapers in
advertising sales and production. This certainly prepared her for the
world of deadlines!

She writes mysteries with romance, thrillers with romance, and
romances with…well, you get it.

Forever a Yooper (someone who hails from Michigan's glorious
Upper Peninsula), Mara now splits her time between the Copper
Country, Las Vegas, and East Lansing, where she is better able to
root on her beloved Spartans.

You can find out more about Mara's books at
www.marajacobs.com

Mara loves to hear from readers. Contact her at
mara@marajacobs.com

www.ingramcontent.com/pod-product-compliance
Lightning Source LLC
Chambersburg PA
CBHW031712170626
46808CB00005B/1713